MURDER
MAKES TRACKS

by the same author

A HEALTHY BODY

GILLIAN LINSCOTT
MURDER
MAKES TRACKS

St. Martin's Press
New York

860221

Library of Congress Cataloging in Publication Data

Linscott, Gillian.
  Murder makes tracks.

  I. Title.
PR6062.I54M8   1985   823'.914   85-1750
ISBN 0-312-55311-0

First published in Great Britain by Macmillan London Ltd.

First U.S. Edition

10 9 8 7 6 5 4 3 2 1

MURDER MAKES TRACKS

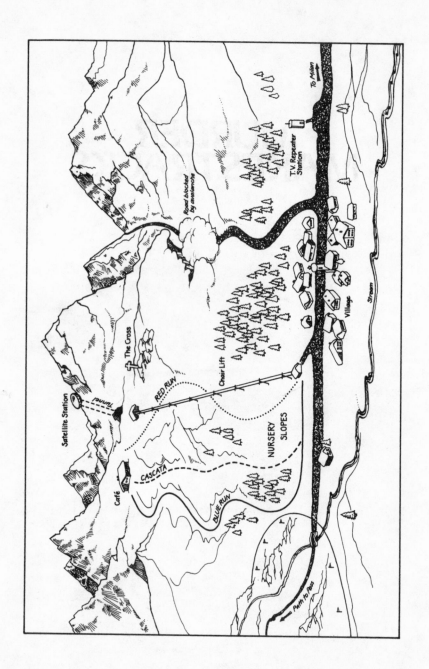

Satellite Station

Café

The Cross

Road blocked by avalanche

RED RUN

CASCATA

BLUE RUN

Chair Lift

NURSERY
SLOPES

Path to pass

T.V. Repeater Station

To Milan

Village

Stream

PRELUDE

'At least they've got their headline,' the first journalist said. 'Horace Hent goes into Space.'

The second journalist parked the glossy file of press releases and photographs under his chair and scooped up a gin and tonic.

'Or into bankruptcy. He's under-financed for satellites.'

The press conference was about to begin and the party from Hent Communications was negotiating its way through palms and tubs of hydrangeas on to the platform, Horace Hent already gleaming with triumph and looking more like a successful retired jockey than the head of Europe's fourth largest communications group.

'Anyway,' said the first journalist, 'he's trying to do it on the cheap. He's taken over a second-hand earth transmission station somewhere up in the Alps.'

'That'll suit his megalomania.'

They watched as the platform party got settled and a huge picture of a communications satellite was projected on to the screen behind them.

'Who's the red-haired woman next to him?'

'That's his wife.'

'No, it isn't. I saw his wife on that trip to Paris two years ago. She's a big blonde.'

'That was two years ago.'

7

Hent got to his feet and the picture on the screen behind him switched to a large map of Europe, cross-hatched in various colours.

'Oh God, here we go. Napoleon's next campaign.'

'Ladies and gentlemen, this is a historic day for us . . .'

The journalists sighed and began scribbling.

Bruin read a report of the press conference in the *Guardian* financial pages at coffee time next morning, in the staff room of the Alderman Kibbalts comprehensive.

'Here, Fuzz, something else for the communications project.'

She read it, asked if she could cut it out, then paused with scissors at the ready while she studied it again. She asked another male teacher, who was marking books with his back to the rest of the room, 'This place where he's got the satellite station, isn't that where you go skiing, Ray?'

He said 'Yes' unenthusiastically without turning round, but she wasn't discouraged.

'I wonder if we could take a party there this winter. They could do some skiing and have a look at the satellite station at the same time.'

Bruin said cautiously, 'After what they did to that hotel in Sardinia . . .'

She swept it aside. 'That was Sardinia. This would be different.'

A week later a letter of enquiry arrived at the offices of a travel firm specialising in school parties. One of the firm's newest members, Nimue Hawthorne, looked up from her ferry timetables to see what the woman in charge of her department was groaning about.

'Oh no, it's Alderman Kibbalts. They want to go skiing this time.'

'Is that bad news?'

'Almost certainly yes. After that affair in Sardinia I said we'd never have them again.'

'But?'

'Exactly. Times is hard. But if we do take them on I'm sending someone from here out with them to see fair play. You ski, don't you, Nimue?'

CHAPTER ONE

Birdie watched their feet, hers enclosed in red plastic, his in black and grey, moving silently ten feet above the snow-plastered pine trees. He still found this way of travelling unreal, like the moment when you realise one wmore gulp is going to tip the scale from sober to drunk. Not that he was drunk now: stone sober with the cold air blasting the inside of his lungs and his eyes dazzled by rainbow points of light on the fresh snow below them. More than a foot of it had fallen overnight. On the newly flattened snow of the piste, brightly coloured skiers darted and turned like tropical fish in a great white aquarium. Up here, with about five minutes more of chair lift before he'd have to stand on his skis again, he could almost convince himself that next time he'd be turning and darting with the best of them. But the past week, his first skiing holiday for seven years, had taught him that among the tropical fish he was no better than a long grey carp. Still, as far as he was concerned, skiing wasn't the main point of the holiday. He glanced at Nimue sitting beside him, smiling to herself with small white teeth glowing white against her brown face, dark eyes flecked with the reflection of the snow.

He said, 'Eight days – you realise this is the longest time we've been together since last summer?'

She nodded. 'Nice, isn't it? Worth tolerating the little

11

brutes for?'

'Yes.'

God knows the little brutes took a fair amount of tolerating, although the village was doing its best. It was an Italian Alpine resort, far from fashionable, but showing stoicism in the face of school parties. At Nimue's suggestion Birdie had scraped together two hundred pounds, done his pre-ski exercises and flown out to join her for a fortnight.

He looked at her again and looked away, trying to judge how much she meant it when she agreed it was nice to be together again. He said experimentally, 'It's a pity there's not more time like this.'

'I'll be back in England next month', she said. Which was fine as far as it went, except their flats and their jobs were two hundred miles apart with meetings confined to weekends or the occasional days off from the gym where he put plump businessmen through their anti-coronary routines. Eighteen months ago she'd asked him not to rush things. He thought his progress since then, if you could call it progress, had been as slow and quiet as the motion of this chair lift. The question was whether it was getting him any further up the mountain. They were past the pine trees now, above the open snow plain that lay between the end of the forest and the top of the chair lift. It was covered with the little rounded hillocks that skiers called moguls and had to pretend to enjoy even if they didn't. Birdie didn't. For one thing, his ski technique wasn't up to negotiating them with any style; for another his cartilage trouble was giving him hell, though he tried not to keep on about it to Nimue. In another minute or so the long wooden hut that ended the chair's upward progress would come into sight and he'd have to concentrate on getting off the thing smoothly. Even on a ski lift, time mattered.

He looked at her again, but she'd twisted round in her seat, staring back the way they'd come.

'There's been about a foot of it overnight down there; that means more at the top. Should be some fresh powder.'

He sighed. When it came to the sea or mountains or moorland that made the background to some of their time together, he could share this eagerness of hers. But excitement over snow was a different matter. For him snow brought memories of pensioners slithering over pavements and traffic snarl-ups in grey towns, something to be negotiated rather than enjoyed. Still, he was trying hard.

'That's great,' he said. Then, conscious that there wasn't much of the ride left, he rushed in,' I think I could get a job in London by the summer.'

She seemed absorbed by the sight of a pair of skiers having mogul trouble below them and he couldn't see her expression, only a curve of neck and cheek and her long black pigtail.

He went on, 'If I did, we could start looking for that flat together.'

'There you are, he's lost his ski. I knew he would.'

He took hold of her pigtail and pulled, very gently. 'Nimue love, did you hear a word I've been saying?'

Her head came up and her eyes met his, unresentful but surprised. 'Of course I did. That would be great if we could.'

She'd said that when they'd discussed it before and come to the conclusion that more time together was something they both wanted, something to work towards over the various obstacles of their separate lives. Only to him it was becoming more urgent with every parting, and he wanted some reassurance that she shared the urgency. Their chair clicked and rattled past the last of the pylons

13

that supported its cable and began the shallow glide down towards the shed at the top of the ski slopes. In the shed a wheel ceaselessly drew the chairs in and paid them out again on their journey back down to the valley.

He said, 'Time passes, you know.'

She smiled and said in a quavering old woman's voice, 'And we're neither of us getting any younger, are we, dearie?'

It was meant as a joke, but it touched a sore point. 'It's different when you're twenty-nine. At forty-three you really mean it.'

A shade of anxiety on her face. 'Why should it be different?'

'Forty-three minus twenty-nine, that's fourteen years' difference.'

'Birdie, you're just being daft.'

A touch of her father's Yorkshire in her voice when she said 'daft' that always fascinated him by its contrast with her mother's dark skin and black hair. The word was often an endearment between them, but he thought he heard a touch of impatience in it this time. He'd timed it wrong again, trying to talk about the future when all she wanted to do was make tracks in the new snow.

Their skis were only a few feet above the snow now. She swung the heavy safety bar back and he sighed and made himself concentrate on fitting his skis into the deep ruts made by other alighting skiers. A lift attendant watched impassively from his kiosk at the front of the shed. It was, if you kept your mind on it, a simple enough procedure. Skis down on the snow, straighten up, push and glide away to the left, while your empty chair went straight on into the shed to keep its appointment with the big wheel. But if you got it wrong you landed in a heap on the snow, with the next chair

14

swooping down at you and the attendant behaving like something out of Italian opera. It had happened to Birdie once this holiday, and once was enough. They were level with the attendant's kiosk now, and the sign that told them in three languages to get off. Straighten knees, ski on snow, take it steady. Nimue, who'd been sitting on the outside, smiled at him and glided effortlessly away. He tried to follow, to stand up and glide after her – and remained sitting exactly where he was. A shout from Nimue, a louder shout from the lift attendant, and the chair was carrying him inside the long shed, taking him out of the sun and into the half dark and he couldn't do a thing about it. His first thought was that he'd had some kind of muscular seizure. He shouted, tried again to get up. The clanking of the chairs sounded as loud as a train and perhaps twenty yards away at the end of the building a huge horizontal wheel drew them towards itself. Birdie made another almighty effort to get up and it was only then that he realised what had happened. His anorak was stuck firmly to the seat of the chair. The clanking was louder, the wheel perhaps ten yards away and the cable throbbed towards it like a live artery. Birdie ripped open his zip, wriggled out of the anorak and slid in a heap on to the concrete floor. As he did so, the machinery gave an even louder clank and the wheel juddered to a halt. The attendant had hit the emergency button. And the man was now surging into the shed on a flow of language as menacing as the machinery itself. He was closely followed by Nimue, who looked gratifyingly concerned, and rushed past him to help Birdie to his feet.

The attendant said something to Birdie in Italian and repeated it more loudly. Birdie unclipped his skis with as much dignity as he could manage, trying to explain in English. Nimue, murmuring calming words in Italian,

15

walked over to the chair and tried to pick up Birdie's abandoned anorak. She called the attendant over to look.

'Superglue, I suppose,' Birdie said.

She nodded.

'He says a school party came up a little while ago and . . .'

'Alderman Kibbalts school?'

'I'm afraid so.'

Birdie walked over and tugged at his anorak. It came away with a ripping sound, leaving some of the white wadding exposed. It had cost him two evenings' overtime.

He said, 'I'll bet it was bloody Wayne.'

Nimue thanked the attendant and she and Birdie walked back into the sunshine at the top of the lift.

'It might not have been Wayne.'

'It usually is.'

Wayne Belling, sixteen years old and nearly as tall as Birdie, was alleged to have driven three probation officers into early retirement.

'Where are the little brutes?'

Nimue said, 'I think most of them were going on a tour round the satellite station. I'm surprised they let them in with the problems they've got today.'

The satellite station's problems had been the talk of the resort by breakfast time. The heavy snowfall that was such good news for skiers had brought very primitive communications problems for Hent's technicians, blocking the steep motor road that led from the village and over the pass to the station itself with a minor avalanche. The opinion in the village was that it might be days before the road could be cleared, and until that happened the only way up to the station was by the chair lift on which Nimue and Birdie were travelling, then

16

through a short tunnel – built long ago as part of an abandoned road project – to the station itself. With the opening of Hent's satellite television service only days away it could hardly have come at a more inconvenient time, and was causing some hilarity round the village, where Hent's money was more popular than Hent himself.

From where Birdie and Nimue were standing they could see the tunnel mouth quite clearly, and the path that led up to it from the top of the chair lift, alongside a winching device for bringing crates of equipment down. Birdie wanted revenge for the Superglue, but decided not to spoil a morning's skiing with Nimue by pursuing the Alderman Kibbalts group through there.

'Why do they want to go round the satellite station anyway?'

'They're doing a project on communications.'

'I thought the only project they were doing was on how high they could get the decibel count without knocking over the bloody hotel.'

Disco sessions at the Hotel Soldanella began at about five and went on until midnight. It was one of the penalties Birdie was paying for his cheap holiday.

'They're not all like that. Some of them are quite bright.'

Distance between forty-three and twenty-nine, fourteen years. Distance between twenty-nine and sixteen, thirteen years. Nimue was, after all, nearer their age than his. At least, he thought, this new obsession was improving his mental arithmetic.

He asked, 'Feel like a coffee?'

There was a small café at the top of the ski slopes. He thought relaxing on the terrace, enjoying the view, they might get back to the question he'd posed on the chair lift. But now Nimue knew he wasn't hurt she was keyed up like a horse waiting to race. She loved skiing and resented the delays that kept her from it.

'Birdie love, it's fresh snow. We can't waste it.'

'Which run are we going down?' he asked as enthusiastically as possible. He resolved that anger over his spoilt anorak shouldn't ruin the morning for her.

There were three runs back down to the village from the top of the chair lift, graded blue, red and black in order of difficulty. Blue was the easiest and longest, a series of slow curves through the woods that began on the far side of the café and, like the others, eventually came out at the nursery slopes down in the village. Red, the medium run, went straight down from where they were standing and over the mogul field. At some points it turned under the chair lift but for most of the journey ran well to the right of it. Near the top of the blue run was the line of black discs on posts that marked the start of the third and most difficult, a run called Cascata that even serious skiers treated with respect. Birdie, seeing Nimue looking longingly in that direction, said, 'We could go down Cascata if you like.'

'No. There're avalanche warnings. Anyway, it's a bit much for you yet.'

He knew her well enough to realise that it was a simple statement of fact without any wish to hurt him. Still, it didn't help. Nimue set off down the red run at some speed and he followed, admiring even in his bad mood her ease and freedom on skis, the way she skimmed and danced round the moguls, seeking out the highest ones like a surfer looking for breakers. His way with them was less challenging, more of a live and let live approach. By the time they'd got to the point where the piste plunged down through the pine trees he'd committed only one minor fall and almost skied himself back into a good temper. The next bit of the way down

18

was, in any case, one he always enjoyed: a straight run through the trees where you could get up some speed after the intricate twistings and turnings of the first pitch. It was, too, the place where his height, weight and longer skis gave him an advantage over Nimue. They usually raced it and, if he didn't fall over, he won. He glanced at Nimue.

'Ready?'

And they were off, first side by side, then with Birdie gaining a little. By the halfway point he was twenty yards or so ahead and going strong, snow swishing under his skis, his tall body folded into something like the crouch of downhill racers. Trees flashed past in a blur and he wanted to shout with release and triumph at the speed of it. Then it hit him. Something red and black flashed into his field of vision from the right. He yelled at it, tried to turn out of the way, but it battered into him, sending him rolling down the slope, over and over in clouds of snow. He ended spreadeagled on his back and head downwards, some way from the point of impact. By the time he'd worked out which way was up, Nimue was kneeling beside him asking if he was all right.

'What the hell . . . ?'

'Wayne. Is your leg hurt?'

As it happened, his left ski had released itself by the safety binding, saving his knee cartilage. He found when he got himself upright that the damage was limited to a few potential bruises, but that didn't lessen his shock or anger.

'It would be bloody Wayne, wouldn't it? What did he think he was doing?'

'He was coming along the traverse.'

'He should bloody well have slowed down.'

'Of course he should. There's a warning sign.'

Wayne and two friends were standing up the slope and

19

watching. The usual two friends, a tall West Indian boy, Joe, and a thin white lad with acne, Sidney. As Birdie dusted snow off himself they began skiing down towards him, Joe carrying Birdie's lost ski and Sidney grinning all over his face. Wayne wore a faintly bored look, as if it had nothing to do with him. Birdie yelled at him, 'What the hell were you doing?'

'Sorry. I was going too fast to pull up.'

He didn't sound at all sorry, and he managed to give the impression that Birdie had been moving at a dinosaur pace in comparison with his own superior speed.

Nimue said, 'That's no excuse. Skiing's about being able to stop as well as just belting along.'

'Yeah. Well, I'm sorry.'

He didn't sound convincing, but Birdie noticed that the apology had been a little less perfunctory when aimed at Nimue.

Meanwhile Joe was making more practical amends by helping Birdie fix the lost ski to his boot. The mechanism was giving some trouble, but Sidney watched, smirking, and did nothing useful. Wayne went on talking to Nimue and had obviously put Birdie and the collision out of his mind already.

'. . . going at eighty miles an hour yesterday. Sidney timed it on his calculator.'

Nimue said, 'I'd check that calculator. You couldn't do more than forty on this gradient.'

'Yeah?' He seemed not at all embarrassed at being caught out, even deigned to ask Nimue a direct question.

'What's the fastest you done then?'

'About sixty, but that was on a specially prepared course.'

'Yeah?'

Birdie heard the revolting youth offer Nimue a cigarette and get it turned down in surprisingly polite terms, given her dislike of the things. It struck him that most of the girls in the school party, who tended to congregate giggling in corners when Wayne was around, would probably have traded years of their lives for a similar mark of favour.

'Tell you what,' Wayne said to Nimue, 'I'll race you down.'

By now the ski was back in place. Joe moved away and joined his friends but they seemed in no hurry to move off, smoking cigarettes on the far side of the piste. Nimue smiled at Birdie, turning away from Wayne.

'No thanks. We'll ski at our own pace.'

The unfairness of it made Birdie furious. Bloody hell, he'd been going much faster than bloody Wayne, faster than Nimue. Now they were all giving the impression that he was some sort of geriatric relic who ought by rights to be pulled quietly along on a toboggan.

'I bloody well don't want to ski slowly.'

'I just thought you might be a bit shaken up, that's all.'

He could tell from her tone that she was trying hard not to be impatient, which added to his suspicion that he was being coddled.

'I'm not shaken up. All that's happened is I've been knocked flying by some blasted juvenile delinquent on skis.'

And if Wayne heard that he was welcome to it. Birdie dug his sticks into the snow, intending to turn his skis down the slope and leave all four of them standing. One ski co-operated at once and turned downslope but the other remained stubbornly pointing at right angles across the piste. In his struggles with the first ski, Birdie hadn't noticed that the binding of the other one had been knocked loose by the crash. He collapsed slowly but inevitably on to the snow again and this time Wayne, Joe

21

and Sidney didn't even try to suppress their laughter. Nimue did, which was even worse. Tactfully she helped him to his feet. Carefully she began to adjust the ski binding.

'I can do it,' Birdie hissed at her through tight lips.

'It's a bit difficult.'

'I said I can do it, blast it.'

And that was it. Nimue let go of the ski binding as if it had burned her and got to her feet.

'Oh Birdie, what's got into you this morning?'

Then she said, in a higher and louder voice across the piste to Wayne, 'Come on then. What are we waiting for?'

And she fired herself down the slope like a missile. The three boys threw away their cigarettes and followed her, uttering war whoops, but it was clear even to the sad and furious Birdie that they wouldn't catch up. He felt so hot with anger that he expected the snow round him to melt into a pit. What was more, he'd really needed Nimue's help with the binding because the damned thing still wouldn't do up. He struggled with it, getting hotter still in his thick ski clothes and turning the air blue.

'I wonder if I could help.'

A man was standing beside the piste about twenty feet above him. His voice had a soft Scots accent, the ski clothes were sleek and expensive. He wore neither hat nor goggles, displaying sandy hair, neatly cut, and grey eyes in a tanned face. His eyebrows were pale, a shade lighter than the hair. Birdie immediately tried to estimate his age, and couldn't. He might have been anything between Birdie's age and Nimue's. But at least his offer of help sounded neither amused nor patronising. Birdie wondered how long he'd been standing there.

'I can't get this thing to clip on.'

The man skied down, came to a neat halt beside Birdie and, within seconds, had the binding in place. He said courteously, 'It's an awkward design, a bit old fashioned. They tend to put them on hire skis.'

Whether he meant it or not, Birdie was grateful for the attempt at face-saving, but the next words were disconcerting.

'I shouldn't worry – all part of the emotional hazards of ski holidays.'

'Emotional hazards?'

'Notorious. Far more broken relationships than broken legs. But they aren't covered by insurance policies.'

He glanced at Birdie to see how he was taking it, and added, 'Probably one of the hazards of altitude – like talking nonsense to innocent strangers.'

He held out a gloved hand. 'Aeneas Campbell. I work for Horace Hent.'

Birdie introduced himself, remembering now that he'd seen the man once in the previous week walking along the village street with a small, black-haired man who was parcelled from knees to chin in a coat of piebald pony skin. Nimue had told him then that the parcelled-up man was Horace Hent himself.

'You work at the satellite station?'

'Yes, that's the big one at the moment. You know we start transmission on Wednesday?'

'I think some of the school party are being shown round it.'

Aeneas said grimly, 'One of them has already been helping himself to souvenirs from it.'

'Not . . . ?'

'Yes. The one you called bloody Wayne.'

Birdie sighed. 'What's he done now?'

'Taken a pocket television set. One of the new

23

miniature ones.'

'Pocket television?'

'Yes. I had to chase Wayne out of Mr Hent's office and when I checked a few minutes later the pocket television was missing and Wayne and friends were on their way back through the tunnel.'

'You asked him for it?'

'Yes, and he denied ever having set eyes on it.'

'So what did you do?'

'What could I do? I could hardly strip-search him on suspicion, so I decided to ski down behind them and see what happened. Then I saw him crash into you and decided you had enough problems.'

'Thanks.'

'As his teacher, I thought . . .'

Birdie said in alarm, 'I'm not his teacher. I'm just staying at the same hotel.'

'And the girl you . . . er . . . were with?'

'Nimue's not a teacher either. She's from the travel firm.'

But being grateful to Aeneas for his help with the ski he said, 'I'll mention it to one of their teachers if you like.'

Aeneas accepted and suggested they should ski down together. They went at a decently fast pace, though not at Nimue's breakneck speed, and only stopped once. That was when Aeneas spotted something in the middle of the piste. He picked it up and showed it to Birdie – a rectangular box with a TV screen about half the size of a postcard.

'Someone might ask Wayne how that got down here.'

At the bottom of the run, as they negotiated crowds of toddlers on the nursery slopes, Aeneas suggested they should have a coffee in the café across the car park at the bottom of the chair lift. As there was no sign of Nimue,

Birdie accepted and they found seats on the narrow balcony.

'In the sun,' said Aeneas, 'and I can look out for Allana.'

'Allana?'

'Mrs Hent the sixth.'

He sipped his creamy coffee and looked at Birdie.

'What happened to the first five? All emotional ski casualties?'

'No. Mrs Hents one and two were before my time. Mrs Hent the third went after a stand-up quarrel at a White House reception. Mrs Hent the fourth distracted his putting once too often on the ninth green of a golf course near Shannon. Very handy for catching the plane to her lawyer in California. Number five just went.'

Birdie said, 'It must come expensive.'

'We charge most of it to the publicity budget. Helps the image to be seen with a new woman every two years or so.'

Birdie couldn't quite tell from the tone whether Aeneas was laughing at his boss. He suspected he probably was and that talking like this to a new acquaintance might be the man's revenge for running Hent's errands – such as chasing schoolboys to recover his electronic toys. He asked, 'Always young?'

'Average age at divorce twenty-two years and three months.' He added, 'Allana's twenty-one and ten months.'

And Hent, when Birdie saw him in the street, had looked nearer fifty than forty.

Aeneas asked, 'Is that disapproval on your face, or envy?'

Birdie decided that one didn't need an answer. He asked instead, 'Do you get many parties round your satellite station?'

25

From the man's face, he was reluctant to drop the topic of Hent and his wives, but he accepted the diversion with good grace.

'No, and this will be the last. Too many security problems.'

'Because of Wayne?'

Aeneas shook his head. 'More serious than that. This is a very competitive business, you know.'

He let the remark hang in silence for a few seconds, then seemed to tire abruptly of the game of trying to impress Birdie. He twisted round in his seat, looking down the main street of the village.

'I wonder where Allana's got to. I suppose she's buying up half the village as usual.'

His smile at Birdie seemed clearly this time to be mocking either his employer or his own subservience.

'That's one of the little problems of our road being blocked. Allana can't stand the chair lift. She flatly refuses to travel on it alone, so I've got to wait for her.'

He looked back at the mountain and the chairs continuing their endless journey up and down it.

'For some reason, it seems to scare her out of her wits.'

CHAPTER TWO

The main street of the village was quiet, with skiers a thousand feet away up the mountain. In another half hour or so it would fill as they descended in swarms for lunch but Nimue had it to herself. She felt drained and miserable now her annoyance with Birdie had faded, and a little ashamed of herself for not resisting Wayne's challenge. She paused at the window of a ski shop to stare at some striped woollen hats, wondering whether to buy one for Birdie as a peace offering. The idea of his puzzled, patient face under one particularly lively specimen in pink and tangerine stripes made her feel like bursting into tears. She glanced up, angry with herself, and saw a smiling and surprised face looking at her from inside the shop, across the window display. The face was mouthing her name and an arm snaked out among the anoraks and sweaters to beckon her in.

'Allana.'

Nimue was inside the shop in a bound, the cow bells on the door scattering notes at random.

'Allana, what on earth are you doing here?'

'On earth or up in the skies.'

Allana hugged her, eyes sparkling, laughing out of sheer pleasure at their meeting. The Dublin accent was as strong as when Nimue had last heard it four years ago, when it was more or less fresh from what Allana claimed

27

to be the fifth consecutive convent school to expel her.

'Where've you been all this time?'

Nimue's answer would have been complicated, but luckily Allana never waited for answers.

'Anyway, we're a long way from the Ideal Home aren't we?'

And Allana grabbed a pair of woollen socks from a display basket and polished an imaginary window.

' "Flossyfliss for that extra glow." Remember?'

And Nimue thought Allana had indeed acquired extra glow, though probably not from Flossyfliss. Her vitality had always been enough to light up a foggy city but now there was a new gloss about it. Her copper-beech hair was beautifully cut, the curves of her breasts hugged by a brief jacket of white mink above black ski pants.

'What was yours? Deep fryers, wasn't it?'

'Cabbage shredders.'

Allana whirled round and dropped the socks on to a small pile of gloves, hats and sunglasses that a bemused assistant was sorting out at the counter. She and Nimue had met while demonstrating home appliances on adjoining stands when both were at a financial low point. Allana, Nimue remembered, had fizzed her way up from that low point almost immediately, using contacts she made at the exhibition to get a publicity job with a plastics firm or, as she put it at the time, 'going into public relations'. Apparently public relations had prospered, but finding Allana at a modest Italian ski resort was a surprise. St Moritz or Gstaad would be more likely to satisfy her need for sociability. Even in the little ski shop she'd become an instant event. She practically danced round it, pausing every second or so to hug Nimue again or pick up some new toy from the baskets of ski accessories.

'Aren't these fun?'

28

These were fluffy ear muffs in fluorescent colours.

'You must have some. Let me get some for you.'

And in spite of Nimue's protests that the last thing in life she needed was a pair of green fluffy ear muffs they joined the pile on the counter. She managed at last to ask Allana if she was on a skiing holiday.

'Dear, no. You know how I hate exercise.'

All that energy, Nimue remembered, resisted any attempt to channel it. She was surprised and pleased that Allana seemed to have found and kept a good job.

'No, we're here because of the opening of the satellite station. You know, television twenty-two thousand miles out into space and back. Tremendous fun.'

Which presumably explained the prosperity. Public relations for a telecommunications firm might just be a job fast-moving enough to match Allana's demand that life shouldn't keep her standing around.

'Is that part of the Horace Hent empire?'

Instant dramatic gloom.

'Darling, he's the only fly in the ointment.'

She stared at a display of small snow shoes, oval meshes of leather straps.

'Could you get up the mountain on those? I hate that chair lift.'

'No,' said Nimue firmly. 'They're just for padding around.'

It was just like the old days, giggling round shops trying to persuade Allana not to spend all her hard-earned pay on lace boots or designer T-shirts. She'd usually failed then and she failed now. Allana unhooked a pair of snow shoes and added them to the heap on the counter, talking about Horace Hent all the time.

'He's unscrupulous and he uses people and he's getting fat and he's totally obsessed with money . . .'

'Aren't all multi-millionaires?'

29

'And he does put out the most awful crap. I mean, look at this satellite thing.'

She waved an arm in the general direction of the mountain top.

'All those beams to outer space and back again, but when you see what they'll be putting on them you do wonder if it's all worth it after all.'

'Well, at least you seem to be enjoying it.'

'While it lasts.'

There was nothing gloomy in the way she said it, just Allana's certainty that although nothing lasted, the thing that came next would be even better.

Nimue said, 'And you don't necessarily have to like your boss.'

This, unexpectedly, brought Allana to a halt. She said in a puzzled voice, 'My boss?'

'Horace Hent.'

A peal of laughter and another hug.

'But darling, he's not my boss. I'm married to him.'

Nimue could hardly find words.

'You . . . married Horace Hent?'

Allana smiled at the assistant and produced a sheaf of credit cards.

'Why not, darling? Everybody else was doing it.'

Up at the satellite station, the white transmitter dish gleamed in the sun, dwarfing the collection of concrete cubes that housed the control room and storage sheds. Beneath it about a dozen of the Alderman Kibbalts group listened, more or less attentively, to Bruin, a plump young teacher with a round earnest face and small moustache.

'. . . so the signal's fed to here, then it's beamed up to the satellite in geostationary orbit at the Equator. It hits the transponder . . . Do you all remember what a

30

transponder is?'

Most of them murmured yes, a few said no, and he began to explain conscientiously all over again.

At the back of the group a girl with a dyed sunburst of hair whispered to her friends, 'I'm fed up with this. Shall we go?'

'Yeh. Wayne and the others have gone off already.'

Three of them, Brenda, Monica and Cathy, walked along the tunnel towards the more familiar side of the mountain and the skiing grounds. Just before it opened out into the sunlight there was a large rectangular chamber cut into the rock wall, which was used to store bundles of slalom poles and the metal boat-like stretcher that carried ski casualties down the mountain. The three of them settled on the stretcher, giggling as it rocked under their weight.

Brenda said, 'I'm fed up with bloody satellites.'

'Still, it's better than ski school.'

'Yes. I thought ski instructors were supposed to be dead good looking. Ours is about two hundred.'

'Past it,' said Cathy, giggling.

Brenda looked at her, narrow-eyed. 'They're never past it. Not even at two hundred.'

Cathy went red, and there was the silence that usually followed Brenda's rulings on sexual matters, broken by Brenda herself. 'But he's not worth bothering with.'

'Who is worth bothering with? Bruin the Ruin?'

Brenda shook her head thoughtfully.

'Mr Reeve then?'

Giggles from the other two. Ray Reeve was the other male teacher with the party.

'What about the big tall bloke, the one with the woman from the travel firm?'

Brenda said nothing.

Monica objected, 'He's too old. He must be over

31

forty.'

Cathy said wistfully, 'She's got a smashing figure. Dead thin.'

For a while they sat there in silence. rocking gently on the stretcher. Then suddenly there was somebody blocking the light at the end of the tunnel. Footsteps thudded on the hard packed snow of the tunnel floor and a man walked quickly past the niche where they were sitting without noticing them, and on towards the satellite station.

As his steps echoed from further away Monica said, 'That was Mr Reeve.'

'Yeah. What's he doing up here?'

The tunnel had been built in the 1930s as part of a grandiose road project that Mussolini never finished. As well as the tunnel itself and the niche where Brenda and her friends were sitting, his engineers had blasted a cavern from the living rock at the far end. Nearly half a century later, suitably adapted, it had come into its own as Horace Hent's office on this latest frontier of his empire. From the tunnel, all there was to see of it was a metal door. Ray Reeve stopped at the door and knocked on it, glancing out at Bruin and his party still gathered under the transmitter dish. He frowned and looked away quickly. A speaking box beside the door invited him to come in.

A transition to thick white carpet that sank under the weight of his boots, to neon lighting, banks of video equipment and small tables with sprays of flowers in white pottery vases. And the owner of it all sitting behind a desk of glass and tubular metal. He looked, at first, too small for the room – a compact man with very black hair and a bland face that seemed to balance like an egg on the polo neck of his fawn cashmere sweater.

Only his eyes were sharp and restless. He didn't get up when Ray Reeve walked in, but waved his hand at a heated coffee jug on one of the small tables and invited him to help himself and sit down. The teacher poured coffee unhurriedly and sat himself down on a leather sofa, facing the desk. The only thing on its shining surface was a black ring binding file of the kind that collects by dozens in teachers' common rooms. It looked out of place among the luxury.

Hent said, tapping it with a finger, 'That's a good presentation.'

'Thank you.'

But Ray Reeve was wary and unsmiling.

'Yes, I've seen a lot of presentations by professionals that aren't as good as this. It gets straight to the point.'

Ray Reeve said, 'Are you going to back us?'

The man behind the desk looked at him long and hard, like a surgeon wondering where to cut, and slowly shook his head.

'Why not?'

'You haven't persuaded me that this place has got room for another ski school.'

'But it's growing all the time. Five years ago there was just one drag lift, now look at it.'

'Everything's got its optimum commercial size. As a ski resort, I think this place has reached it . . .'

'It hasn't even started. The promotion's . . .'

But Hent's attention was already withdrawn, his mind somewhere else.

'If you can get somebody else to back you, the best of luck. I just don't think it's viable.'

As Ray Reeve walked back along the tunnel he was too deep in his own thoughts to give much attention to the two people who passed him from the other direction: a middle-aged couple in matching ski suits of pink and grey, walking hand in hand. He stood aside for them, but didn't reply to their polite 'Good morning'.

At the end of the tunnel, above the mogul field, a young man in the uniform of the local ski school was waiting for him. As soon as he saw Ray Reeve's face he said, in English, 'No luck then?'

'No.'

'I'm sorry, Ray. I think it could have worked.'

'It would have worked.'

'And there's no hope of getting the money from anybody else?'

'We've gone through all that.'

Silence. The two men stared down over the slopes, at the skiers skimming round or falling between the little hillocks.

After a while the Italian said gently, 'At least you still have your school teaching.'

From below, sounds of conflict rose in unmistakable Alderman Kibbalts accents.

'He took my skis.'

'I didn't touch your fucking skis. They're useless anyway.'

'If you don't get those sodding skis off in just five seconds I'll stuff them up your . . .'

Followed by yelps and the thwack of ski sticks on anoraks.

'Yes,' said Ray Reeve. 'I've still got my school teaching.'

Back along the tunnel, the middle-aged couple had reached Hent's office. This time he stood up and poured coffee for them while they complimented him on his furniture and talked about their home in America until, more or less politely, he asked why they'd insisted on seeing him. The women smiled at him as if he should

34

have guessed.

'Mr Hent, we want to use your satellite station to spread the word of God from the mountaintops.'

CHAPTER THREE

Birdie clumped downhill, with his skis over his shoulder, back to the Hotel Soldanella. He was wondering whether to keep his promise to Aeneas Campbell to tell one of the teachers about the theft of the miniature television, and if so, which one. From what he'd seen of the three of them over the past week Ray Reeve wouldn't be interested and Bruin seemed, even without this, to be permanently submerged in the tide of events. The young man had spent the past week trying to cope, with almost undiminished good temper but decreasing effectiveness, with stolen stuffed ptarmigan, broken pin-ball machines and hats, goggles and ski sticks that went missing again as soon as they were found. It seemed cruel to add to his burdens. Which left Fuzz. Fuzz, real name Frances, in her thirties and by far the most competent of the three, was the one who took over when Bruin failed, pacifying the owner of the stuffed ptarmigan and repairing the pin-ball machine with her manicure set. And in spite of her efficiency – perhaps because they dimly realised that somebody had to be efficient if their lives were to stay reasonably comfortable – the kids seemed to like her. And that was how she referred to them: 'the kids', combining her efficiency with a great deal of tolerance for them. Her attitude was that they might be difficult but given the sort of backgrounds they came from, the world should be grateful they weren't a good deal worse. She wasn't likely to get excited about a toy stolen from an outrageously rich man, but she'd probably be the best person to tell.

He left his skis and boots in the porch and walked on stockinged feet through the reception area. Clamour from the dining hall suggested the Alderman Kibbalts group were already being fed, so he went to the bar in search of Nimue. He found her there, deep in conversation with Ray Reeve over glasses of hot spiced wine, and her smile when she saw him was as warm as if she'd already forgotten their quarrel that morning. She was at the bar in an instant getting him a glass of wine. As she put it on the table beside him she whispered, 'Sorry, love.' Then, aloud, 'Ray's had some bad news. Hent won't back his ski school.'

She found it easier to talk to the man than Birdie did because of their shared skiing expertise.

Ray said, 'He was just stringing me along. I don't think he was really considering it at all.'

He drank a great gulp of the wine, and Birdie thought he looked not so much depressed as shattered. This dream of starting a new ski school had been more than a commercial venture.

'Five years I've been planning it, ever since I first came here and saw the potential of the place. And the ten best instructors from the old ski school were ready to give in their notice and join us next season.'

He took another angry swig of wine.

'Hent probably spends more on his drinks bill than what we were asking.'

Birdie made a doomed attempt to be consoling, 'At least you can still bring your school parties out here.'

Ray choked and coughed.

'That's exactly what I want to get away from. Look at

37

it. Six months of badgering their families for money and making lists of their revolting shoe sizes and arguing over insurance, and when we do finally get out here they twist their bloody ankles at the rate of about three a day and most of them have as much interest in skiing as the rats in the biology laboratory.'

'I'd assumed it was your idea.'

He shook his head. 'Fuzz talked me into it. Developing their potential and so on.'

He swirled the dregs of the spiced wine savagely round his glass.

'If I'd had the same chances at their age I'd have made the British ski team. And are they grateful?'

The answer to that was all too obvious, so Birdie left Ray Reeve moaning to Nimue and went to find Fuzz. Some kind of pasta eating competition seemed to be in progress in the dining room, but he forced his way through it and found her distributing second helpings, a spaghetti strand in her hair.

'Could I have a word with you? About Wayne?'

But there was sombody else competing for her attention. The girl from the reception desk had also found a way through the pasta maze to tell Fuzz she was wanted on the phone.

'For me? Did he say who it was?'

The girl from reception didn't know, and with an apologetic shrug at Birdie, Fuzz followed her out of the room.

'Sorry about this. See you later.'

Birdie went to rejoin Nimue in the bar, but when they looked for Fuzz at reception and in the dining hall a few minutes later there was no sign of her. He decided the case of the television could wait till evening, particularly as Hent had got it back anyway. After the Hotel Soldanella he was longing for some fresh air and quiet.

'What about going back up the mountain for lunch?'

Food cost more up there, but it was worth it for the peace. He had to include Ray Reeve in the invitation but was relieved when he refused. They left him staring gloomily into the steam of a fresh glass of wine. When Nimue asked him casually what he was doing in the afternoon he said, without enthusiasm, that he'd probably look for some powder snow above the Cascata.

As soon as they were settled on the chair lift Nimue said, 'I'm sorry about this morning. It was snow madness. When there's fresh snow and sun I just want to go fast and feel it under my skis and . . . I'm sorry, love.'

'I didn't mean to spoil it for you.'

'Anyway, after lunch we'll find some fresh powder, just for us, and I'll show you what it's like. It's a whole world better than being on the piste.'

He slipped an arm round her and his hand brushed against green fluffy ear muffs.

'Ears cold?'

'No, that was Allana. I'm just wearing them in case she asks if I did.'

She'd told him about the meeting with Allana in the ski shop and now, snuggling against him, filled in some of the details.

'. . . and she's just as crazy as ever. God knows what Horace Hent makes of her. I can't imagine her married to a man like that.'

'She probably won't be for long.' And Birdie passed on what Aeneas Campbell had told him about Hent's rapid turnover in wives.

She stared at him. 'What a peculiar man.'

'Aeneas or Horace Hent?'

'Both of them, but Hent especially. It's like an ogre in a fairy story drinking virgins' blood. Not that Allana's exactly that, but . . .'

39

The chair lift came to a halt, leaving them suspended high above the pine trees. Their chair moved gently up and down on its supporting cable like an indolent yo-yo. Five minutes or so later it started again and the delay was explained as a series of orange containers swung past them on the downward side, all marked with a double H.

Nimue said, 'They're using the lift to get things up and down for the satellite station, while the road's blocked.'

'Did Allana tell you what it's all about?'

'Apparently they're running a satellite service to cable networks in Western Europe, especially where there are a lot of British or American expats.'

'I wouldn't have thought that was much of a market.'

'Allana says it all depends on the advertising.'

They were near the top of the lift now, almost level with a huge wooden cross that topped a rocky outcrop on their right-hand side. Birdie had noticed what seemed to be a competition among the devout of the Alps to put these crosses in the most inaccessible places possible. But two visitors at least had made their way across to it, a couple dressed alike in pink and grey ski suits.

Nimue said, 'Shall we stroll over there before lunch? There's probably a good view down the valley.'

As they got off the lift Birdie glanced inside the shed and saw that the chair with his strip of anorak attached had been shunted into a kind of siding where it hung motionless with other chairs awaiting repair. It still made him angry to think of Wayne. They walked round to the back of the shed, left their skis propped against it and picked up the path to the rocky outcrop.

It was no more than a line in the snow trampled by several pairs of ski boots. As they got nearer the cross they could see that there were three people there. The woman was sitting at the foot of the outcrop with a boy

40

whom Birdie recognised as one of the Alderman Kibbalts lot beside her. The man was standing beside the cross itself and appeared to be making a speech to the valley. As Birdie and Nimue got closer, some words drifted down to them.

'I will lift up mine eyes unto the hills, from whence cometh my help . . .'

It was a sonorous American voice.

'What the . . . ?'

'My help cometh from the Lord, which made . . .'

Then the woman's voice, firmly, 'No, Joshua, it won't do.'

The man turned away from the valley and looked down at her. 'You don't think so?' he asked, in a subdued voice.

'No, Joshua. It hasn't got the elevation.'

She turned and saw Birdie and Nimue who'd stopped some way from the rocks, reluctant to disturb a religious service. The boy saw them too and blushed.

She said, 'Hello. Are you climbers?'

Birdie started to explain about just going for a walk before lunch, but she cut him off.

'I mean, are you spiritual climbers?'

She was, perhaps, in her early fifties – a brown-faced wiry woman with an unexpectedly deep and attractive voice. One glance at Birdie's face seemed to give her the answer she needed, and she went on, 'Joshua and I are surveying.'

'It looks a very nice place,' he said politely.

She gave him a shrewd glance. 'Have you any idea what I'm talking about?'

'No,' said Nimue.

'Always ask. Knock and it shall be opened unto you. Joshua and I are looking for places to build churches.'

It had struck Birdie that it was a part of the world well

41

provided with churches. He said so.

'Not ours. Have you heard of the Fellowship of the Climbers of Mount Tabor?'

'Er . . . I'm not sure we've got it in England.'

She said tolerantly, 'We have many fellow climbers in England. We're hoping to build a church on the summit of your Snowdon mountain.'

Nimue said, 'There's a café there already.'

'Then we'll turn the café into a church. The mountain-tops are for churches, not cafés.'

A large square man had arrived beside them, panting from his descent.

'This is my husband, Climbing Guide Joshua Jones. I'm Barbie.'

'Climbing guide in a spiritual sense that is,' he explained, holding out his hand to them.

Barbie turned to the boy, sitting motionless on the rock beside her.

'And this is the newest young member of our climbing team, Tim.'

Nimue said to him, 'You're with the Alderman Kibbalts group, aren't you?'

He nodded, red and tongue-tied. Birdie remembered that when he'd noticed him the boy had always been on the fringes of the group, never part of it. He skied better than the others, and usually on his own.

'Shouldn't you be down there getting some lunch?'

The boy seemed to take it as a command. He stood up immediately, murmured something to Barbie Jones, and set off for the ski-lift hut.

'He's a fine young man,' said Barbie Jones as they watched the boy march, stiff-backed, along the snow path.

Joshua, meanwhile, was scenting new converts. 'You'll have noticed that the scriptures are full of references to

42

mountaintops. Moses and Mount Sinai . . .'

Barbie made it a duet. 'The Mount of Olives, the Sermon on the Mount, then there's Mount Tabor itself of course . . .'

'We've been to all of them, Barbie and I, with parties of our fellow climbers . . .'

'Then there's the case of Sodom and Gomorrah.'

'But,' Birdie objected, dragging up remnants of scripture classes, 'Sodom and Gomorrah were cities of the Plain.'

Husband and wife beamed at him.

'Exactly. Because they were cities of the Plain they couldn't help but be sinful.'

Birdie felt as if he were sinking in soft snow. Nimue was no help. He didn't know if her silence meant she was trying not to explode with laughter, or with irritated logic.

'So you go round the world looking for mountains to build churches on? It must come expensive.'

'It certainly does, which is why we depend on the efforts of our fellow climbers at base camp.'

'Spiritual base camp?'

Barbie said cheerfully, 'We have our own television channel back home. It's bringing in more fellow climbers all the time.'

And Joshua, less cheerfully, 'We are planning on using television in Europe, but that's not so easy.'

Birdie said, meaning it as a joke, 'Perhaps you should ask Horace Hent for a piece of his satellite.'

And Joshua, darkly, 'We have, this morning.'

'So Horace Hent isn't a fellow climber?'

Joshua shook his head, but Barbie said, as sunny as ever, 'Not yet. But God has His own ways with people who use the mountaintops.'

Birdie and Nimue said goodbye to the spiritual climbing

43

team and walked back towards the hut.

Birdie said, 'You got rid of young Tim quickly, didn't you?'

'Did I? I suppose that kind of thing worries me. I mean, it's all right for them, they've chosen it, but to try to drag anybody in at that age . . .'

But the seriousness didn't last long.

'Did you notice where those two came from? I saw it on her camera case: Plains, Georgia.'

They laughed and he slipped an arm around her.

'Do you realise, Horace Hent's had quite a morning. The road's blocked, then Wayne steals his little television, Ray badgers him for a ski school and those two turn up and start demanding some of his satellite time.'

'Probably an average morning in the life of a multimillionaire.'

They had a good leisurely lunch in the little café at the top of the ski slopes, finishing a bottle of Valpolicella between them and lingering over cups of black bitter coffee, with the idea of sobering up before putting their skis on again.

'You can get drunk on the powder, even without wine,' Nimue said.

The glint was back in her eyes and he told himself to enjoy the snow and the sun and being together, instead of worrying on about jobs and flats and this time next year. The calculator that had lodged itself in his brain tried again to click out that this was easier in your twenties than your forties, but he determinedly shut it off.

'This powder snow of yours – where do we find it?'

Apparently you had to look for it away from the pistes where machines rolled and packed the snow into a compliant carpet, away from the moguls and other people's ski tracks. They found it off to the right-hand

44

side of the red run among the pine trees, just out of sight though not out of sound of the chair lift. This was a relief to Birdie who had a suspicion that powder snow was going to be even less tractable than the other kind and didn't want to prove it under the eyes of the Alderman Kibbalts lot.

Nimue paused, leaning on her ski sticks. 'It's mostly a matter of confidence. You have to point your skis downhill more, weight well back and ski tips up.'

And she set off in slow lazy turns down a slope of small larch bushes, the loose snow blowing up behind her skis like spray from a speed boat. After two or three turns the pace got faster and the turns tighter until she was carving regular S-shapes in the snow round the larch bushes, her body moving as rhythmically as a dancer's. After a hundred yards or so of this, rather to Birdie's relief, she fell in a great explosion of snow, and her laughter drifted to him up the mountain.

'How not to do it. Come on, have a go.'

He pointed his skis downhill and followed, missed the first few larch bushes by a hair's breadth, swerved wildly to avoid a more substantial pine and swooped in a great cloud of snow on down the hill and past Nimue.

'How do you stop?'

Her voice followed him, choked with laughter. 'Turn. You're supposed to turn.'

He tried to turn the way he'd been taught on the piste, and the snow came up to meet him like cumulus cloud swallowing a jet. He lay there, giddy from the wine and the speed, looking up through clouds of snow at thicker clouds gathering in the sky.

Nimue, herself snow-covered, was beside him, and anxious. 'Birdie love, are you hurt?'

He closed his eyes and said nothing, heard her unclip her skis and felt her kneel down in the snow.

45

'What is it? Is it your back?'

He couldn't move far because one of his boots was still attached to a ski, but he could move quickly, hooking an arm round her waist and pulling her on top of him.

'Birdie, you brute, I thought . . .'

He kissed her, and after a while she knelt up, laughing and breathless.

'You are a sod. I thought you'd really hurt yourself.'

'That was preventive first aid.'

He told her he was comfortable where he was, but she persuaded him to get up and they brushed some of the snow off each other, though it still clung like sifted flour to hair, eyebrows and the stitching of their anoraks.

'It doesn't matter anyway,' Nimue said. 'We'll fall over again.'

And they did, leaving soft craters among the larch bushes linked by Nimue's long trails of S shapes and the diagonal dashes that were the best Birdie achieved. But he was happy to be away from the Alderman Kibbalts crowd on the piste and to feel Nimue relaxing. At some point she managed to lose the green ear muffs and said they could stay there till the snow melted.

They decided to end the powder snow session as clouds settled on the pass and small gritty spots of snow began to fall. They cut back through the trees on to the red piste, taking it slowly because the light was failing, and by the time they got to the bottom snow was falling more heavily. There weren't many skiers left on the nursery slopes and most of the chairs clanked in and went back up the mountain empty.

Nimue said, 'Hotel and bed?'

Birdie thought that was a good idea. They stood together at the bottom of the chair lift, luxuriously delaying the moment when they'd turn for home and the billowing white duvet.

The light was getting worse all the time and when they looked up the chairs vanished into mist as if there were no mountain there at all. Then a dark mass loomed out of the mist on the downward cable and resolved itself into a chair full of ferociously striped anoraks: Brenda, Cathy and Monica crammed altogether into one chair, giggling and shrieking as the exit point came into view because their feet and skis were hopelessly entangled.

'Brenda, move yours back. Brenda. Brenda, stop mucking about.'

A wail from the girl in the middle. 'I can't. I'm trying to. Honestly.'

'Stop it, you two. We're going to get all mashed up in the machinery.'

A few yards from the exit point the giggles stopped and the shrieks took over in earnest. The ski attendant – like the one who'd raged at Birdie that morning – swore, dashed into his box and must have pressed the emergency button because the chair came to a halt. He reappeared and dragged Brenda out smartly so that the other two came with her, toppling on the snow in a heap of skis and clashing stripes.

He said to them, in serviceable English, 'Your teachers have told you, you are only allowed to go two in one chair, not three.'

Brenda picked herself up.

'We haven't done it any harm.'

'If you do it again they will take your lift pass away, so you don't ski any more.'

'I don't care. I hate skiing.'

She looked down at her friends.

'Come on, you two. Let's go and get ready for the sodding disco.'

And, giggling again, they skittered off over the snow, with sidelong glances at Birdie and Nimue. As they went, one of them waved at a figure who'd just skied down and was making for the chair lift to go up the mountain again.

'Hello, Tim. You not coming to the disco then?'

Tim didn't answer, just slid along on his skis, head down against the snow, giving no sign that he noticed anybody else.

Nimue whispered, 'Poor Tim. Always on his own.'

The attendant was already back in his cabin, talking vehemently into the telephone. When he saw Tim he pressed the button to restart the chairs but went on talking.

Nimue said, 'He's probably bawling out the attendant at the top for letting them get on three at once.'

They watched idly, arms round each other. Within a minute or so Tim was out of sight as the lift carried him up into the snow. The chairs clanked empty down from the lowering sky and went empty up again, while the attendant in his cabin carried on what looked like an increasingly angry conversation. Then three more customers arrived on the upward side, anorak collars up and caps pulled well down over their ears. They were arguing as they came.

'I just can't see the point in going up again.'

'Yeah, you can't get up any speed in this shit, Wayne. You can't see where you're going.'

'You don't have to see where you're going, do you? You just point your skis downhill and go.'

Joe and Sidney didn't seem convinced, but what Wayne said went. They slotted their skis into the snow ruts and were scooped up by the next chair. As they started their upward journey Wayne moved in to take the next chair and at the same time a single figure, cradling its skis in its arms, came into view on the downward side.

Sidney called down to Wayne, 'It's bloody Reeve, carrying his skis down.'

Wayne gave a war whoop and thumped into his chair. It hoisted him skywards and for a few seconds he and the man descending were on a level with each other, their faces only yards apart.

'What's up then, Mr Reeve? Not skiing down. Lost your bottle, have you?'

Then Wayne followed his friends into invisibility and Ray Reeve swung in to land, his face pinched with cold or anger. He looked even more annoyed when he saw Birdie and Nimue standing there.

Birdie asked, 'Are you all right?' and got a few words thrown at him: 'Binding broke in the powder.'

And without any other acknowledgment Ray Reeve stumped away towards the road.

'Ray's not having much of a day of it either, is he?'

With the visibility getting worse, there didn't seem likely to be any more customers for the upward chair lift. The attendant had put down the phone at last and he came out to unhook the chain that would close off the entrance, signifying the end of the afternoon's skiing.

'Time to go,' said Nimue, glancing up at Birdie.

They bent down to unloose their ski bindings, Birdie having trouble with his as usual but this time accepting Nimue's help, clipped their skis together and glanced once more up the mountain. And, as they watched, one more passenger swung down out of the snow. First a grey blob, that took shape as an individual lounging in a corner of the chair. A pedestrian this one, without skis. A piebald pedestrian. The brown patches on Horace Hent's pony skin coat stood out so that for a while he seemed an assemblage of blotches, then, as the chair swung closer to the snow, the blotches coagulated into his small, relaxed form. The attendant recognised Hent

49

and moved in close to the getting-off point, ready to help the resort's only celebrity alight with dignity. A few yards to go now, with Hent's boots only a few feet above the snow. Time for him to stop relaxing, to make the small effort to stand up, with the attendant there ready to take his arm. Level now with the notice telling passengers to get off, and still Hent didn't move, made no effort to raise the safety bar across his lap. The attendant, with an expression on his face that said it was one of those afternoons, stepped in quickly to do it for him, pushed the bar back with a clang, took Hent firmly but respectfully by the elbow. The elbow moved unresistingly and Hent followed it, sprawling on top of the attendant, bringing them both down on the ridged snow with the next chair swinging towards them. It was Birdie who dashed across to the attendant's box to press the stop button, Nimue who went to the pair on the snow. The attendant stood up, face white, with Hent still sprawled face down at his feet.

'His . . . his heart?'

Nimue took Hent by the shoulders and turned him over gently. His face was pale, eyes closed. The chest of his pony skin coat was decorated with a bizarre badge, a protruding badge of yellow and red feathers. From the coat's hem, runnels of red were already marking the snow.

Nimue said, 'He's been shot. With an arrow.'

Shouts from above reminded them that there were still passengers on the lift, although not yet within sight.

From out of the snow, distant but carrying well, came Joshua Jones's unmistakable voice. 'Hey, you people, you won't go home and leave us up here?'

The attendant, moving in a daze like a man through water, went to the back of his cabin and began to drag

50

out a stretcher.

They brought more police in from Milan. Some of them operated at the biggest hotel in the village, where Hent and the rest of the personnel from the satellite station had their rooms, along with Joshua and Barbie Jones. Others, with their interpreters, moved into the Hotel Soldanella. As darkness fell the chair lift was cranked back into life and men carrying powerful lamps rode up and down it while below them other men on skis made torchlight searches of the piste. The lights, glowing disturbingly from the parts of the mountain where there was usually nothing but pine trees and darkness once the sun was down, were visible all night from the windows of the Soldanella.

The teachers reacted predictably. Ray Reeve, once his questioning by the police was over, simply disappeared. Fuzz was a tower of strength, insisting that she or Bruin must be present at the questioning of any Alderman Kibbalts pupil, squashing the more gruesome of the rumours that flew around, making frantic phone calls to England. Bruin supported her as well as he could, although his expression throughout the night was one of doomladen puzzlement. At Fuzz's insistence he even herded them all in to supper then got the disco going to keep occupied the people not immediately needed for questioning. He'd protested mildly, at first, that it hardly seemed respectful, but Fuzz pointed out briskly that most of them only knew Horace Hent by sight and cancelling the disco wasn't going to bring him back to life. So the events of an evening at the Hotel Soldanella were carried on to the endless pulsation of the disco beat. Now and then one of the seven pupils who had actually been on the lift near the time of the murder would appear at the door of the disco with conscious

51

drama and there would be a surge forward, everyone wanting to know what the police had asked. Brenda, Monica and Cathy – once they'd grasped they weren't going to be prosecuted for riding three to a chair lift – revelled in the attention. Wayne, Joe and Sidney appeared at the disco much later, noticeably more subdued but playing it cool. Tim, as usual, didn't appear at all.

Much of the interest had been in whether anybody had seen the corpse, and on this point Brenda and friends and Wayne and friends were equally disappointing. The consensus in the disco was that Horace Hent had been machine-gunned by the Mafia. But the music went on and, once the stars in the show had been given their few minutes in the spot light, the dancing resumed. At eleven o'clock it was still going strong until it suddenly stopped in mid beat and the ceiling lights were switched on by a hand at the door. Cries of protest arose at what the dancers took to be their teachers' intervention. But the cries trailed off into a tense silence as they saw who was standing at the door. Fuzz, yes, and Bruin behind her, still looking as if he couldn't believe what was happening. But with Bruin and Fuzz, two uniformed policemen and another unknown man in civilian clothes.

The three men advanced silently into the middle of the floor and one of the policemen asked in English, 'Does anyone here own this?'

The man in civilian clothes took his arm from behind his back and held out the thing he was holding so that everybody in the room could see it. A bow. A small crossbow with a polished wooden butt and a trigger like a rifle's, and a fibreglass crosspiece.

'Yeah. It's mine.'

And Wayne stepped forward as casually as if he were claiming something left on a bus.

*

52

The first light was already touching the tops of the mountains when they took Wayne away in the car to Milan. By then they'd searched the room he shared with Joe and found three crossbow bolts with red and yellow feathers in his drawer. They'd questioned Joe, Sidney and Wayne again, taken fingerprints, with Fuzz always in the background vibrating with resentment and anxiety. Frantic phone calls to England had been made from the hotel reception desk, consular staff roused from their beds. Somehow, on the fringe of it all, Bruin, with help from Nimue and Birdie, managed to persuade most of the Alderman Kibbalts party to their rooms, if not to their beds, ignoring questions about whether Italy had an electric chair.

Birdie and Nimue were watching from the window of their room as two grim-faced men ushered Wayne into the back of a car. It drove slowly through the sleeping village, on its way down the valley. Birdie put his arm round Nimue's shoulder and felt her whole body tense and hard. He said apologetically, 'The police had no choice.'

A few years ago he'd still been a policeman, and watching them at work had brought an immediate feeling of familiarity.

She said, 'He says he didn't do it.'

The obvious reply would have been cruel. He knew all too well what Nimue was remembering – a time when she'd been taken away, probably by men who looked much like those, for a crime she hadn't committed.

'Love, it's not the same. Not you and Wayne. He's . . .'

'Guilty?'

A sideways look at him, very different from the one she'd given him just a few hours ago, waiting idly by the chair lift and thinking of bed. A look that made him feel he was talking from the other side of a crevasse, and that

53

feeling made him angry.

'Yes, guilty.'

He thought of Wayne cannoning into him, of the miniature TV set dropped on the piste after Wayne denied having it.

'His sort don't know when they're lying or not.'

'His sort?'

The crevasse widened. He turned away.

'Let's go and see if there's any coffee.'

CHAPTER FOUR

There was coffee, and sitting drinking it were the three Alderman Kibbalts teachers in an otherwise empty dining room. Ray Reeve had reappeared from wherever he'd been during the night and looked every bit as tired as the other two. But he was dressed in polo-neck and salopettes as if it were a normal skiing morning.

Bruin explained for him. 'Ray's going to try and get them off to ski school as usual. We've got to do something with them.'

Outside the light was broadening into a fine, clear morning but the atmosphere inside felt jaded and stale, as if too many people had slept in their clothes. Bruin's face was puffy and mushroom-coloured. Fuzz's eyes were sinking deep pits into her face and she was tearing a bread roll into fragments. From where she was sitting she could see the reception desk and she kept her eyes fixed on it.

'We're waiting for a call from England. They're trying to trace Wayne's father.'

'No mother?' Birdie asked, mildly curious.

She glanced at him as if it were his fault, then back at the reception desk.

'She walked out when Wayne was three. Wayne said his father was working on an oil rig in the North Sea.'

Bruin said mildly, 'That's just the kind of thing Wayne

55

would say.'

Fuzz said, flatly, 'It's natural to fantasise at Wayne's age. It's part of the adaptation process.'

Nimue murmured 'yes', but Reeve, who'd been drinking his coffee as if the conversation had nothing to do with him, made a derisive noise.

'What about shooting people with crossbows? Is that part of the adaptation process?'

He pushed his cup away and marched out of the room, his woollen socks padding on the polished floor.

Fuzz said, 'There goes the voice of justice.'

'Would you call . . . ?'

'Yes, I would. The same sort of justice that pulls a kid like Wayne in as soon as anything happens because he's got a record . . .'

'And a crossbow,' Birdie thought, but was too cautious to say it.

'. . . and interrogates him all night and tricks him into saying things and . . .'

Bruin, on this occasion, had more nerve than Birdie. He said: 'Fuzz, you can't say they tricked him about the crossbow. They just asked whose it was.'

'Yes, but what about the way they kept battering on at them just because they were on the bloody chair lift? And Tim.'

'You have to admit, the easiest way of shooting somebody on a chair lift is if you're travelling on the same chair lift in the opposite direction.'

'Why? It might have been someone on the ground. Or in one of the trees.'

Birdie could think of several reasons why not and so, probably, could Bruin, but he clearly didn't want to take on Fuzz again. The four of them sat there drinking coffee as the dining room filled up slowly with Alderman Kibbalts pupils notably more subdued than usual. There was no sign yet of Sidney and Joe or Brenda and friends, but Tim, hollow-eyed, sat on his own at the end of a table, applying jam to a roll as if marks were awarded for neatness. Birdie doodled on the back of a ski map:

Brenda
Monica } Down
Cathy

He paused, wondering how long it had been between them and the next passenger, then remembered that one of the girls had actually called to Tim as they were walking away. Say three minutes, including the time when the lift had been stopped. He shaded in a three-minute gap then added another name to his list:

Tim } Up

They'd watched Tim out of sight then lingered, what, say three or four minutes before Ray Reeve swung into view, and that had coincided more or less with the arrival of Wayne and friends.

Joe
Sidney } Up
Wayne

Ray Reeve } Down

Then five minutes, perhaps longer, while they'd struggled with his binding and got their skis together. Then:

Hent (Deceased) } Down

They'd gone over it all several times with the police and he was trying to convince himself that he hadn't, out of underlying hostility, left anything out of the account that might help Wayne. But he couldn't in all honesty find anything. The facts looked as damningly clear to

57

him as they did to the Italian police.

Birdie had, from curiosity, timed the chair lift on his first day and he knew it took around twelve minutes to complete its journey. On that basis Tim must have been near the top of the lift, perhaps at the top by the time Hent began his last journey, and Wayne, Joe and Sidney had passed him something like halfway.

Nimue had the advantage of understanding what had been going on in Italian all night. He asked her, 'That crossbow, do you know exactly where they found it?'

'I told you, under the chair lift.'

'I know. The point is, where exactly under the chair lift? Top, bottom, halfway?'

'Just below halfway, in the pine wood.'

It was a relief to him that however often you swung the pointer, it ended up pointing to Wayne every time.

Nimue said, following his thoughts, 'But that's circumstantial.'

In an odd way, tiredness suited her, drawing the skin tighter across her high cheekbones, making her eyes even more dark. He leant close to her, speaking softly so that Fuzz wouldn't hear.

'Love, do you really believe he didn't do it?'

She stared at him, as if the need to ask the question had puzzled her.

'I want him to have a fair chance.'

A man in skiing clothes strode into the lobby leaving the outer door swinging behind him, and walked up to the reception desk. The girl at the desk bent towards him, then pointed through to the dining room. Birdie thought it was yet another plain clothes man, but then he saw it was Aeneas Campbell, face red from the cold air and his eyebrows standing out pale against it. He came over to their table and stood in front of them.

'Is one of you Nimue Hawthorne?'

Fuzz had tensed even more, expecting yet another call on her resources. Nimue glanced at her before replying.

'I am. What do you want?'

'You're Allana's friend?'

'Yes.'

'She wants to see you.'

Nimue was on her feet at once. 'Where is she? At her hotel?'

Aeneas shook his head. 'She's still up at the satellite station.'

'But why? Won't the police let her come down?'

'The police have been trying to persuade her to come down. So have I, so has everybody else. She simply refuses to use the chair lift.'

'Poor Allana.'

'She asked me to come and find you. I thought perhaps you might be able to persuade her.'

Nimue glanced apologetically at Birdie, then dashed upstairs for her anorak while Aeneas slumped into her empty chair and accepted lukewarm coffee. He explained that Allana, along with himself and four technicians, were still up at the satellite station when the news of Hent's death was broken to them. They were clearing up after the afternoon, all except the two nightwatchmen, intending to go down in the next few minutes before the lift closed for the day. Allana had always disliked the chair lift, and her main reaction to her husband's death had been a hysterical refusal ever to travel in it again. The police had to question her there in Hent's office at the end of the tunnel and what little sleep she had was on his big leather sofa.

'We all tried to persuade her, but she says she'll stay up there till the snow melts if need be.'

Fuzz showed a tendency to add this problem to her list. She said accusingly to Aeneas, 'Couldn't you fly her

59

out by helicopter?'

'Not today and probably not tomorrow. There's still too much wind up at the top.'

Nimue reappeared in anorak and boots. She stopped briefly at Birdie's chair. 'I'm sorry, love, but I can't leave Allana on her own. Do what you can.'

A touch on his shoulder, then she and Aeneas Campbell were gone, setting the door swinging again.

Birdie turned over in his mind her words, 'Do what you can'. He had, unfortunately, no doubt at all what she meant by them. Do what you can for bloody Wayne. Although he knew the reasons for her concern, part of him resented that she should be so bothered about the wretched boy. He couldn't help dwelling on the boy's youth, his arrogance, the fact that Nimue stood, in the great tract of time that divided himself and Wayne, marginally closer to sixteen than to forty-three. And even that wouldn't have mattered so much, except for the feeling that it wasn't so much a tract of time as a canyon, with an unbridgeable divide somewhere around that halfway point. Fuzz had said with certainty that it was natural to fantasise at Wayne's age, and Nimue had immediately agreed with her. But, trying to think himself back to Wayne's age, he couldn't remember any such difficulty in distinguishing between what was real and what wasn't. Had he forgotten or did that canyon really mark some change in the nature of adolescence, with him on one side of it and Wayne and Nimue on the other? It was an idea he found much more worrying than anything that was happening to Wayne. He sighed, gulped his cold coffee, and tried conscientiously to carry out her instructions.

'Tell me about this crossbow.'

A short, embarrassed silence, then Bruin said, 'We slipped up there a bit.'

'You mean . . . you knew he had one?'

'No, but we should have guessed. You see, he's fairly obsessed with weapons, and some fool showed him this piece in a magazine about how you can buy hunting crossbows without a licence or anything. The next thing we knew, he was carrying this mail order catalogue around.'

'Openly?'

'Well, secretly but meant to be seen, if you understand what I mean. Part of Wayne's on-going campaign against authority.'

'Um. So he bought this crossbow?'

'We didn't know that, did we, Fuzz?'

She shook her head, clearly wanting no part in the conversation.

Bruin went on, 'But we should have suspected it. The three of them had their heads together on the coach from Milan, and I thought then they'd smuggled something through Customs.'

'Did you guess it was the crossbow?'

'No. I assumed it was probably Scotch or cigarettes.'

'So when did you know they had this crossbow with them?'

'When Wayne claimed it in the disco.'

Fuzz suddenly came back to life. 'I don't see why they're sure it was that crossbow that killed Hent.'

Bruin said, 'It was the same sort of bolt as the ones in his drawer.'

'Aren't they all the same?'

Bruin caught Birdie's eye, and committed the disloyalty of an exasperated look. Birdie realised that he and the young teacher were in much the same boat, virtually under orders from women who, for whatever reasons, wouldn't accept Wayne's guilt. He was filled with a need to get away from the hotel's oppressive

61

atmosphere, and it seemed only humane to take Bruin with him.

He suggested, 'Shall we take a ride up in the chair lift? See if it makes things any clearer?'

'Will they be running it?'

'We can go and see.'

Fuzz said she had to wait at the hotel in case Wayne's father phoned, so Bruin and Birdie set off up the street together, gulping in stinging lungfuls of mountain air. It took more than a murder to disrupt the economics of a ski resort and the lift was carrying skiers skywards as if Hent's body had never come swinging down. The only sign that anything had happened was a small group, composed mainly of Alderman Kibbalts pupils, standing as close as possible to the landing point and looking for traces of blood. Bruin ignored them, but as he and Birdie were waiting in the chair queue, added some morbid curiosity of his own.

'The chair he was in . . . do you think?'

'No,' said Birdie firmly. 'They've probably got it in the sidings at that shed at the top.'

Alongside, perhaps, the other chair with his fragment of ripped anorak. It was a shock to realise that less than twenty-four hours ago that had been the darkest suspicion attaching to Wayne. From that, through theft of the miniature television to murder seemed meteoric progress in crime.

As they shuffled into place and waited for the chair, Birdie noticed that Bruin's feet were in training shoes.

'Don't you find those a bit slippy?'

'Yes. Fuzz said I should get proper walking boots, but they're awfully expensive.'

It occurred to Birdie that Bruin probably got even less for worrying over the Alderman Kibbalts lot than he did for reducing the waistlines of middle-aged businessmen

62

at the gym. The chair swung at them and he managed to bundle Bruin into it.

The pine tree tops were glistening under fresh snow and the sun was bright again.

'Better than yesterday afternoon,' Birdie said. 'Did you have trouble with the visibility?'

Bruin and Fuzz, questioned routinely by the police along with everyone else, had explained that they were skiing together on the blue run and didn't hear about the murder until they got back to the hotel. Birdie suspected, from Bruin's plumpness and physical awkwardness, that he was an inept skier. Bruin confirmed it.

'With my sort of skiing it doesn't matter if you can see or not. You still fall over.'

Birdie looked carefully at the chairs passing them on the downward side, mostly empty because at this stage in the morning skiers were going up the mountain rather than down it. He filled one of them, in his imagination, with the pony skin-parcelled figure of Horace Hent. The chair was higher than they were, perhaps about twenty feet above the pine trees, and descending towards them on a shallow gradient. As it swung closer the height difference levelled out, so that for six seconds by Birdie's stopwatch it was travelling towards them only a few feet higher. As it passed it seemed so close that Birdie thought he could almost have touched a person in it, although in reality there were probably fifteen feet or so between them. Bruin, following his look, said, 'Near enough to shoot somebody.'

'You'd need a steady aim, but yes.'

'Wayne's probably got that all right,' said Bruin, rather bitterly. Birdie wondered if he too envied the boy's assurance.

Bruin added, 'But he'd see you taking aim.'

'There wouldn't be much he could do about it though,

would there?' As he said it, Birdie had an idea of the desperate loneliness of Horace Hent in those last few moments when the parcel of his life had come apart. For all his papers and his television channels and his money and his wives he'd have been as remote from help, suspended in a chair high above the snow, as in the middle of the Antarctic. He imagined Hent watching as Wayne on the upward chair came into view, seeing the crossbow, wriggling sideways perhaps, curling into a self-protective ball, but quite powerless to stop that bolt thudding into him.

He said to himself, 'Hent was shot in the chest. Right in the chest.'

Bruin nodded.

Birdie said, reluctantly, 'But that doesn't make sense, does it? If somebody in this chair just coming down were pointing a crossbow at you, you'd instinctively try to do something, wouldn't you?'

Bruin gave an alarmed glance at the oncoming empty chair, glanced at the snow twenty feet beneath as if estimating the possibility of jumping, then crossed his arms over his chest and hunched into a ball. In that position, anyone wanting to kill him must surely aim for the head rather than the chest. Bruin unfolded himself slowly, but while in a hunched position his mind seemed to have been moving fast.

'But would everyone react the same way? I mean, if you thought the person was just fooling about and you felt angry, for instance, you might go like this.'

He spread his arms theatrically, chest exposed, wagging a finger at the descending chairs. And Birdie agreed that, though less convincing, this too was possible. It was a fact that Hent had reason to be angry with Wayne because of the stolen television. Supposing he'd taken the crossbow to be a silly joke and found out only in the last split second of his life that it wasn't.

The chair lift had dipped a little and was now travelling about ten feet above a gulley of fresh snow.

Bruin said, 'It would be just possible, wouldn't it, to shoot somebody and then jump off the chair here so that you never got to the top of the lift. The snow would break your fall.'

'But you'd still have to get on at the bottom, and you'd leave a great pit if you jumped. Anything moving through deep snow leaves as many tracks as a hamster in a bowl of trifle.'

They rattled past one of the pylons that supported the cable. It had small metal rungs set in it, for use by maintenance men. Bruin tried again.

'An acrobatic type might climb up a pylon and shoot from there as the chair went past.'

'Yes, but he'd still have to get to the foot of the pylon through soft snow.'

'I see what you mean. Same point about the tracks. So it still looks like Wayne.'

He sounded as much relieved as regretful.

They were above the ski grounds now and past the last pylon, with skiers twisting and crashing in the mogul field below them. The long wooden hut was coming into view, and the ramp leading from it to the tunnel mouth.

Bruin said, thoughtfully, 'I suppose that's where they winch the crates up and down.'

'Yes.'

Birdie's mind wasn't on it. He was thinking of Nimue, wondering whether he'd see her appearing at the mouth of the tunnel with this friend of hers, the bereaved Mrs Hent. He had no doubt of her ability to sort out that little problem. He hoped she'd register, at least, that he was conscientiously going through the motions in the task she'd set him. Bruin was still talking.

'Supposing he was shot in the tunnel or the satellite

65

station. You could winch the body down the ramp and load him on to the chair already dead.'

'Two reasons why not. I reckon he was no more than a few minutes dead when he got to the bottom. Anyway, wouldn't the attendant up here notice if somebody started loading corpses on his lift?'

'But it wouldn't take that long. Maybe no more than a minute or two.'

Again, Birdie had to admit that might be the case. But it still left the problem of the attendant.

Bruin persisted, 'But if somebody walked him up to the chair with an arm round his shoulders . . .'

'You'd be running an impossible risk.'

'I suppose so.' Bruin thought about it a bit more and added, 'And you can't get away from the fact that Wayne owned the crossbow and the crossbow was found under the chair lift.'

When they'd got off the chair, Bruin suggested half-heartedly that they should question the attendant but they were handicapped by a shortage of Italian. Birdie pointed out too that this would be the first thing the police would have done, and they'd clearly discovered nothing that dissuaded them from arresting Wayne.

'What next?'

'Coffee.'

Outside the café door a class of Alderman Kibbalts pupils was getting itself organised, under the eye of a young Italian instructor. Most of them were struggling inefficiently with ski bindings and a few were trying to push each other down a snow bank. Tim, his skis already on, ski sticks in hand, stood some yards off, watching them without interest.

Birdie said, 'I'd like a word with him. I'll see you inside the café.'

He walked over to the boy. 'Hello, Tim. There are a

couple of things I'd like to ask you about yesterday.'

The boy nodded obediently, licking lips which Birdie noticed were slightly wind-chapped. He wore no ski cap but his thick, light-brown hair nestled neat as a cat's fur round ears and forehead. His cheeks were still childishly plump in an otherwise thin face.

'We saw you get on the chair lift ten minutes or so before Hent's body came down.'

Tim nodded again.

'And you've told the Italian police that Hent was still alive when your chair passed his chair?'

Another nod.

'Were you far up the lift when you passed him?'

'Near . . . near the top.'

Tim's eyes were worried and nervous. It could hardly be lost on him that his evidence helped to build up the case against Wayne.

'So he'd only just got on the lift then. How are you so sure he was alive?'

'He . . . he looked at me.'

'How did he look? Worried? Smiling?'

'No. He just looked.'

Birdie tried to choose his words carefully. Tim was a less tough character than most of the Alderman Kibbalts lot, and he didn't want to give him unnecessary nightmares.

'You don't think he could have been dead already? Just propped up there so that he looked as if he was alive?'

'No. His eyes were open.' Tim added, with more life in his voice, 'Anyway, he couldn't have been dead when I saw him, could he? Wayne got on the lift a long time after I did.'

Then he blushed at finding himself speaking so vehemently to an adult and looked away. Birdie felt sorry for him.

'Thanks, Tim. Your class seems to be moving off.

Hadn't you better join them?'

The others had got themselves into some sort of order and were following the instructor in an unsteady line over the snow.

'It doesn't matter. I can catch them up easily.'

It was said factually, without arrogance, and turned out to be true. Tim set off after the others in a controlled swoop that made their efforts look by contrast like a line-up of the seven dwarves.

Only two tables were occupied inside the café. In one corner Bruin was guarding two cups of coffee, Birdie's with the saucer upended over it to keep it warm. In the other corner, as far away as it was possible to get, the three girls who'd travelled down together in one chair the afternoon before talked and giggled with their heads together. Bruin seemed to be doing his best not to notice them.

He asked Birdie, 'Anything interesting from Tim?'

'Nothing new. He's a quiet sort of lad, isn't he? We saw him with those American missionaries yesterday.'

Bruin was unsurprised. 'The spiritual climbers. The woman, Barbie, came to Fuzz practically as soon as we arrived and said did we want to bring a party of kids to see a video about mountains at their hotel.' He smiled, but guiltily, at even a mild disloyalty to Fuzz.

'Fuzz jumped at it—she thought it would be about skiing. She took about a dozen of them down after dinner one evening and wasn't too pleased when it turned out the video was all about churches. Nor were they.'

'What happened?'

'Most of them walked out, but Tim was impressed and stayed on. His mother's a bit of a religious nut too, so I suppose he felt at home.'

Birdie glanced over at the group in the corner.

68

'Shouldn't Brenda and the others be at ski class?'

'I suppose they're too tired after last night.'

Bruin still didn't look towards the group, and Birdie suspected that he found the girl pupils hard to deal with. He suggested, 'I think I'll have a word with them. After all, they were up here yesterday afternoon.'

'But you told me they got down long before Hent's body.'

'Still . . .'

But Birdie didn't have to make the first approach. The girls had noticed him looking in their direction, and there was a little flurry of nudging and giggling before Brenda got up and walked over to him.

The walk was really something. There weren't many tables in the small café, but she managed to sway among them as if negotiating a slow slalom course, accompanied by muffled giggles from her two friends, before coming to rest beside Birdie.

'Is it true you're a detective?'

'No.'

'Monica says she saw you talking to Tim just now.'

'Yes.'

'You trying to clear Wayne's name?'

Birdie felt like saying that would be a job for an earth-mover. He restrained himself.

'I'm just trying to find out what happened.'

She nodded, looking down at him and narrowing her round eyes, as if he'd confirmed something she suspected.

'Aren't you going to ask us questions then?'

'All right. Why don't you ask your friends to come over.' He thought he caught a muffled groan from Bruin.

Brenda said, 'Will you buy us another coffee? We've run out of Italian money.'

By the time he got back from the counter with three

more cups, Brenda, Monica and Cathy were rearranging the chairs round the table with maximum noise. It was, too, a process that seemed to bring buttocks and thighs, taut in their ski pants, as close as possible to their teacher at every opportunity. Bruin looked as if he was not enjoying it and Birdie thought suddenly of his own daughter, who must be very much the same age as Brenda. When he'd last seen her, a fortnight earlier, her preoccupations were tennis and O-levels, in that order. At least, so it had seemed. He tried to put that distraction out of his mind.

'You three were up here yesterday afternoon?'

Brenda was spokeswoman. 'That's right.'

'Skiing?'

'No, just messing about.'

A scattering of giggles from the other two.

'Where?'

'Everywhere.'

'In the café?'

'We had a look in.'

'Who was in here when you looked in?'

Silence, then: 'That old American woman. The mad one. She was waiting for her husband.'

'Anyone else?'

Cathy, the plump one, put in helpfully, 'There weren't many people up here because of the weather.'

'When you were mucking about up here, could you always see the top of the chair lift and that ramp up to the tunnel?'

Brenda again: 'Yeah, I suppose so.'

'But you weren't looking at them all the time?'

'No.'

'Did you notice anything coming down that ramp?'

They looked at him as if he were mad, shaking their heads.

'How long were you up here?'

'Dunno.'

'Did you see Mr Hent at all?'

They even giggled about that, and seemed in no hurry to answer it. At last Brenda said, 'We saw him in the morning, when we were looking round the satellite place.'

'But after that?'

Giggles, and more head shakes. He tried another tack.

'You got into trouble for all coming down in the same chair.'

Brenda said, as she'd said to the attendant, 'We didn't do it any harm.'

'But there must have been an attendant up at the top as usual. Didn't he try to stop you?'

They glanced at each other.

'He was in his little hut thing. Listening to the radio.'

'So he didn't notice?'

'He did once we'd got on. He came out and started shouting at us in Italian, but he couldn't do nothing about it because we'd already started.'

'But you're certain there was an attendant there?'

'Yeah, of course.'

Brenda had managed to push her chair so close to Bruin that she was practically sitting in his lap. It was pity for him, as well as irritation with the girls, that made Birdie decide that things had gone on long enough.

'Thank you for helping. I'm sorry to have interrupted your morning.'

This abrupt ending to the scene left Brenda open-mouthed. She was just getting into her stride. Bruin's relief on the other hand was obvious. He stood outside the café door with Birdie, letting the breeze blow on his sweating forehead.

Birdie said, 'Do you get the impression they were

71

lying to us?'

Bruin looked alarmed at the idea. 'About what?'

'I don't know what about. I just got a strong impression there's something they're not telling us.'

'I wouldn't say so. They're always like that.'

'Doesn't it depress you sometimes, the thought of dealing with that for the next thirty-five years of your life?'

Such a bleak and numerical summary of a teacher's career had apparently never struck Bruin before, and he wrinkled his forehead trying to respond to it.

'I don't know. I mean, most of them are OK, and even when they're not there's always the hope that the next batch will be better.'

Birdie thought of an endless succession of Waynes and Brendas stretching down the years and realised Bruin was looking at him anxiously.

'I'd better get back down. Fuzz might be needing help.'

Birdie watched him slipping and sliding along the path to the chair lift, then took the higher track up towards the tunnel mouth. Nimue still hadn't reappeared and he decided it was time to go and find out what she was doing.

CHAPTER FIVE

'It's not that I'm not sorry about him,' Allana said. She was pacing, in black-stockinged feet, around the deep pile carpet, sandals abandoned on the rug, fingers twisting in the gold chains round her neck. Nimue was curled into a corner of the big leather sofa, watching her.

'It's not that I'm not sorry at all. There was always, you know, so much life about him, even if it wasn't the kind of life you liked.'

Nimue nodded. To one as restless by temperament as Allana, it probably seemed a personal insult that death could put a stop to anything she'd known.

'That was what attracted me to him at first. I know you think I only married him for his money . . .'

Nimue made a protesting noise.

'No, well, I did a bit. But I wouldn't have done it if I hadn't liked him at the start. He was, you know what I mean, good crack.'

She flopped down suddenly on the rug, her head on the sofa, touching Nimue's knee.

Nimue said, 'You need sleep. If I take you down to the hotel and stay with you . . .'

'It's no good Nimue. I'm not going down in that lift.'

'But it might be days before they get the road to the village open.'

'I'll stay here till the snow melts if I have to. I'm not

73

going on that chair lift.'

Nimue said gently, 'But it wasn't the lift that killed him.'

'But if he hadn't been on the lift that boy, what's his name . . . ?'

'Wayne.'

'Why did he do it? I asked the police why he did it, but they wouldn't tell me.'

'I think their idea is he'd just got the crossbow and he wanted to try it.'

'That's mad,' said Allana.

She moved her head from side to side as if to escape the thought of it.

Nimue said carefully, 'You know Wayne denies doing it?'

'Do you believe him?' Allana was kneeling on the rug now, looking up at her.

'I don't know. It's . . . it's just the feeling of how helpless you are if you really haven't done something but everybody thinks you have.'

A fleeting smile came over Allana's face.

'Oh, I know. In the convent once the nuns thought I'd smuggled in some Maltesers and I hadn't and I was furious, even though I'd done a hundred worse things they never found out about at all.' Then the cloud came over again. 'I felt like that when the police were asking me questions last night. As if they thought I'd killed him.'

'But you were nowhere near the chair lift at the time, were you?'

'Of course not. I kept telling them I was in this room all the time.'

Tears began running down her cheeks, and Nimue knelt beside her on the rug and held her while she sobbed.

74

'I suppose they thought I married him for his money so I probably killed him for his money. Do you think that was it?'

'Of course not. They were questioning all of us.'

'I thought it would be fun, all that money. I thought if you had so much money you wouldn't have to think about it all the time – you know, not like wondering whether you could afford the one pound fifty tights or make do with the sixty-five pence ones.' She gazed into Nimue's face as if the most important thing in the world was to get her understanding about the tights.

'But it doesn't work like that. He was thinking about money all the time. As if he had to have all the money in the world and all the newspapers in the world and all the televisions in the world. Then there wasn't enough in the world and so he has to go out into space, has to have his bit of satellite. Then he'll want a whole satellite to himself, then a lot of satellites, then . . .'

She was talking about him as if he were still alive, pouring out months of resentment, until she realised what she was doing.

'Oh, I didn't mean . . .'

She pounded on the sofa with her fists, sobbing, 'No, I did mean it. It doesn't make it different because he's dead.'

Nimue hugged her silently and after a while Allana said, in a calmer voice, 'It was the same with women. He'd see one he wanted and for the next few days there'd be nothing in the world except getting her. You know, one day I was a publicity assistant in his office in London, and three days later there I was sitting at a dinner table with him, an Italian prince and an American presidential candidate, and I'm the one he's listening to.'

Which showed, Nimue thought, a sound grasp of psychology on the part of the late Hent. Allana would never tolerate being ignored, even for a president.

'You know, you think you're something special, but you find out later from all the other wives that it was just the same with them.'

Nimue asked, surprised, 'You've been comparing notes with his ex-wives?'

Another fleeting smile, as when Allana was remembering annoying the nuns. She scrambled to her feet, taking a key from her pocket and fetched a plump yellow envelope file from a case in the corner. She delved into it and fanned out a handful of letters. Some were handwritten on various colours of paper, some typed, some airmail forms. 'It's a sort of club. We call it the GBH club.'

'Grievous bodily harm?'

'No. Getting Back at Hent.'

She tidied the letters back into the file and replaced it in the case.

Nimue asked, 'You mean all Hent's ex-wives write to each other comparing notes about him?'

'More than that. We discuss what to do about him.'

'Like what?'

'We were planning some fun – like buying up shares in some of his companies and voting against him at meetings and things like that.'

Nimue knew from the old days that Allana's idea of fun usually amounted to serious breach of the peace, but in those days it was never worked out in advance.

'Did you dream up all this?'

'Oh no. One of the others wrote to me about it the day after the wedding. I thought it was in poor taste at the time. Two months later I wrote back and asked could I join.'

Allana settled back beside Nimue on the rug. 'Darling, you're looking all shocked and disapproving. You don't

76

expect us to fight like cats just because we were all married to him?'

It had always been one of Allana's talents to make the maddest course of conduct sound like the only sensible thing to do – as long as you were with her.

Nimue said, 'I suppose you didn't tell the police about this GBH club?'

'Darling, why on earth would they be interested?'

Birdie made his way up the steep path from the chair lift shed to the tunnel mouth. Planks had been pushed into it as rough-and-ready steps but now they were almost covered with snow, their projecting edges glossed with thin films of ice, more slippery than the trodden snow around them. Even if you admitted the possibility that Hent had been killed somewhere up in the satellite station or the tunnel, that the murderer had managed to load him on to a chair within minutes of his death, unnoticed by the attendant, there was still the question of how he'd managed to manoeuvre the body down this slippery path to the chair lift unseen. There'd have been skiers not far below and anyone could have looked out of the café window. The visibility was quite bad at the time, but not bad enough to cover such a risk. Once again, the more you looked at it, the more you came back to the chair lift and Wayne. But with resentful stubbornness, Birdie would go on testing it until even Fuzz and Nimue had to accept Wayne's guilt. He walked along the tunnel, turning the idea over in his mind. The floor was of hard beaten snow, with deep ruts scored where they must have manoeuvred the crates along to the ramp. They gleamed in the light of electric bulbs along the roof. At some points small streams had worked their way through the rock and solidified into ribs of green ice down the walls. Almost as soon as he was inside the mountain the tunnel turned so that the daylight was lost. Its length surprised him. He'd been walking for about two minutes before it turned again and a circle of daylight appeared at the far end. Not knowing about the door that led to Hent's sanctum he walked past it and came out into the light below the great transmitter dish. Aeneas Campbell was talking to a technician in the control room, but came out when he saw Birdie.

'Nimue's still in there with Allana.'

Aeneas looked as tired as everybody else did that morning, but there was a heaviness about him, a stunned way of moving that suggested grief as well as tiredness. And Birdie realised with a shock that this was the first sign of grief he'd met for Horace Hent. He said, 'I'm sorry.'

Aeneas just said 'Yes,' and looked at him, weighing the words as if they meant something. Then: 'It seems . . . rather a waste.'

He began walking slowly with Birdie back towards the tunnel entrance.

Birdie asked, 'Has Mrs Hent agreed to come down with Nimue?'

'I don't know. I left her to it.' His tone said very clearly that he'd had more than enough of Allana Hent. Birdie wondered if, with Hent's death, she was now his boss. He looked at the vast white dish and the dark mouth of the tunnel.

'Will she inherit all this?'

Aeneas stared as if he thought Birdie were weak in the head. 'Good heavens no. It's a multi-national company, not a semi in Hendon.'

'But she'll get something. I mean, more than if they just divorced?'

'I imagine she'll inherit a substantial part of his

78

personal estate – which should be enough for a girl who used to be one of his typists.'

'You think she married him for his money?'

Again a look suggesting that Birdie hadn't even started on the facts of life.

'They all did. He felt safer that way. He knew where he was.'

They were back at the tunnel now. Aeneas stopped just before they stepped out of the sunlight into the darkness and turned to him.

'So if you're suggesting that Mrs Hent might be a helpful diversion, you're probably right.'

Birdie gaped at him. 'Diversion?'

'If the defence are thinking of lining up a list of people who might have wanted to kill him, there'd be no shortage.'

Birdie said, alarmed, 'But I'm not defending Wayne. I'm just trying to get clear what happened.'

Aeneas went on as if he hadn't spoken. 'A man like Hent attracts enemies. Only none of them happened to be on that chair lift at the material time.'

And he led the way into the tunnel. Birdie, following, recognised war had been declared, and couldn't find it in his heart to blame the man. In his mind, however unfairly, Birdie and Nimue were associated with the school party. At the steel door Aeneas paused.

'If you want to ask Mrs Hent anything, I'd be obliged if you'd do it as tactfully as possible. Frankly, all I'm concerned with at the moment is getting her down.'

He opened the door and the shock of the luxury of Hent's adapted cavern, after the rock and ice of the tunnel outside, was succeeded by another shock of seeing Nimue on the sofa with Allana's head resting on her shoulder, eyes closed. Allana looked ridiculously young like that, almost as young as the girls in the

Alderman Kibbalts party, and there seemed a schoolgirl intimacy about the two of them, so that the abyss in his mind opened up again, the feeling of exclusion from part of Nimue's life. But she smiled and looked relieved when she saw him.

Aeneas said flatly, 'Allana, Mr Linnet wants to talk to you.' And Allana's eyes flew open, scared and resentful.

This hadn't been at all Birdie's idea, and he recognised it as part of the man's hostility and grief. Aeneas was out to rub their noses in Wayne's guilt and seeing Birdie, however unfairly, as on the boy's side, was going to embarrass him as much as possible. It occurred to him that the idea of hurting Mrs Hent might also be part of it, and he decided he didn't like the polite Aeneas Campbell much after all. But, having been pushed into it, he'd flounder on. It might at least show Nimue he was taking the task she'd set him seriously. So when Aeneas asked, 'Do you want me to stay?' he paid him back in his own coin and said politely that he did, if it was no trouble. Aeneas sat himself at Hent's desk.

Birdie asked, 'What was the last anybody up here saw of Mr Hent?'

He knew the police would have gone over this many times in the long night, so wasn't surprised when Aeneas replied promptly, 'I was the last to see him, at about twenty past three that afternoon. We'd been discussing something in the transmission room and I walked halfway back along the tunnel with him, carrying on the discussion. When we'd settled it, I went back to the transmission room and he went on towards the chair lift end of the tunnel.'

'What sort of mood was he in?'

'Normal. Concerned about one or two technical points with the first transmission tomorrow, but nothing that couldn't be sorted out.'

Three twenty, and Hent's body had arrived at the bottom of the lift around a quarter to four. With an old policeman's instinct, Birdie had checked his watch at the time. That allowed him twenty-five minutes after parting from Hent to walk the rest of the way along the tunnel and down to the shed and make the twelve minute journey down the chair lift, alive or dead. So it had, if Aeneas was right, taken thirteen minutes for Hent to walk halfway along the tunnel and down the admittedly slippery path to the lift. That seemed to Birdie a surprisingly long time. But then Hent might have slipped or had trouble with his boots, or even stopped to talk to somebody on the way.

'Did anybody else see him on the way down?'

Aeneas shook his head. 'Not as far as we can find out, or the police.'

Which brought Birdie to the point that had been troubling him.

'What about the attendant. Wouldn't he have helped him on to the chair?'

Aeneas said, 'Normally, yes he would. But I gather from the police he was on the telephone at the time.'

A gasp from Nimue. She said to Birdie, 'Of course, don't you remember? He was having a shouting match with the attendant down at the bottom about letting Brenda and Cathy and Monica get on at the same time.'

A look of gloomy smugness on Aeneas' face. Once again the Alderman Kibbalts party were in the wrong. Birdie turned to Allana. She was very much awake now, still leaning on Nimue but with eyes fixed on him.

He said, as gently as possible, 'And what was the last you saw of him?'

Her voice was quiet and he had to lean forward to catch it.

'At lunchtime. Aeneas came up with me in that

81

horrible chair, and Horace had asked me to bring him up a packed lunch from the hotel because he was working.'

'You brought the lunch?'

She nodded. 'For all three of us. Wine and smoked salmon sandwiches. We had it in here while Aeneas and Horace talked.'

And, from her tone, while Allana sat bored in the background.

'And then?'

'And then they went on through to the transmission room and I stayed here and wrote letters.'

'Did Mr Hent look in to tell you he was going down?'

She shook her head. 'He'd leave that to Aeneas.'

'So you didn't see him again until . . .'

She said flatly, 'I didn't see him again.' She closed her eyes and let her head flop back on to Nimue's shoulder.

Birdie persisted, 'But he must have walked past this door when he went along the tunnel. Wouldn't you have expected him to look in?'

The eyes opened and looked at him with hostility. 'Why should he? He flew off to China last month and didn't even tell me he was going.'

'So relations between you and your husband weren't close?'

'Oh, for God's sake,' she said to Nimue, 'who is this? He's worse than the police.'

Nimue patted her shoulder and said Birdie was trying to help, but Allana would not be soothed.

'It's like sending a marriage guidance counsellor to a funeral. You want to know why my husband and I weren't close?'

'That isn't the point. All I wanted to know was whether . . .'

Birdie was feeling hot with embarrassment under his thick ski clothes and felt Nimue should be doing more to

82

help him. After all, she'd got him in to this. Allana jumped up.

'Show him that interview, Aeneas. You know the bit I mean.'

And as Nimue made a wry, apologetic face at Birdie, Aeneas slotted a cassette into the video set by the wall, with the skill of someone who'd done it many times before.

Allana said, watching intently, 'It was an American chat show, last year.'

Aeneas started it at the exact point where the interviewer leaned back in his chair and said to the camera, 'Now, Horace, let's turn to your private life. How many wives is it so far?'

'Six,' said Hent.

'As many as King Henry the Eighth. Was that all part of the plan, Horace?'

'No plan of mine, Mel. You might say God or evolution or something planned it that way.'

'Er, God or evolution, Horace?'

'Or whoever arranged it that women are past their best by the age when most men get started.'

A choking sound from Nimue, and Allana walked over and turned off the video.

'I threw a silver teapot through his television screen when I first saw that.'

Nimue said, 'In the circumstances, that was quite mild.'

'It was a Georgian silver teapot.' Allana rounded on Birdie. 'Are you still surprised that I wasn't waiting out there to kiss him goodbye?'

'Er, no. Just one thing surprises me.'

'What's that?'

'Why you didn't walk out on him after throwing the teapot.'

83

Allana looked at him pityingly. 'Why should I make things that easy for him?'

Later, as he and Nimue were travelling down on the chair lift, Birdie asked, 'What the hell is she playing at?'

In spite of persuasion from Aeneas and Nimue, Allana had flatly refused to travel down with them. The most she'd do was provide Nimue with a list of clothes and food that should be sent up to her from the hotel.

'I don't think she's playing at anything, at least not more than usual. She's genuinely scared of this thing.'

'But she hated Hent's guts.'

'That wouldn't make any difference. Allana's got a very vivid imagination.'

Birdie was silent.

Nimue said, 'You don't like her, do you?'

'I certainly don't understand her.'

'There's not that much to understand about Allana. That's the nice thing about her. She's got all the simple, uncomplicated demands of life that most people grow out of at about seven – lots of nice things happening all the time and everybody happy and loving her.'

'That's all very well, but you can't have that when you're grown up.'

'Allana used to manage it.'

The chair hummed downwards on its cable, with the sun shining across the valley and into their eyes.

Birdie asked, 'Do you think Allana would be capable of murder?'

'Oh yes.'

The speed and conviction of Nimue's reply surprised him. She went on, 'If anybody seriously annoyed her and there happened to be a gun or something lying handy, that would be it.'

'So if she got her hands on . . . ?'

A picture was developing in his mind of Allana standing there in the tunnel, shouting to Hent to make him turn. But Nimue was still treating it lightly.

'The thing is though, she'd be totally incapable of covering it up once she'd done it. Instant repentance, floods of tears and not a dry eye in the jury box.'

'So you think if she killed Hent, she wouldn't keep quiet about it?'

'Judging from what she was saying, she'd go coast to coast on American television about it.'

But Birdie still wasn't happy. The sense of exclusion he'd felt when he'd seen Nimue and Allana sitting together on the sofa wouldn't go away and was hardening into a suspicion of secrets kept. He said stubbornly, 'But something doesn't add up here. A woman with the temperament you're describing would have been up and away from him months ago. She stayed.'

Silence from Nimue.

He persisted, 'I think there was a reason, and I think she told you something about it.'

Nimue shifted uneasily in the chair.

'There . . . there is something. But it's nothing to do with the murder.'

'How can you know that?'

'I just don't see how it can, and I promised her . . .'

The uneasiness boiled into sudden anger. 'Look, Nimue, either you want me to investigate this or you don't. But if we have to rule out Wayne on the basis that he's only a teenage hoodlum and rule out Allana because she's got a sweet, childlike temperament – I mean if adults only need apply, I'm giving up this whole damned thing here and now.'

'I never said we had to rule out . . .'

'I'm beginning to think there's some sort of conspiracy going on to make me feel guilty for being an ordinary

85

mature male adult, and I've had just about enough of it. First you and Fuzz and bloody Wayne, now you and Allana . . .'

'If you'd just stop shouting at me for a moment . . .'

'I'm not bloody shouting.' He stared at the snow passing beneath them.

Nimue said quietly, 'Allana and the ex-wives have got some daft kind of secret society going. They call it Getting Back at Hent.'

'Bloody hell. What do they do?'

'I'm not sure they've done anything yet. From what she was saying there were plans to buy up his shares and make trouble on the stock market and so on . . .'

'On the alimony he gives them, I suppose.'

'I suppose so, but I don't see . . .'

'All right, we won't go into that. How many wives did he say on that interview?'

'Six.'

'So there're six Hent wives somewhere around the world plotting sabotage, is that it?'

'I don't think it's as serious as you make it sound. I mean, if they're all like Allana they're probably getting a terrific kick out of what they might do and that will be all it comes to.'

'But supposing they're not all like Allana. Bloody hell, five of them. They might be anywhere, doing anything.'

'Well, they weren't on the chair lift yesterday, so I don't see that it's relevant.'

He thought for a while.

'I suppose she didn't tell the police about this?'

'No. She didn't think it was relevant either.'

'They ought to know about it.'

Nimue looked alarmed. 'Birdie, you can't. I promised her.'

'You can't pick and choose the facts you give them.'

'You can't tell them. She'd think I'd betrayed her. Birdie, promise me . . .'

He gave way to the desperate appeal on her face.

'Love, you can't . . . All right, I won't go out of my way to tell anyone. But if it comes up again . . .'

'It won't. I don't see how it could.'

The chair lift swung on down.

CHAPTER SIX

It was lunchtime back at the Hotel Soldanella, and the usual pandemonium. Judging by the noise from the dining room the shock of Wayne's arrest had not deprived the Alderman Kibbalts party of its collective appetite. Nimue was pounced on by Fuzz even before she had time to get her anorak off and hustled away to speak Italian into the telephone on the reception desk. Birdie, taking refuge in the bar, found Bruin already there with a glass of wine. He jumped up guiltily when the door opened, but relaxed when he saw it was Birdie.

'I should be on duty in the dining room, but I need something stronger than water to get through this afternoon.'

'What's happening?'

'Fuzz says I've got to take Sidney and Joe out skiing.'

On normal afternoons the Alderman Kibbalts party had no ski classes and were left to practise where they pleased – which for at least half of them involved slipping off to the café with the Space Invader machine. But the more competent skiers formed pairs or small groups to go up the mountain, and Sidney and Joe were planning to do exactly that. Which, Bruin explained, was fine from one point of view as they could hardly be expected to sit around all the time feeling bad about Wayne. On the other hand, since the two of them were still not completely cleared of complicity, the Italian police had exacted a promise that the teachers would not let them out of their sight. Without that promise, Bruin said, the two of them might well have joined Wayne in the car down to Milan.

'The obvious thing would be for Ray Reeve to take them skiing, but he flatly refuses to have anything to do with them. And Fuzz is too busy, which just leaves me.'

Birdie could understand Bruin's gloom. From what he'd seen, Sidney and Joe would ski him off his feet and enjoy doing it.

He offered impulsively, 'I could take them if you like.'

After all, he'd have to question the two of them at some point, and this would be as good an opportunity as any. Bruin was instantly grateful.

'Would you really? You ski better than I do, and being an ex-policeman and so on . . .'

How did people always find that out, Birdie wondered. Were there numbers tattooed on the back of his neck? But he accepted Bruin's thanks and a glass of wine. A few minutes later Fuzz put her head round the door and Bruin jumped up and jogged apologetically back to his duties, saying as he went, 'I'll tell them to meet you out in the lobby at two.'

Birdie finished his drink and went out to find Nimue, still by the reception desk with anorak on and hire car keys in her hand.

'Love, we're still having problems finding anyone on the telephone. I'm going to drive down to our office in Milan and use the telex.'

She looked so tired that he had to fight the urge to pick her up and carry her off to bed.

'Does it have to be you?'

'It's my job after all. I'll be back late tonight if I'm lucky. Tomorrow morning if not.'

'Don't get avalanched.'

'Oh, the main road down the valley's all right. It's only the one up to the satellite station that gets avalanches.'

He went out with her to the car, kissed her and waved her off with a heavy feeling in his stomach. After their disagreement over Allana he was saddened by even this short absence without a chance to make it up under the duvet. At least, he supposed, he could plod on with the work. Looking at his watch and finding it was slightly more than an hour before he was due to meet Sidney and Joe, he decided to walk through the village to the Hotel Montagna Bianca and try to find the two American missionaries. According to Brenda and friends, Barbie Jones had been in the café the afternoon before. It was just possible she might have been looking out of the window towards the chair lift. And they had, after all, been the next ones down after Hent's body on the chair, though too far behind to be in crossbow range.

He found them without too much trouble in the hotel's very up-market snack bar. Stuffed eagle owls, stoats and hawks loomed out over the diners from shelves on the pine-wood walls and a glass case over the bar was stuffed with silver cups and photos of grinning skiers. The spiritual climbing team were lunching at a gingham-covered table, tucking into succulent pizzas the size of hubcaps and glasses of orange juice. They greeted Birdie politely and sympathised with him about yesterday's events as if there'd been a death in the family.

Barbie said, 'Where did the young man come from?'

It took Birdie some moments to realise she was referring to Wayne.

'Er, not far from Birmingham, I think.'

She leaned eagerly across the table to him. 'Is Birmingham on a plain?'

'Yes, not many mountains around there.'

90

She glanced at her husband. 'Just what we thought, wasn't it, Joshua?'

Joshua had just carried a forkful of pizza looped with festoons of melted cheese to his mouth and he munched happily, signalling with his eyes to Birdie that he'd answer when he'd swallowed.

'That's so. Why don't you sit down and join us, Mr Linnet?'

Birdie settled on a spare chair, and a girl in a white lacy blouse and red skirt immediately appeared and handed him a menu the size of a newspaper. He ordered red wine and spaghetti carbonara and started asking questions. If they found this surprising, they gave no sign of it.

'You saw Horace Hent yesterday morning. Did he seem quite normal then?'

Joshua smiled gently. 'Well, Mr Linnet, it's not easy to judge that because Barbie and I had never met Mr Hent before. If you're asking me if he displayed any apprehension, the answer is no.'

'He refused to let you use his satellite, I gather.'

'That is so.'

'Angrily?'

'No, but then we'd given him no cause to be angry. We asked him to use God's mountains for God's work and he, for his own reasons, refused that proposition.'

Birdie asked, genuinely curious, 'You really expected he'd let you use his station for religious broadcasts?'

Barbie answered that one. 'If you don't ask for miracles, Mr Linnet, you don't get them.'

'But this time you didn't get one.'

'Sometimes, Mr Linnet, you have to make many attempts to climb a mountain.'

He abandoned that line of questioning. 'Mrs Jones, you were at the top of the chair lift yesterday afternoon?'

She nodded. 'We both were.'

'Can I ask you what you were doing there?'

They showed no resentment at the question. Barbie said, 'Joshua was doing some more spiritual surveying, near the place where you met us yesterday. I was feeling cold so I went to wait for him in the café.'

'Was there anybody else there?'

'No, but three English girls looked in.' A hurt expression came over her face at the memory of Brenda and friends. 'I believe they may have come from the plain of Birmingham too.'

Birdie agreed that spiritual climbing was unlikely to be one of Brenda's hobbies. He asked, 'When you were in the café, were you looking out towards the top of the chair lift at all?'

She nodded. 'Some of the time. I was looking out for Joshua. I knew he'd be coming from that direction.'

'You could see the top of the chair lift from the café, in spite of the snow?'

'Yes.'

'Did you see anything at all of Mr Hent?'

She shook her head.

'Did you see him or anyone else coming down the path from the tunnel?'

'No, but I wasn't watching all the time.'

Birdie's lunch arrived, steaming spaghetti with flecks of egg and little nuggets of bacon. He tried to wrap it round his fork and go on asking questions at the same time.

'When did you leave the café?'

'Soon after the girls from Birmingham looked in. I saw Joshua coming, so I went to the door to meet him.'

Birdie turned to Joshua and a carefully wound forkful of spaghetti escaped and slithered back to his plate.

'If you were walking from that little hill with the cross

92

you must have passed right behind that chair lift shed.'

'Yes, that's so.'

'Did you see anything of Mr Hent?'

'No.'

'Or of anybody else?'

'No. I noticed some people still skiing, but they were lower down.'

Birdie managed a cautious mouthful and let it glide down his throat before attempting his next question.

'When you'd met your wife at the café you went over to the chair lift, right?'

He nodded.

'Now, from my memory down at the bottom, you two were travelling about fifteen chairs behind Mr Hent. Did you see him at all, either getting on the chair, or on the way down?'

Barbie shook her head. 'Fifteen chairs is quite a lot of space, Mr Linnet. He'd have been out of sight over that dip down to the woods before we got on.'

Birdie agreed with her. He'd tried to work it out the last time he travelled down in the chair with Nimue. About twenty yards between one pair of chairs and the next; three hundred yards between Hent's chair and Joshua and Barbie. There was nothing incredible about their story that the first they knew of Hent's presence on the lift was when they swung in to land beside his dead body at the bottom.

He finished most of his meal, with Barbie and Joshua chatting politely as if he were just there on holiday, about the snow, about the work that was still going on to try to clear the road to the satellite station. Barbie had heard it might take another two days because a lot of rock had fallen as well, which meant, Birdie thought, another two days' imprisonment for Allana. He ordered more orange juice for Barbie and Joshua and more wine

93

for himself, gloomily noting that the orange juice was freshly squeezed and cost four times as much as the wine. They wanted to know if he was skiing that afternoon, and he glanced at his watch and told them he was taking out Wayne's best friends, which brought the conversation back to murder. Barbie said she hoped they wouldn't keep Wayne in custody in a flat place like Milan. Joshua took a more severe view.

'We've heard a lot of criticism from Europeans, Mr Linnet, about our gun laws in the United States, but it seems to me the way you let your young people have crossbows is every bit as bad.'

Birdie said this was hardly a typical case. It was a matter of just one boy and one crossbow.

Joshua raised his voice a little. 'I'm afraid that's not so, Mr Linnet. Barbie and I know of one more boy from your party with a similar weapon, and by no means a bad boy either.'

Birdie choked on his wine. From their expressions, Barbie and Joshua seemed to have no idea of the importance of what had just been said.

'I'm sorry, this is very important. Are you telling me that you met another boy from the English school party with a crossbow?'

They nodded. The seriousness of it still didn't seem to have sunk in, and they were staring at him with friendly but puzzled expressions.

'Who? When and where?'

'Outside the café, Mr Linnet. On that same day.'

'Which boy was it?'

'The nice quiet one who's so interested in our work. Young Tim.'

Birdie said, trying to take it in, 'You're saying you met Tim with a crossbow outside the café?'

'That's so.'

94

His attitude was making them take it more seriously, and the puzzlement on their faces was growing.

'When exactly?'

Barbie answered for them. 'Well, I can't say exactly, but it must have been just after lunchtime. You remember we met you up there?'

Birdie nodded. It seemed a tired world away now, but he could remember meeting Barbie and Joshua and young Tim near the cross, and Nimue suggesting that the boy should go for lunch.

Barbie went on, 'Tim went down for lunch, remember. But he must have come up again quite quickly, because less than an hour after that I got cold and Joshua took me over towards the café and, just at the back of the ski-lift shed, there was young Tim fitting a crossbow together.'

Joshua corrected her. 'He'd already got it together. The crosspiece was on, there was even the bolt in it.'

'What kind of crossbow; did you notice?'

Joshua said, 'Small hunting type with a wooden stock.'

Birdie said nothing. That had been a description of the bow to which Wayne laid claim in the disco.

Joshua, reading his expression, said reassuringly, 'We took a very firm line with him, Mr Linnet, didn't we Barbie?'

'Yes, we told him he must take it down straight away and give it to one of his teachers.'

Birdie asked, 'And did he do it?'

Barbie again, 'Oh yes, Mr Linnet. I'm sure he did. Tim struck us as a very serious and polite young man.'

And that had been it. They'd simply gone on their way to the café, leaving Tim with a crossbow ready to use, in the blithe confidence that he'd simply do as he was told. And no, they hadn't told the police because they couldn't see any necessity for it. It was, Birdie thought,

95

all of a piece with their optimism in thinking a man like Hent would hand over satellite time for the asking. He sunk his head in his hands, with Barbie and Joshua watching anxiously, obviously still unsure what the fuss was about.

'Let's get this straight. If all this happened about an hour after we met you, we're talking about a time round about half past two, right?'

They thought about it for a while and agreed with him, although they were still infuriatingly vague about time. Which meant, Birdie thought, that Tim would have had plenty of time to ski down to the bottom in a leisurely way with the crossbow under his anorak. He and Nimue themselves had seen him there, getting on to the chair lift again, his anorak done up to the chin. And, ten minutes or so after that, Tim's chair had passed Hent's – who by Tim's account was still alive at the time. Somewhere in his mind at the back of all this was Wayne's face, grinning with triumph. The message seemed to be getting through to Barbie.

She said, with the first trace of uncertainty, 'Perhaps we should have done more, but Tim seems such a trustworthy young man.'

It was five past two before he parted from them, and he ran back up the hill to the Hotel Soldanella, his lungs protesting at the thin air. Joe and Sidney, with their ski boots on, were waiting for him in the lobby, but he rushed past them and found Fuzz, as usual, waiting by the phone at the reception desk. She started to thank him for agreeing to take Joe and Sidney skiing but he cut her off.

'Where's Tim? I need to speak to him.'

She didn't know; thought Tim had gone off on his own as usual, but whether walking or skiing nobody seemed to know. She was sure he'd be back around half past four for tea. Birdie was on the point of telling her why it was so urgent, but just stopped himself. So far all he had was Joshua and Barbie's story – the next thing must be to speak to Tim. He'd have been perfectly willing to sit there in a chair in the lobby waiting until Tim came back, and after the run uphill his muscles would have welcomed the rest. But Fuzz was having none of it. He'd promised Bruin to take Wayne's friends skiing and skiing they must go. She promised to tell Tim that Birdie wanted to see him as soon as the boy got back.

So that was it. Up the chair lift again, which was becoming as familiar as the bus to work, with Joe and Sidney carried up about twenty yards in front of him, just as they'd been in front of Wayne the afternoon before. When he arrived at the top Joe nodded at him and said, 'Let's go.'

It sounded like a challenge and it was. The two boys went off like snow hares along the narrow path from the chair lift and went straight on down the red run. Remembering how Wayne had cut him up in front of Nimue, he was grimly determined to keep up with Wayne's friends. Luckily at this point it seemed to be simply a matter of slotting his skis into the tracks made by others and letting them run. Soon he was gaining on the smaller and lighter Sidney; a twitch of the skis that had never worked so well before and he was past the boy, brushing the sleeve of his anorak, and thundering along in the track of Joe. His eyes were watering, the cold air was stinging his face and the hiss of his skis on the snow reminded him of the sound from the wheels of his touring bike on a good road in summer. For a moment he forgot why he was there and enjoyed the sheer animal pleasure of the thing. He even wished Nimue could see him.

It couldn't last. A few hundred yards further on, Joe

turned up-slope and came to rest by one of the red marker posts. Birdie, close behind him, tried to follow and wiped out in a cloud of snow with a crash that juddered the mountain. But in terms of losing face it didn't matter so much because Sidney followed him a few seconds later in an even more spectacular fall, rolling twenty yards or so down the mountain, shedding ski poles and goggles as he went. Joe and Birdie helped pick him up.

'Great snow,' said Joe, grinning at Birdie.

And Birdie was disconcerted to find himself grinning back and saying yes, great snow. He even felt grateful to Sidney for being overtaken and overturned. He said to himself, 'Forty-three one, sixteen nil,' then told himself to grow up and concentrate.

As they waited for Sidney to gather himself together, he said to Joe, 'I want to stop somewhere and have a talk with you both.'

'There's a hut down here a bit. We usually stop there for a smoke.'

The next bit of the run was the awkward bit, narrowing between the trees and humped with moguls. His suspicion that Sidney was a devious individual was confirmed by the boy's skill with the fiddly things. He skidded round them, not fast but neatly, while Joe and Birdie with their more straightforward approach came variously to grief. Each fell down his own mogul, then collided and fell down the same mogul, then Birdie hit a tree and Joe got the tip of his ski stuck in a snow bank, while from a flat patch below Sidney yelled advice and sarcasm.

'Bloody hell.'

The tree and Birdie's skis were unscathed, but dozens more moguls waited for him to open negotiations with them. Accusing himself of middle-aged caution Birdie simply pointed his skis downhill and let fly. He skimmed over the first mogul in his path, rocketed off the second, then skittered like an aircraft propeller on the third before landing with an almighty jolt almost at Sidney's feet.

'Hey man, a helicopter turn.'

The cry came from Joe, up-slope.

'A what?'

'We've been trying to do that all week, haven't we, Sidney?'

'Forty-three two, sixteen nil,' thought Birdie unfairly, and hoped they wouldn't expect him to demonstrate it again. Luckily the next bit was a straightforward down-hill run and the three of them arrived at a wooden hut beside the piste, panting from the speed and more or less at the same time.

The hut was a simple wooden cube, probably used by foresters in summer but empty now. There was a wooden platform at the front of it and Joe and Sidney took their skis off and settled down on it, backs against the wall. They produced cigarettes and offered one to Birdie as he sat down beside them. From the platform they had a view down over acres of pine trees to the valley, where a small stream ran black through fields of snow. Opposite, the high peaks were already glowing gold in the afternoon sun and Birdie thought he could hear, from the next valley, the crack and rumble of an avalanche. Below and to their right were the crowded nursery slopes, and the hut where the chair lift ended.

For a minute or two Birdie sat and watched the two boys as smoke from their cigarettes drifted straight up into the still air. They weren't exactly hostile, but now the passing fellowship of skiing was interrupted they weren't responding to him either. They'd have sat like that, smoking their cigarettes and staring down the valley, if he hadn't been there. Whether they intended it or not, they gave the impression that what he was and what he wanted had nothing to do with their lives.

He asked suddenly, 'Did Wayne have the crossbow under his anorak?'

Joe shook his head slowly, and Sidney said, 'No, he'd never taken it out anywhere. Not here, I mean.'

Joe said, 'Even at home we just took it up the sewage farm shooting rats.'

Birdie was annoyed, not because they might be lying but because they so clearly didn't care whether he believed them or not.

'You're not trying to tell me you went to all the trouble of smuggling the thing out here and never took it anywhere.'

Silence, then Sidney said reluctantly, 'Just in our room. We just took it out and put it together and so on in our room.'

Birdie looked at Joe. 'Were you there too?'

'Yeah, we were just sort of playing about with it.'

'But what were you planning to do with it?'

'We were going on a hunting trip, up in the woods.'

'Just the three of you?'

'Yeah.'

'And you're definitely telling me that neither Wayne nor either of you had it with you on the chair lift?'

They nodded.

Joe said, 'We told the police that too, but they didn't believe us.'

Birdie wasn't surprised. He went on, 'The crosspiece comes off, doesn't it? He could have broken it down and put it under his anorak, or those dungaree things.'

Joe said, 'Salopettes. And he didn't. I should know, I was there with him when he was getting changed.'

There was just enough reaction to suggest to Birdie that he might get further by annoying them.

100

'You say you were.'

'Well, I sodding was. I mean, what's the good of you asking us things we've already been asked if you're not going to believe us when we tell you?' He threw his glowing cigarette butt off the platform and into the snow.

Birdie said, 'If you think Wayne didn't kill him, don't you want to help prove it?'

Sidney asked, 'What's the point? I mean, he's going to get done for something he never did sooner or later, isn't he, so what difference does it make?'

Birdie shouted, 'The difference of whether he really did it or not.'

They both turned to him with surprised looks on their faces, as if his shouting was unprovoked violence.

He said, trying to force a way through their passive hostility, 'Just for now, I'll take your word for it. You say none of you had the crossbow on the chair lift. When did you last see it before the murder?'

Joe said, 'The night before.'

'Where?'

'In our room. Wayne had this idea we should practise putting it together in the dark.'

'For night operations,' Sidney added.

'So you just sat there with the light off, taking it apart and putting it together?'

They nodded.

'Was anybody else there?'

'Wayne wouldn't trust anybody else,' said Joe.

Sidney said, as if taking an interest against his will, 'There was somebody else, but only for about a minute.'

'Who?'

'Tim.'

Birdie tensed, but the boys didn't seem to notice. Joe said casually, 'Yeah, that's right. He wanted to ask if

101

you'd got his socks or something.'

Sidney explained, 'I had to share a room with Tim, and he knocked on the door of Wayne's room and came in wanting to know if I'd seen his socks. I told him they were on the floor behind the radiator and he went out again.'

He began to laugh. 'There was Wayne sitting on the bed with the crossbow in his hands and Tim looking sideways at the wall, nearly twisting his neck off pretending he hadn't seen it.'

'You said the light was off. Perhaps he couldn't see it.'

'There was a light in the corridor,' Sidney said. 'He saw it all right.'

'So Tim went off to look for his socks. And when you'd finished playing around with the bow, what happened to it?'

Joe said, 'Wayne put it back in his drawer.'

'And that was the last you saw of it till the police showed it to you after the murder?'

They nodded.

Joe said, 'They told us they found it under the chair lift. I don't know why it had to be Wayne who put it there. Anyone could've put it there.'

'That's what I mean,' mumbled Sidney. 'They'll always get you for something if they want to.'

But Joe's passivity was slipping a little. He appealed directly to Birdie. 'They said all our fingerprints were on it. Of course they'd be on it – we'd all been playing about with it.'

Sidney contributed another grumble. 'Anyway, whoever shot him would be wearing gloves, wouldn't they?'

'I suppose so.'

Sidney turned on Birdie savagely. 'What do you mean, you suppose so? I mean, you're the one who's supposed to know, aren't you? You're the one asking all the bloody questions.'

Joe said, 'Cool it, Sidney. He's only trying to help Wayne.'

Which made Birdie feel instantly guilty. He said to Sidney, 'If I knew, I wouldn't be asking the bloody questions, would I?'

He and Sidney glared at each other. Another avalanche cracked and rumbled in the distance. In spite of the sun, Birdie was already beginning to feel the cold through his ski clothes. He stood up and walked about the platform, his boots making a hollow sound on the planks.

'Was Hent alive or dead when he passed you?'

Silence behind him.

He swung round on them. 'You must know that. Either he was alive or he wasn't.'

Sidney said, 'We didn't notice.'

'Oh come off it.'

Joe insisted, 'We didn't see him.'

'You must have seen him. I watched you getting on that lift, just a few minutes before he fell off it. You must have passed each other.'

Joe said, 'We never said we didn't pass him. We just said we didn't notice him.'

'But surely if you're going up in a chair lift you can't help noticing the people coming down?'

'Not always,' said Joe. 'Not if you're talking or thinking about something.'

In fairness to them, Birdie paused and thought about it. He'd been up the chair lift several times a day for the past week, and could he honestly say he'd noticed the people coming down every time, any more than you notice the people sitting opposite you in a bus? Yesterday morning, for instance, when he'd been deep in conversation with Nimue, he wouldn't have noticed a

103

polar bear. And Hent, slumped in the corner of the chair, hadn't looked obviously dead. Even he and Nimue and the attendant had been deceived at first. He still didn't trust Sidney and Joe, but in this respect he couldn't prove they were lying.

The shadow of the opposite mountain had begun to touch the wooden platform. The three of them stepped back onto the snow and began sorting out skis and sticks. Of all the questions fumbling around in Birdie's mind, the most insistent was this matter of Tim. Sidney and Joe, as far as he could gather, had read no significance at all into Tim's glimpse of the crossbow. But then they hadn't heard Barbie Jones on the subject.

He asked as they were doing up their bindings, 'Have you thought who might have killed Hent?'

'The Mafia,' said Sidney instantly. 'He probably hadn't paid his protection money.'

Birdie tried not to sound sarcastic. 'Worked out how they got to him on a ski lift?'

'Yeah, well, we were talking about that. Supposing you had a powered hang-glider, and you cut the engine at the last minute so that . . .'

And at intervals on the way down Sidney improved on that and other theories until the quiet slopes and skies were humming with hang-gliders and assassins in skidoos and ski jumpers hovering impossibly in mid air. By the time they'd got to the bottom Birdie felt he'd had more than enough of it and wanted to go off in search of Tim, but they were determined to go up again. They didn't, of course, consult him about it and just announced that they were going. Since he'd taken on the responsibility of delivering them back to the hotel there was nothing for it but to follow them up again in the lift and keep an eye on them.

At least, that was the idea, but his feet had hardly

touched down at the top of the lift before another unwanted responsibility intruded. A voice hallooed from up the slope between the lift and the tunnel entrance and, looking up, he was more than a little annoyed to see Allana, red hair flying, torso hugged by her white mink jacket. She made signs and sounds indicating that she wanted to speak to him and began to flounder down the slope in elephantine steps. Birdie saw that she was wearing snow shoes strapped to her fur boots. Sidney and Joe were watching too with some curiosity but more impatience. He hesitated, torn between the need to keep them in sight and the urgency Allana was signalling.

Joe said, 'We'll go on down. See you back at the hotel.'

'Yeah,' said Sidney. 'We're not going to run off, are we?'

And they turned to go, but Sidney made a small concession, shouting to Birdie as they went. 'We're going down the blue run this time. You can catch us if you want to.'

Birdie was pretty sure it was meant sarcastically, but had no time to brood on it because Allana was almost upon him, puffing and panting but making surprisingly good progress on the snow shoes.

She said, without any preliminaries, 'Have you brought them?'

He stared. 'Brought what?'

'Nimue was going to fetch some clothes and things for me from the hotel.'

He explained about Nimue having to go off to Milan in a hurry and suggested that she'd bring the things up next day. That, apparently, was a grave disappointment.

'Oh, what'll I do?'

Birdie suggested rather brusquely that she could solve

it by coming down in the chair lift with him then and there – having given up all hope of keeping Sidney and Joe in sight – but she wouldn't think of it.

'I'm practising with the snow shoes, but I don't know; would they go down the whole mountain?'

Birdie thought not. He passed on Barbie's guess that it might take two days to clear the road to the satellite station.

'Oh, what'll I do?'

He was beginning to get the idea that he was expected to do something about it, and resented it. She'd been, he thought, ready enough to shut him out from that closeness she had with Nimue, so why should she expect help from him now? She stood there staring at him out of big grey eyes that looked tragic but with a spark deep down that mocked her own sense of drama. He didn't know what to make of Allana and that unsettled him into clumsiness, even brutality.

'Why didn't you tell the police about this Getting Back at Hent wives' club?'

The grey eyes went quite cold.

'You don't know about that.'

It wasn't an appeal; more like a flat statement that he didn't know because she wasn't willing for him to know.

He said, 'You can't decide what people know or don't know.'

'You're not to tell anybody about that. Not anybody.'

Again, it was a simple statement of fact. She didn't wish it to be told, therefore it wouldn't be told. He remembered what Nimue had said about her friend's simple demands of life.

'It may have to be told,' he said. And he skied away from her, leaving her standing there on snow shoes. He thought she called to him, but he didn't look back.

The track to the blue run went past the café and

106

Birdie, who knew he'd very little chance of catching up with the two boys, decided he needed a toilet and coffee shop. And, in the coffee queue, he found himself standing next to Ray Reeve. Left to himself, the teacher probably wouldn't even have spoken, but when Birdie said hello he grunted a reply. With the prospective meeting with Tim now at the front of his mind, it seemed to Birdie a good idea to do a little preliminary ground-work. Barbie Jones, by her account, had told Tim to give the crossbow to a teacher. It was, after all, possible that the boy had done exactly that.

He said, 'Yesterday afternoon, you were skiing on your own?'

'Yes. For God's sake, I've told the police that about a dozen times.'

Birdie said humbly, 'I'm sorry, I'm just trying to get it clear. Did you see Tim at all?'

'Tim? Why on earth would I have seen Tim?'

'It's not so impossible. You were skiing that afternoon and so was he.'

Ray Reeve said slowly, as if speaking to a moron, 'I've told everybody who was interested, I was skiing in the powder near the start of the Cascata. I wasn't likely to meet Tim or anybody else there.'

Which, even to somebody of Birdie's limited skiing knowledge, made sense. Skiing in the deep powder snow, away from the prepared pistes, was something for the experts. He'd found that when he'd tried it with Nimue the day before. And yet there was something nagging at his mind about it, something that told him there was another question he should be asking Ray which had nothing to do with Tim. He pressed on at random, trying to find it, as the coffee queue inched forward.

'You came down on the chair lift because your binding

107

broke?'

'As I've also told everybody a dozen times.'

Ray's jaw was jutting and his voice so angry and quiet that it was close to a hiss.

Birdie said, 'Does that mean your ski came off?'

'Yes.'

'When you were actually skiing in the powder?'

'Yes.'

'So you fell over?'

Ray's jaws unclamped and he shouted in a voice that had everybody in the queue turning to look at them. 'What an imbecile question! If a ski comes off when you're flat out in powder snow of course you fall over.'

'I only . . .'

'Jean Claud Killy would fall over, Franz Klammer would fall over, anybody would bloody fall over.'

The girl behind the counter pushed two cups of coffee cautiously towards them.

Birdie said, as pacifically as he could manage, 'And get covered with snow.'

'When you fall over in powder you do tend to get covered in snow, yes.'

The voice was back to a near hiss. They paid for their coffees separately and carried them in silence to the same table. Deciding that he'd gone far enough, Birdie changed the subject, explaining that he'd been skiing with Joe and Sidney and they'd gone ahead down the blue run.

'As long as they stay off the Cascata,' Ray said. 'It's closed because it could avalanche.'

He drank his coffee scalding hot in two gulps, got up and went without saying another word. Birdie sat there, drinking slowly, unconscious of the bustle and ski chat around him. The thing nagging at his mind had now come out in the open, and he didn't know quite what to

108

do with it. He'd learnt one thing about powder snow the day before, and that was if you fell over in the stuff it was like fine flour. It got down your neck and stuck to stitching on your anorak and your eyebrows and the woolly fibres of your hat, and it was hours before you got rid of the stuff. If anybody fell in powder snow then signs of it would be on him till it melted. And Birdie, from old professional experience, had a trained memory. He'd seen Ray Reeve get off the chair lift the day before – presumably not long after his fall in the powder. And as far as he could remember, examining his mental picture carefully, Ray Reeve had been no snowier than any other skier. He told himself he shouldn't make too much of it, that Reeve's ski vanity might have been great enough for him to brush off every particle of the stuff before going down on the lift. But it bothered him. His coffee had gone cold. He left it and went outside to find his skis, remembering how Ray Reeve had looked after Hent had turned down his ski school.

CHAPTER SEVEN

Outside the whole range of peaks had turned pink from the setting sun and there were fewer people on the mogul field. The shouts of homing skiers drifted up to him from below among the pine trees. It was getting towards the end of the skiing day, and Birdie wished he hadn't lingered over his coffee so long. There'd be only just time to ski down to the village before the light went, and Tim should be waiting for him back at the hotel. Well, it would do the boy no harm to wait because he had a lot of explaining to do. Birdie skied along the well-worn tracks away from the chair lift and the café, towards the start of the meandering blue run down to the village. After a few minutes of easy running, with not another skier in sight, he came to the shadow-filled snow bowl where the piste started on its steeper downhill course. It looked unfamiliar in this light and he reminded himself he'd have to keep his mind in gear because this was the start of the experts' Cascata as well as the easy blue run. Still, there shouldn't be any confusion because, as Ray had told him, the Cascata was officially closed. There was the black marker where the piste tipped itself over the edge of the bowl and out of sight and, stretched across the trail, a length of fluorescent netting on posts and the chequered black and yellow board signifying danger. Off to the right a less challenging-looking track curved round the top of the bowl, marked with a blue blob on a post. Birdie rested on his ski sticks for a while, then set off along the blue marked path, a broad track in the snow.

At first it was all he wanted it to be, curving gently along the shoulder of the mountain with a view down to the valley and the village where the lights were just coming on. The snow was soft and easy to turn on, the breeze from the peaks blew cool on his face and it was totally quiet. Even the skiers below him couldn't be heard any more. He coasted along, waiting for the path to take a downward turn. When it did, his troubles started.

It turned sharply, so that instead of following the curve of the mountain he was suddenly facing straight down into the valley. And, having brought him to that point, it disappeared. Instead of soft snow marked by earlier skiers' tracks he found himself on an icy hump with the soft snow skimmed away by wind and only the hard, polished stuff left, broken here and there by small teeth of grey rock. And no indication at all of where the track was supposed to go. Then to his relief he saw another of the marker blobs on a post over to his right— a relief that lasted for only a few seconds because as he got nearer, side-slipping cautiously on the hard snow with a dismal rasping sound from his ski edges, he saw that instead of the familiar blue, the marker was unmistakably black. And that meant he'd somehow, goodness knows how, stumbled on to the experts' only run, the Cascata that even Nimue talked about with respect and Ray said was closed because of avalanches.

'Bloody hell!'

There was only one sensible course: to get off the damned thing and climb back to wherever he'd taken the wrong turning. But that wasn't as easy as it sounded.

111

The icy snow that had been uncooperative when he skied down to the black marker became positively hostile when he tried to get back up again. He tried it sideways, digging his ski edges in, but time after time they refused to bite and he slithered further down. Twice he fell heavily, banging exactly the same place on his elbow each time, trying to ignore the protests from his unreliable knee. After a few minutes of this, sweating and furious, he was only a few feet further up than when he started. He paused to consider. At this rate of progress it would be night before he got back on to the blue run. And if he couldn't get back there was only one alternative – he'd have to go on down.

'Bloody, bloody hell!'

And not another skier on the mountain. It had become completely silent and deserted. The café and the chair lift, only a few minutes' skiing time away, belonged to another world. He stood there breathing hard, telling himself it was skiable, other people had done it, so why shouldn't he? Point your skis down the mountain and go, with gravity at least on your side. He waited for his heartbeat to steady and noticed gloomily that it seemed to be taking longer than usual. Altitude or age? Before he'd come on this damned holiday the question wouldn't even have occurred to him. He felt he'd aged from mature to pensionable in just over a week, which was no frame of mind for the most challenging run of his short skiing career. He told the mountain aloud, 'I'm forty-three, I'm fit, and I'm bloody well going to do it.'

Judging by the fact that he fell twice more in the next hundred yards, the mountain was unimpressed. On the second fall, finding that he was slithering in a fairly orderly manner, he went with it and arrived at the next marker post on the seat of his ski pants. It was unheroic but practical and he might have gone on like that all

112

the way down if the mountain hadn't thrown another obstacle at him. Below the black marker it looked, at first sight, a lot easier. There was a broad corridor of snow between two ridges of rock pinnacles that looked almost as easy as the nursery slopes. He started off with some confidence, to find that the failing light had deceived him and he was in a mogul field steeper and more malevolent than anything in his experience. He made the discovery when he was lying on his back with one ski off and his elbow giving him hell from its third thumping. The whole slope was nothing more than a mountain range in miniature. After three or four more falls he realised that the peaks were a little less sharp at the sides of the snow corridor and, at a pace varying from conciliatory to runaway, sometimes on his skis, sometimes on his buttocks and, it seemed to him, most of the time on his battered elbow, he skied, cursed and slithered down to the next marker.

From there it was at least encouraging to see how much of the mountain he'd already negotiated. The lights in the village were much closer, standing out against the dusk that already filled the valley. From that point the black markers led straight down a narrower slope as the ridges of rock closed in steeply on either side. Birdie thought he recognised this feature from the chat of expert skiers in the bars. They called it the gun barrel, and snatches of what they'd been saying about it floated discouragingly into his memory.

'. . . having to do really tight parallel turns.'

'Get it wrong and you break your skis on the rocks – or your neck.'

'Bloke got killed there last year. Went straight down it and . . .'

Birdie stood and looked at it, and the more he looked the more he was certain he couldn't do it.

'Geronimo.'

The shout startled him so much that he glanced sideways, expecting to see Sidney or Joe rushing past him, mocking his caution and his middle-aged wobbliness. But they weren't there; no Joe, no Sidney, nobody. Just his own skis hissing as they gathered speed and the sound of his own voice echoing back from the steep grey rocks on either side.

'. . . onimo . . . imo . . . O . . . Oh God.'

Something in his mind had hijacked him, flung him down the gun barrel, and there he was ripping down that long corridor of snow like an opening zip fastener and there was nothing whatever he could do about it. It was beyond him, far beyond him, to be travelling over snow at that speed and in failing light, but even further beyond him was the possibility of stopping. He simply didn't know how to. In a moment of pure madness and frustration he'd started the bloody skis running and the only thing he could do was stick with them.

'Till death do us part,' he thought.

Then he couldn't think any more; couldn't see. The speed had driven everything from his mind and the only sense still working was hearing: full of the hissing of skis against snow that got louder and louder until it filled the whole universe and there was nothing but skis on snow that wouldn't stop till they'd hurled him out of time and space.

Which happened quite soon. There was a thunderous shock and speed, mountain, skis, dissolved into a huge whiteness, an explosion into nothingness. And Birdie lay there, not existing, until the whiteness at the end of the world dissolved itself into water and began to drip inside his anorak. He stood up cautiously, up to his waist in the stuff. His legs, as far as he could discover against the weight of snow, were unbroken. His elbow was giving

114

him hell but that was nothing new and the general feeling that he'd been kicked in the chest by a cart horse would probably go away in time. The amazing fact was that he'd come through the gun barrel. The long streak of snow between its rock walls was now above him, so nearly vertical that he felt sick to look at it. He hastily looked away and down, and found to his relief that he was almost back on the nursery slopes. He could see skiers down there, even hear their voices. They were shouting and waving to somebody. Shouting and waving to him. Were they enquiring about his health? Congratulating him? Light-headed with relief he felt around in the soft snow for his skis. They were easy enough to find, though his gloves, goggles and one ski stick had been swallowed up so deeply that only the spring thaw would disclose them. But the Cascata had apparently done its worst and all that was left between him and the safety of the nursery slopes was one sweep of mountain, quite steep by his normal standards but nothing compared with the thing up above him. He started across it with some confidence, wishing that his audience down on the nursery slopes would stop shouting. It was deeper snow than he'd expected but quite soft and biddable, parting easily to let his ski tips through. He tried a turn, clumsy but functional, and increased his speed. They were still shouting at him down there and he took it to be encouragement, even admiration perhaps. He had, in the relief of getting down, quite forgotten the avalanche warning. Another turn, then a long traverse. He thought after he turned that he heard a small crackling sound and hoped his binding wasn't going to give way like Ray Reeve's. And now he was so close to the nursery slopes that he could hear what they were shouting: shouting to him to go faster. And it seemed the snow wanted him to go faster too because it was suddenly doing odd things

115

under his skis, slipping away from them like a vast horizontal escalator, and those shouts from below were . . .

'Avalanche!'

'Bloody hell.'

He never knew afterwards how he'd done it. Ray Reeve told him later that what saved him was his decision – not that he was conscious of making any decision – to keep skiing as fast as he could on the same course. If he'd turned, Ray said, the thing would have been on top of him and he'd have drowned in a wave of snow. As it was he simply kept going, with the escalator slipping away beneath him, hit the firm edges of the nursery slope and rolled over and over while the avalanche spilled ton upon ton of snow just a few yards away. It was the slowness of the thing that horrified him as much as its force. Long after he'd got to his feet and been clucked over by spectators the snow was still moving with the sluggishness and menace of an elderly crocodile. An unstoppable surge of millions of miniature snowballs like globules of polystyrene from a packing case. On the slope above it was just light enough to see the triangular gash it had made in tearing itself away.

Ray Reeve said, 'You did that, your tracks, skiing across the top of it.'

He was standing there on the nursery slopes, a small crowd of people round him. Among them Birdie noticed Sidney and Joe, even their impassivity shaken by that crawling heap of snow.

Birdie said, 'I meant to come down the blue run.'

Ray Reeve sounded furious, as if it was all Birdie's fault.

'Somebody changed the markers at the top. One of the ski instructors has just brought a class down the blue run, and he noticed.'

116

Birdie's eyes went straight to Sidney and Joe. They were the ones who'd told him they were going down the blue run. They'd had more than enough time to change the markers while he was talking to Reeve and drinking coffee.

Sidney said at once, 'It wasn't us, if that's what you're thinking.'

And Joe, 'The markers were OK when we were there.'

He looked long and hard at them but knew he could prove nothing. It was all of a piece with the Superglue on the chair lift, but this time it could have ended with the breath crushed out of him, or of somebody, by that slow-moving monster behind them.

Then he thought, 'Me or somebody', and wondered whether it had been meant exclusively for him. After all, there weren't many skiers still up the mountain at that time in the afternoon and the more experienced of them, or the ones skiing with instructors, would immediately notice what had happened. And if it had been intended especially for him, who else other than Sidney and Joe knew he'd be going down the blue run? Possibly quite a few. Anybody, for instance, who happened to be within earshot when Sidney called back to Birdie, inviting him to follow them down. And, of course, Ray Reeve. And if you started thinking like that it became more than a possibly fatal piece of devilment and became altogether more worrying. He turned from Sidney and Joe to find Ray Reeve looking at him.

'Are you all right?'

Birdie said he was, which was more or less true. Every bone and muscle in his body was throbbing or aching, the clothes inside his anorak were soaked with sweat and melting snow and his remaining ski stick had been swallowed by the avalanche. But looking up the moun-

117

tain to where the white slick of the gun barrel gleamed in the last of the light, he was amazed to have got down alive and more or less unmaimed. Ray, after another glance at Birdie, skied quietly away towards the road and the rest of the crowd melted away. Only Joe lingered to say, 'It really wasn't us this time.'

Then he too was gone, leaving Birdie to shuffle without ski sticks over the snow, like a battered battery chicken.

At the hotel there were three urgent objectives: to get dry clothes round him, a drink inside him, and then tackle Tim. He saw Fuzz as he went in and decided not to waste time telling her about the avalanche.

'Did you tell Tim I wanted to see him?'

'Yes.'

'Where is he?'

Fuzz didn't know, but said she'd look for him.

Her lack of urgency surprised him until he remembered that she knew nothing about Barbie and Joshua Jones' account of the crossbow. He almost told her about it, then postponed it till after his meeting with Tim. She was so protective of the kids she'd probably insist on being present at the meeting if she knew about it, and that wouldn't help at all. He asked her to send Tim up to his room when the boy appeared, squelched into the bar for a glass of grappa and carried it upstairs with him to change.

He found he was wet to the skin, had to strip off everything and towel himself vigorously, then root around in drawers for dry underwear and a polo-neck. He was dressed but sockless when he heard footsteps on the stairs to the room, then somebody stopped outside the door. His first thought was Nimue, back early from Milan, and he was halfway to the door when the person

118

outside knocked on it gently. Not Nimue then.

'Who's there?'

No answer, but a sound like a giggle or perhaps a nervous intake of breath, then a girl's voice.

'It's me. Can I come in?'

'Who?'

'Brenda. I want to tell you something. About yesterday.'

He opened the door and Brenda walked in, dressed in a tracksuit of shiny mauve satin that strained over buttocks and breasts. The legs of it were too short for her, revealing round calves and plump little feet, pink as fondant sweets. She stood in the middle of the the room staring at him, and he was the one who felt awkward.

'Well, aren't you going to ask me what I know?'

She moved behind him to shut the door, then went to sit on the side of the bed.

'You are a detective, aren't you?'

'I told you in the café, no.'

'But you are trying to prove Wayne didn't kill that Hent bloke?'

Birdie could have done without this, but if the alarming child had something to say there was no point in discouraging her. He waited, and she looked up at him expectantly, smoothing the tracksuit over her plump thighs. 'Well, go on then.'

He said, 'Shall we go and talk about it downstairs?' He was beginning to see why Bruin was so ill-at-ease in the girl's company. The thought of his own daughter didn't help.

She said, 'If we talk about it downstairs, all the others will hear, won't they?'

He sighed and moved as far away from her as he could get in the small room, till his back was pressed against the wood panelling.

119

'What is it you want to tell me?'

She looked round the room, taking in his discarded and damp clothes.

'Got any cigarettes?'

'No.'

It handicapped her, not having a cigarette to draw on, but she did her best, narrowing her eyes and tilting her head to one side.

'You know up at the café this morning, when you asked us what we were doing yesterday afternoon?'

He remembered his feeling then that the girls weren't telling the whole truth.

'You said you were just mucking about.'

'Do you want to know what we were really doing?'

'Has it got anything to do with the murder?'

'It's cold in here, isn't it? Can I get under your duvet thing?'

'No.'

She swung her legs up on the bed and tucked the duvet round them. A challenging stare at him, then, 'That's for you to decide, isn't it?'

He breathed deeply. 'Look, Brenda, get on with it. Either you've got something to tell me or you haven't.'

She looked at him, hugging her knees, head on one side.

'So tell me, what were you doing when you said you were just mucking about?'

'Come over here,' she said.

'What?'

'Over here. I don't want to shout it out to the whole world, do I?'

He moved two steps closer, then looked hastily away because she'd managed to pull down the V of her tracksuit top to the level where it was more an invitation than a neckline.

120

'Look here, you little . . . I mean, look, Brenda, I don't know what you're playing at but . . .'

'Shhh,' she said, and he froze because there were more steps on the stairs. Surely Nimue this time. He leapt for the door and reached it just as somebody tapped on it.

'It's me. Fuzz.'

There was nothing for it. He opened the door wide and watched Fuzz's face, waiting to see her eyes widen as they took in Brenda at ease on the bed. But her expression was one of weariness.

'It didn't take you long, did it, Brenda? You know what I told you after the last time.'

Birdie said, too quickly, 'She said she wanted to tell me something about yesterday.'

'There's always some excuse.'

She turned to the girl. 'Get out. I'll see you later.'

Brenda went, but didn't speak to Fuzz or glance at her. At the door though she paused, looked directly at Birdie, and said goodbye in a voice that could have come straight from a commercial for after-shave.

'Out,' said Fuzz.

The door closed and the bare feet padded away downstairs. Birdie, face red, stared at Fuzz who looked, if anything, even more strained and worried than usual.

'I know how it looks. I swear to you, I didn't invite her and I didn't lay a finger on her.'

'You don't have to tell me that. I know Brenda.'

He said awkwardly, 'Thanks for the rescue.'

She didn't smile.

'I didn't know she was here. What I came to tell you – nobody seems to know where Tim's got to.'

121

CHAPTER EIGHT

Birdie knocked on the door of Tim's room and, getting no answer, opened it and walked in. It was tidy as a monk's cell, with two hand-knitted woollen pullovers neatly folded on the chair and a paperback about St Luke beside the bed. A room that could have belonged to anyone from fifteen to ninety. Birdie was puzzled at first to find no trace of Sidney there because he'd said he had to share with Tim, then he was aware of voices from the room next door. By the sound of it, Sidney had wasted no time after Wayne's departure in moving in with Joe. He moved closer to the wall and heard Joe's voice first, low and reasonable.

'. . . can't blame him if he thinks we did it. After all, we were the ones who'd told him where to go.'

And Sidney's, louder and petulant: 'He's just going to keep picking on us. Everything that happens, it's going to be us.'

Birdie wondered if they'd guessed who was knocking on Tim's door and were staging the dialogue for his benefit. He left Tim's room, closing the door firmly behind him, and knocked on the next one. It was promptly opened by Joe.

'Have you seen Tim?' Birdie asked them.

They both shook their heads.

He said to Sidney, 'I thought you shared with him.'

'When Wayne went I thought I'd come in with Joe.'

From Sidney's casual tone, nobody would have guessed that Wayne went under police escort. Birdie thanked them and left and, as he closed the door, caught the looks of surprise on their faces. They'd expected more questioning. Downstairs Fuzz was at the reception desk, trying to deal with questions from half a dozen of her pupils at once. She saw from his face that he hadn't found Tim and suggested another check on the disco. It seemed an unlikely place for Tim but Birdie spent ten minutes looking for him among the strobe lights and the bludgeoning beat. He poked his head into the lounge that had become the school common room, but none of the card players there had seen Tim either.

By now it was close to six o'clock, when the Alderman Kibbalts party had its early dinner, and quite dark outside. Birdie went back to Fuzz. 'When you told Tim I wanted to see him, did he say anything?'

She thought hard. 'Not that I can remember.'

'Did he look worried?'

'Tim always looks worried.'

Birdie suggested they should try ringing the Hotel Montagna Bianca, in case Tim was with Joshua and Barbie Jones. They got Barbie on the phone, who was concerned but said they'd seen nothing of Tim since spotting him on the ski slopes that morning. By this time Bruin had arrived and Fuzz suggested that he should go with Birdie and check some of the more likely places around the village. The two of them zipped themselves into anoraks and stepped out together into the sharp, starry night, with the cold already turning the water on the pavements back to ice.

As they walked down the hill to the village centre Bruin said, 'It's not like Tim to go off.'

'I think perhaps he didn't want to talk to me.'

123

They walked a few more steps in silence, then Birdie said, 'Yesterday afternoon, when you and Fuzz were skiing together, did you see Tim at all?'

Bruin's face was screwed up with thought. He said slowly, 'No, I don't think so. Not that I can remember. Is it important?'

There seemed no need to ask the next question. If Tim had come up and presented them with a stolen crossbow, Bruin would infallibly have remembered it.

'No, it's probably not important.'

Bruin glanced up at Birdie's face, 'Is . . . is Tim something to do with all this?'

'I just don't know yet.'

Silence again. Birdie had decided not to mention anything about what Barbie had said until he saw Tim himself. He didn't want Bruin, or anybody else, putting the boy on his guard.

They looked inside the first café they came to. A group of Italian boys were playing with the machines but there was no sign of Tim. They tried to ask, in makeshift Italian, if the proprietor had seen him, but the answer seemed to be no. The next café, opposite the church, contained several men in ski instructors' anoraks drinking grappa, plus Ray Reeve. They were talking gloomily in Italian and Birdie thought they were probably the consortium who'd had their hopes of a ski school dashed by Hent. Ray Reeve seemed annoyed to see them, but used his good Italian to find out from the proprietor that no boy of Tim's description had been seen. Ray didn't seem interested and didn't even say goodbye when they left.

'That man really is a sod,' Bruin said.

At Birdie's suggestion they looked in the church, without result. They tramped on, past shop windows full of multi-coloured ski gear, to the furthest café, a little box of a pizza house at the far end of the village. Again, nobody could remember seeing anyone who looked like Tim. They tramped in silence back through the village and up the hill to the hotel, to be met by an anxious Fuzz at the door.

'Any sign of him?'

'No.'

'Oh dear, perhaps it was him she saw then.'

Her efficiency was so badly shaken that it took a few minutes to get the story out of her. While they'd been gone, she'd been making enquiries for Tim around the hotel. One of the girls serving dinner lived in a farmhouse at the top end of the village, in the opposite direction from where Birdie and Bruin had been searching. She'd been walking in to work as usual at about four o'clock and she remembered passing a boy answering to Tim's description soon after she left home.

Fuzz said, 'She thought he was one of ours, but she wasn't sure. Anyway, the point is he was walking away from the village towards the pass.'

Birdie and Bruin exchanged worried looks. To all intents and purposes the village ended at the Hotel Soldanella. Beyond that the road narrowed and ran on upwards past a few small chalets and farmhouses, before climbing steeply over the pass into Switzerland.

Birdie asked, 'Where could he get up that way?'

'Nowhere. The girl said the road's blocked by snow just past her house. The cross-country skiers use it sometimes, but that's all.'

She stared at Birdie, expecting him to do something. 'But if he was trying to get away from you . . .'

Put like that it sounded as if he'd hounded the boy out into the snow. He sighed, feeling the battering his body had taken from the Cascata, crushing down the idea of hot bath and good dinner.

125

'I'd better go and find him then, hadn't I?'

'I'll come too,' said Bruin.

With Fuzz looking like that, they couldn't say anything else. She'd obviously have liked to go with them, but somebody had to look after the rest of the party and, as Bruin pointed out, there was always the chance Tim would turn up while they were away. They borrowed a large torch from the hotel owner and once more stepped out into the cold.

The moon had risen over the mountains and the snow reflected and diffused its light. For the first half mile or so they were walking along clear road, with grit-studded snow banks crowding gradually closer on either side. Then the tarmac surface gave way to hard trodden snow and there was a strong smell of warm cow on the air. The small house on their left was probably where the waitress from the hotel lived, and if she was right Tim had passed that way about four hours before.

'Little idiot,' Bruin said.

He was making heavy going of it in his unsuitable shoes and, although around fifteen years younger than Birdie, he was plump and untrained. After the farmhouse there were just two more wooden chalets, shuttered and empty, then the snow banks fell away and they were looking at a long expanse of snow stretching upwards until the mountains closed on it, with the black gash of a stream running through it. The only signs of humanity were a line of small red flags marking a course for langlauf skiers, and the tracks they'd made in the snow.

'We're not supposed to walk on the langlauf tracks,' Bruin said.

'Somebody already has.'

Birdie pointed to a line of footprints, some of them on the ski tracks, some to the side of it. He switched on his torch and, walking on the ski tracks, they followed the footprints over the snow. The valley became narrower and the ground rose gently so that they could see the lights of the village below them. To their right among the pine woods Birdie could make out the deserted nursery slopes and, above them, the white gash of the Cascata. Bruin, punctilious as ever, was trying not to spoil the ski tracks, walking to one side of them in the soft snow, puffing and floundering. If Birdie's mind had been less full of Tim, of Sidney and Joe, or Ray Reeve, he might have paid him more attention. As it was, he'd almost forgotten about Bruin until a shout from behind warned him that the teacher was in trouble. He turned and saw him kneeling in the snow, his face twisted with pain.

'A ditch or something. Can't get my foot out.'

Cursing, Birdie turned back to investigate. He bent down and by leaning on his shoulder Bruin was able to free the trapped leg. It came out wet and dripping with mud.

'I think it's sprained.'

He looked up at Birdie like a hurt child. 'What shall I do?'

'Get back to the hotel.'

It sounded brutal, but Birdie thought he could only deal with so many problems at a time. He uprooted one of the marker flags from beside the tracks.

'You can lean on this. If you just follow our footprints back you can't go wrong.'

Bruin looked doubtfully at the uprooted flag and at Birdie. The anarchy of disturbing an official marker seemed to bother him almost as much as the sprained ankle.

'But will you be able to manage on your own?'

Birdie just stopped himself saying he'd manage a damned sight better on his own. Instead he reassured

127

Bruin and watched him set out, limping heavily, on his way back across the snowfield to the village, clutching the red marker flag like a lance and pennant. He at least should come to no great harm, but for Tim, if he'd struggled up towards the pass, it was a different matter. The footprints led on, still following the ski tracks. It was getting colder, with Birdie's breath hanging in a cloud in front of him and the snow crust cracking and rustling under his feet. The moon was so bright that he switched the torch off, deciding he might need it more later. In less than a mile the ski tracks ran out. At least, they stopped heading up the valley and looped around the outermost of the red marker flags before heading back for the village. As far as the ski resort was concerned, this was the edge of civilisation. But the footprints went straight on, sunk deep in the fresh snow, with here and there a mark that might be a handprint beside them where the walker had stumbled. The valley narrowed to a point where there was just room for a few yards of snow on either side of the stream. It was fringed with a few scrubby bushes, their lower branches glossed with ice from the spray, but under the snow the water was still running, sounding urgent and cold. Birdie shivered and thought that Tim – if the tracks were Tim's – must have been in a deep panic to come out here on his own. And from that point the going was much more difficult. Every ten steps or so Birdie found himself plunging into depressions that brought the snow up to thigh-level and sent him pitching forward to leave his own large hand-prints on the snow. After a few hundred yards of this he was sweating in spite of the cold. And Tim, he remembered, was a thin, insubstantial-looking lad. He tried calling his name, not loudly because the narrowness of the valley and the silence made any words sound cataclysmic.

128

'Tim? Tim, are you there?'

Nothing but the sound of the stream, even louder now. Up ahead it poured itself down a steep slide of grey rock and beyond that the mountains met and closed off the valley completely, or seemed to. In summer, he'd been told, there was a good path for walkers over the pass, but in these conditions even mountaineers would think twice about it.

He pressed on as far as the foot of the waterfall. The stream spread across the slab, caught into ice at the edges but fast-moving in the centre, and tipped itself into a dark green pool that made him ache with cold even to look at it. The tracks he was following went straight to the edge of the pool, and Birdie's heart turned over.

'Oh ye gods.'

He inched as close to the water as he could, expecting any second that the snow would give way and fling him in, eased himself on to his stomach and slid forward, snow scooping down his collar, until he was looking into the pool. Then a sigh of relief so deep it left a little melted scar of snow under his face. Nothing there but round, grey stones. Cautiously he got to his feet. It was darker in this cleft in the rocks than on the snowfield and he used his torch to look for the tracks, partly obscured by his flounderings. But now he knew Tim hadn't gone into the pool it was easier to read them. Tim – or whoever had made the tracks – had stood by the pool trying to work out some way of getting up the waterfall. There was even a small crust of snow at the bottom of the rock slab as if the person had tried to get a foothold there and withdrawn when he saw or felt the ice covering it. The fact that the person had even considered such an unpromising route was, to Birdie, proof that his strength and judgment had been failing fast. He'd been at the end of his tether and couldn't climb the waterfall, so where

129

had he gone? There wasn't much choice. If he couldn't stick with the stream any more and hadn't gone back on his tracks, the only possibility would be to climb up the side of the valley, hoping to rejoin the stream at a point above the waterfall. And, shining the torch around, Birdie found this was exactly what the tracks did. They went off at right angles to the stream steeply up the valley and from then on, rather than occasional palm prints in the snow, the person had left larger, body-sized impressions and, at one point, an untidy pit where he'd gone deep and had to dig himself out. As he followed, himself tiring, Birdie grew more and more appalled at the panic which must have filled Tim to have driven him to this terrible floundering in the snow.

He stood still and called quite softly, 'Tim, are you there?'

And because the message of failing strength had been printed so clearly on the snow he was hardly even surprised when he heard a weak shout from higher up, a boy's voice, shrill and alarmed. 'Who's there?'

'Is that you, Tim?'

Silence.

'Stay where you are,' Birdie shouted, still not knowing exactly where the boy was.

The tracks turned parallel to the valley and stopped at the foot of a grey crag made up of layers of shale. The layers protruded in thin, crumbling steps, cemented with bands of ice, with the occasional jagged vertical flake that seemed designed for impaling things. Winter or summer, it would have been lunacy to climb it.

'Tim, are you there?'

No answer, but not far above his head something rattled and a shower of ice and shale chippings cascaded down the face. Then there was a sob of fear and more scrambling. Rock fragments rained down round Birdie,

130

making deep pock marks in the snow.

'Tim, for goodness' sake keep still.'

And from above a voice desperately level, rationing its last scrap of control, said, 'I'm stuck.'

'Bloody hell.'

Birdie looked up and around and found the shale uninviting at every point. In daylight a slim person might be able to scrabble up a few feet of it before disaster hit, but it would never take his weight.

'I can't hold on.'

The boy was frankly sobbing now and in deep trouble. Not just chippings but whole plates of shale were crashing down.

'Stay there.'

Which was, Birdie realised, a bloody stupid thing to say, but what else was there? He lodged the torch behind a flake of rock so that he could see what he was doing – not that it improved things much – and pushed his gloves into his pockets. By stretching up to his full height he could just manage to hook his fingers on to what looked a comparatively reliable piece of shale. Then, trying to convince himself it was no worse than doing pull-ups at the gym, he took the weight of his body on his arms and shoulders. This brought his feet clear of the snow, and then it was a case of jamming his body against the shale to spread some of the weight while stretching up with one arm for a hold anything better than suicidal. All this brought more stones clattering down and he thought he could hear sobbing from above him, but there was nothing he could do about that. Another pull upwards, until the next band of shale crumbled under his fingers, and he was clinging to the jagged face with nothing other than chin, elbows and a few millimetres of boot sole.

'I . . . I can't hold on,' said Tim's voice from above him.

131

'You and me both,' thought Birdie.

He wasn't sure how he found the purchase for his next move upwards. Judging from the raw state of his chin later, that might have done most of the work. But whatever the mechanics of it, one hand closed round a pinnacle of rock that was spiky but firm, while the other tried to take a grip on something unexpectedly smooth and rounded. The toe of a boot. The toe of a boot that kicked.

'You little . . .'

His fingers closed round an ankle and, mostly by the rock spike but partly by Tim's feebly thrashing foot, Birdie dragged himself up beside the boy.

'What the hell were you trying to do?'

Tim had got himself stuck on a shelf a few feet wide and, as the kick proved, was in no immediate danger of falling. Above the shelf the rock face bulged out, looking even more brittle than below and entirely unclimbable. He was sprawled along the shelf, his left arm firmly hooked round a piece of rock. His face in the moonlight was the colour of condensed milk and Birdie's anger cooled when he looked at him. The boy was so cold and scared he didn't know what he was doing. He stared at Birdie, wide-eyed and unspeaking.

'What were you trying to do?' Birdie repeated more gently, but still got no answer.

He sat down beside Tim and made him release his hold on the rock. It had in any case been too small to give anything but psychological support.

'What have you done with your gloves?'

'Lost them.'

The reply was almost inaudible. The fingers of both hands were bluish white. Birdie rubbed them till Tim gasped and wriggled with pain, then drew his own warm gloves over them.

132

'Are you hurt?'

He had to repeat the question twice before he got even a shake of the head.

'Well then, we're going to get you down this and go home. It's not as bad as it looks.'

Which was untrue. He knew it would be even worse going down.

'I'll go first, then I want you to step on to my shoulders. Understand?'

He wasn't at all sure the boy did understand, but he was seriously worried about exposure. Tim was already sick from cold and exhaustion, and to stay where he was all night might kill him. He explained what he wanted again, then got down the rock face in what was more a controlled and painful slither than a climb. It was perhaps fifteen feet from Tim's perch to the snow. Birdie pressed his face and arms against the rock.

'Ready, Tim? Just lower yourself down.'

It was a process of verbal hypnosis. Birdie's arms were aching and his legs quivering with the strain before the boy could be persuaded to let himself hang by his hands from the ledge and then slither the short distance that separated his feet from Birdie's shoulders.

'Just let yourself slide down. Pretend I'm a drainpipe or something.'

It was like talking to a ten-year-old, but even that seemed to be beyond Tim's understanding or strength. He simply collapsed backwards, bringing them both down into the snow, winded but otherwise unharmed.

'Good lad.'

But Tim's eyes were closed and he was breathing heavily. Birdie slapped both cheeks and the eyes opened, but they were dull and unfocused.

'Tim, we've got to walk.'

But Tim didn't seem to understand and Birdie had to

133

lump him down as far as the foot of the waterfall in a fireman's lift, thankful that he wasn't as solid as Wayne or Joe. At the trampled snow by the pool he put Tim back on his feet and supported him.

'Tim, old son, you've got to walk. I can't carry you all the way.'

He stripped his own anorak off and put it round the boy's shoulders, talking to him as he pushed the unresisting arms into the sleeves and zipped it up.

'That's the hardest part over, Tim. Just walking now.'

He held Tim's arm tightly and guided his feet into the tracks they'd made on the outward journey.

'That's it. Left and right. Left and right.'

By the time they got to the marker flag at the far end of the cross-country course Tim's condition had improved. His eyes were focusing and he was able to manage one-word answers to some of Birdie's questions. By now Birdie himself, in ski pants and thin sweater without gloves or anorak, was getting badly chilled, but once on the langlauf tracks they made better progress. Tim even managed to walk unsupported. Once or twice Birdie caught the boy glancing at him in a way that showed his mind was beginning to move again.

It was past ten o'clock when they got back to the road.

Birdie said, 'Soon be home now.'

Tim looked up at him. 'I didn't want to see you.'

His face was sharp and bloodless, framed by the collar of Birdie's anorak.

'I know.'

They began walking down the road towards the lights of the village.

Birdie said, 'It was about the crossbow.'

'Yes.'

'Where did you get it, Tim?'

Tim stopped and looked at him, apparently surprised

the question needed asking.

'It was Wayne's.'

They began walking again, past the deserted chalets, past the farmhouse with its smell of cows. Birdie had to force himself to ask the next question, to ask any more questions, when the answers came with such exhausted simplicity.

'Why did you take it?'

'I went in to ask Sidney something. They were playing about with it.' His tone was flat as if it didn't matter or had happened a very long time ago.

'But why did you want it?'

'They never let me do things. They think I'm different. I just wanted to . . . try what it was like.'

Their steps thudding on the frozen road were louder than their voices.

'When did you take it?'

'Just after lunch, when they'd gone off skiing.'

'After lunch yesterday?'

'Yes.'

'And Mr and Mrs Jones saw you with it and told you to give it to a teacher?'

'Yes.'

And Birdie couldn't put off asking the next question any longer. 'But you skied down with it and got on the lift again, didn't you? And then you shot Mr Hent with it.'

'No,' said Tim in the same calm, flat voice.

Birdie stopped and took him by the shoulder. 'Tim, for goodness' sake, say it now and get it over.'

But suddenly there was a light back in Tim's eyes and, under two layers of anorak, his shoulder came alive and wriggled in Birdie's grip.

'No, no, I didn't. I knew you'd think I did. That was why . . .' And he twisted out of Birdie's hands and,

135

incredibly, tried to run back up the road towards the mountain. Birdie ran after him and caught him as he was falling and the boy collapsed against him, limp and gasping with sobs.

'I didn't. I didn't kill him.'

Birdie said, holding on to him, 'You had the crossbow. You were on the chair lift.'

'No, not when I saw him. I didn't have it when I saw him.' He was now shivering violently and Birdie knew he should get him indoors quickly, but this chance wouldn't come again. He held him against his chest, feeling the thin body vibrating like a wire cable.

'What had you done with it then? What had you done with it?'

'I'd . . . I threw it away.'

His eyes closed.

'Did you give it back to Wayne, then? Did you give it back to him?'

The eyes opened, very close to his own, and Tim repeated more strongly, 'I threw it away.'

'Where did you throw it?'

'On the snow.'

'Where? Where on the snow?'

But Tim wouldn't, or couldn't, say any more. His eyes closed again and his head flopped sideways. Faced with the inhumanity of choking answers from a boy in a state of near collapse, appalled at himself for what he'd done so far, Birdie could only hook an arm round Tim's shoulders and half support, half carry him the last few hundred yards back to the Hotel Soldanella. And once through the door an explosion of warmth and light and noise, with Tim being taken from him and Fuzz staring with reproachful eyes, and everybody wanting explanations and pressing hot wine and coffee on him.

In the middle of it all somebody passed on a message

136

from Nimue saying she'd done all she could in Milan and would be back in the morning.

CHAPTER NINE

He woke to find her standing by the bed and daylight coming through the small uncurtained window.

'Hello, love. What time is it?'

'Nearly ten.'

He got out of bed to hug her, every muscle creaking and protesting from the strains of the day before. When she had a chance to look at him properly, she gasped.

'Birdie love, what have you been doing to yourself?'

He looked down at his legs and chest and found they were patched with bruises and knew from the feel that part of his face had been rubbed raw by the shale.

'Some of it's from the avalanche and some of it's from Tim.'

She sat down suddenly on the bed, still wearing boots and anorak. 'What's been going on?'

Her face, when he told her about the Cascata and the avalanche, made him more aware of the danger than he'd been at the time. She listened without saying a word, hands clenched together.

When he'd got himself back to the nursery slope she said, 'It could have killed you, you know that?'

He sat down beside her and put an arm round her.

'Yes, but it didn't. Look, it's hardly even dented me.'

But she didn't laugh. She hugged him quickly then started pacing round the small room.

138

'If it was Joe and Sidney I'll tell that school never to let them near a mountain again, or anywhere else.'

'They deny it of course.'

'Well, who then?'

'I'm not sure, love. I'm just not sure.'

She looked at him for a few seconds, then pulled her suitcase from under the bed and started rummaging in it.

'What are you looking for?'

'The bruise stuff and some antiseptic for that face.'

She made him stretch out on the bed while her long fingers massaged cream into overstrained joints and lightly over bruises.

When she'd finished she said, 'And what's this about Tim?'

He told her every detail he could remember. It was, in its way, an offering to her, showing that he'd been trying to do what she wanted while she was away.

She said, 'You could feel there was something odd about Tim.'

For some reason, perhaps the memory of the moment when he thought the boy might have drowned in the mountain pool, Birdie felt a need to defend him.

'He's not so odd. He just doesn't react in the same way as the rest of them.'

Nimue didn't reply. She began stripping off her jumper and ski pants and he hoped, in spite of his mass of bruises, that she was going to get into bed with him, until she explained, 'I didn't even have time to wash in Milan. Before we do anything else I want to change.'

He sighed a little to himself at whatever it was they had to do, but for the moment he was content to watch her, neat and unselfconscious as a cat, while she sponged down in the small washbasin. It was as she was standing on one bare leg, carefully soaping the other foot, that she delivered the shock.

139

'You'd have been far too exhausted to go to the police last night.'

'The police?'

At first he genuinely didn't know what she meant. She changed feet.

'About Tim taking the crossbow.'

Until then it hadn't occurred to him. As far as he'd thought about the next step at all, it was simply discussing what he'd learned with Nimue. He'd been too preoccupied with what was happening at the time to think beyond that.

'It must be the most important bit of evidence so far.'

He couldn't deny that, but a protest was growing inside him, all the more insistent because he knew he couldn't justify it.

'You think we ought to tell them today?'

She turned round to stare at him. 'Have we got any choice?'

Surprise at having this sprung on him made him clumsy. 'You weren't always so set on telling the police things.'

He realised from the way her shoulders slumped over the washbasin that it had been worse than clumsy, it had been cruel, dragging up a time they'd both prefer to forget. But her voice when she replied was carefully calm. 'It's not just a case of citizen's duty. It's a boy locked up when he needn't be.'

'Let's face it, love, it's not the first time Wayne's been locked up and I don't suppose it will be the last.'

She seemed to be concentrating on soaping her toes and said quietly, 'I went to see him last night.'

'Where?'

'This children's hostel place just outside Milan. It's . . . quite comfortable.'

'And what did he have to say?'

140

'That he didn't do it.'

'Well, he would, wouldn't he? I still think . . .'

She went on, looking down at her foot, 'He said it as if it wasn't important, as if he didn't expect anybody to believe him. He was just sitting there in this little room, and they'd got him some English motor cycle magazines and he was just . . . so passive.'

Birdie nodded, remembering Sidney's 'He's going to get done for something he didn't do sooner or later'. It was their passivity that scared him, a refusal to feel guilty about anything because they didn't accept that there was any justice. Tim at least wasn't passive. He'd vibrated with misery and guilt. He said, 'It would be worse for Tim, being arrested and locked up.'

'It's bad for anybody.' She came and sat down beside him on the bed to dry her feet, but didn't look at him. 'You can't say it doesn't matter about Wayne being locked up because you like Tim and you don't like Wayne.'

'It's not a matter of liking Tim. I'm not even sure that I do like him very much.'

'Then why are you trying to protect him?'

He'd been trying over the last few minutes to answer that for himself, ever since it became clear that the events of the previous night had some hard implications by daylight.

'It was just so pathetic, pinching this crossbow as if it would somehow magically make him like all the rest of them. Then it goes wrong and he nearly kills himself from exposure because he feels guilty.'

'Does feeling guilty make it all right then?'

'No, but you can understand people who feel guilty. The thing about Wayne and his like is that they don't. It's as if they had a piece of their brain missing. You just can't understand them.'

141

Silence.

'Do you see what I mean?'

She said, 'Or is it that people who don't feel guilty are a threat to the way you see yourself?'

The more he thought about that, the more it worried him. He remembered the weight of Tim over his shoulders, the sprawled desperate marks in the snow. Was it just the fact that Tim was so much a child still, so obedient to adult authority, that made him hesitate to surrender the boy?

Nimue had seen the worry on his face. She said more gently, 'I'm sorry, love, but they're both the same age, they're both sixteen. We can't play God with them.'

He said sullenly, 'It could still be Wayne. If Wayne saw Tim with the crossbow and made him give it back, then threatened him later that if he told anybody . . .'

'Yes, it could still be Wayne, but it could be anyone else too. It opens the whole thing up. If the police know Tim was carrying the bow around that afternoon, they'd release Wayne.'

'And lock up Tim?'

'It would depend whether they believed him, wouldn't it?'

'I'm just not convinced Tim did it.'

She walked across the room to replace the towel on its rail. 'All right, perhaps Tim really did throw it away and somebody else picked it up. That would be for the police to decide.'

He had a vivid picture of Tim shut up in a room with detectives and interpreters, stammering out his story unconvincingly, a story that cold and exhaustion had first wrung out of him.

He admitted, 'In their place I'd think he'd done it.'

'Yes. He admits to stealing the crossbow, he passed Hent on the chair lift, we've only got his word for it that

142

Hent was alive when they passed.'

'You see, you think he did it.'

'Birdie, I just don't know. But what I do know is that we can't keep it to ourselves.'

He pleaded, 'Let's wait another day. Just one more day.'

'But Wayne . . .'

'They wouldn't release him straight off anyway. It would take them at least a day to check.'

'And what are you going to do with the day?'

'Go on poking around. Try to come up with something.' Try against all hope to find a way out of this maze that seemed to be leading him and Nimue away from each other. Try, before the hedges of the maze turned into brick walls.

'Perhaps you're right about why I'm reacting like this. Only I'm asking you, begging you, just to give me another twenty-four hours.'

She said, 'It's somebody else's time I'm giving.'

'Thank you.'

'And Birdie, if we haven't got any further by this time tomorrow, I'm going to tell the police about Tim, you know that?'

He nodded. She began moving purposefully round the room, gathering up clean clothes.

'Anyway, with luck Tim might have told somebody else about it by now.'

That simple way out hadn't occurred to him. The last he'd seen of Tim was when the boy was being helped upstairs to his room by Fuzz, with Bruin limping along in their wake.

'Could you have another talk with him this morning, see if he'll tell you anything else?'

'Not if Fuzz knows about it. She already blames me for last night.'

Nimue, now in plum-coloured corduroys and clean white sweater, admitted this was a problem. But she, unlike Birdie, seemed full of energy and ready to go, although she could have snatched only a few hours' sleep in Milan.

'I get on all right with Fuzz. Shall I have a word with her and see if she'll let me speak to him?'

It would be insane protectiveness to keep Nimue from Tim.

'That's a good idea. Thanks.'

'See you downstairs in half an hour.'

Nimue began looking for Fuzz at her usual station by the phone on the reception desk but there was no sign of her. But Bruin, sitting on an armchair in the lobby reading a paperback with his injured ankle propped on a stool, thought she'd be upstairs in Tim's room.

'She got a doctor to him this morning. Apparently his temperature's a hundred and two.'

Nimue climbed to the first-floor corridor, deserted now that most of the Alderman Kibbalts group were out skiing, and tapped on the door of Tim's room. It was opened a crack by Fuzz and, over her shoulder, Nimue caught a glimpse of Tim, flushed of face and heavy-eyed. Fuzz looked relieved when she saw it was Nimue and came out to the corridor, closing the door gently behind her.

'I think he'll sleep now.'

The two women walked side by side down the stairs to the common room, with Fuzz stumbling from tiredness.

'I wonder if there's any coffee.'

With a little persuasion in the kitchen Nimue was able to produce not only coffee but rolls and cherry jam. She got Fuzz settled in an armchair within sight and sound of the telephone and poured the coffee with plenty of milk.

144

'Did you see him?'

Nimue nodded.

'How was he?'

'Quiet. He wants Joe to send him his leather jacket.'

Fuzz sipped coffee, eyes on Nimue's face, hungry for any information.

'And I got the telexes sent off. They'll ring from Milan if his father gets in touch.'

'Poor kid.'

Nimue didn't know whether that sigh was for Wayne or Tim or all the other poor kids in Fuzz's professional life. She asked, 'How's Tim?'

'Like a blown fuse. The circuit gets overloaded and that's it.'

Nimue thought that Fuzz herself, although unquestionably a heavy-duty circuit, was in danger of blowing a fuse. She was almost glad that her reluctant promise to Birdie stopped her from adding the latest facts about Tim to the overload. But she did ask about Tim's repeated claim that Hent was alive when their chairs passed.

'Do you think Tim's telling the truth?'

'Tim's truthful.'

'Always?'

Fuzz said in an angry voice, although her anger didn't seem to be directed at Nimue, 'Why does everyone keep on at him? He could have died from exposure last night.'

'That wasn't Birdie's fault. He couldn't know Tim would react like that.'

'He should have guessed. Tim's a walking mass of guilt. First his screwed-up mother, then when we manage to get him away from her for the first time in his life he walks straight into two religious maniacs out here, and now all this. Tim just can't go on taking it.'

'But it is important. If Tim really is telling the truth

about that, then it makes things worse for Wayne.'

Fuzz nodded, pushing the palms of her hands hard against her forehead. This was obviously not a new problem to her.

'Oh, that bloody man.'

And Nimue began to defend Birdie, explaining over again that he had no choice but to question Tim, until it dawned on her that Fuzz wasn't talking about Birdie.

'No, bloody Hent. Why did he have to do this to them?'

Nimue suggested gently that Hent could hardly have planned to get himself murdered. Fuzz sighed, took her hands away from her forehead and slumped back in the chair.

'No, but it's all of a piece, isn't it? I mean, there are his bloody newspapers and videos and telly programmes pushing lies to the kids about everything that matters, all the money and the grabbing and the violence. Then he gets himself killed and it all spills over into real life – but it still doesn't seem real.'

'Until you think of Wayne down in Milan.'

Fuzz nodded, but she was looking straight ahead of her as she spoke and not at Nimue, as if she could fire her own anger out into space with no transmitter except its own force.

'They eat people, Hent and the rest. Rich people telling lies and getting richer for it, and poor bloody kids are supposed to tell the truth all the time.'

It was clearly not the time for any more questions about Tim's truthfulness. Accepting this, Nimue tried to reply to what Fuzz was saying. 'I don't like his papers either, but do you think they have as much influence as all that? Aren't most people a bit tougher to eat?'

Fuzz shook her head and put down her empty coffee cup. 'Don't you believe it. He even ate us once.'

146

'Ate you?'

'We had a family help unit attached to the university I was at. We started this neighbourhood paper to tell people about their rights and so on, and it really took off. Then we needed money to keep it going, so we went to Horace Hent.'

'But why, if you didn't like his papers?'

'He didn't have any papers then. This was fifteen years ago. He'd made his first five million out of petrol additives and was still laying claim to a social conscience. So he funded us, and before we knew where we were he'd turned the paper into the most useless sort of give-away advertising sheet and he just went on from there.'

'What did you do?'

'Dropped it like the piece of filthy bog paper he'd made it and went on to other things. I was in my last year at university by then anyway.'

Nimue thought how a succession of Waynes and Tims and Brendas had got the same fierce commitment that Fuzz had once given her families project.

'Poor Fuzz.'

Fuzz gave her a weak grin. 'Oh, it's all part of the learning curve, I suppose. But it makes me furious when they get at the kids.' She became efficient again, asking Nimue how long the telexes would take to reach England, looking longingly at the reception desk telephone. Nimue advised her, probably uselessly, to go upstairs for a few hours' sleep and went out to the porch to meet Birdie.

As they walked together down the hill to the shops Nimue told Birdie about her lack of success with Fuzz. 'I'll have another try when she's calmer, but I don't think I'll get anywhere. If you as much as suggest that one of her kids might be lying, you get a blast about the sins of

147

everyone else.'

Birdie was showing some signs of sympathy for the late Hent. 'All right, he was a bit of a sod. But have you noticed, everybody disapproved of him, but they were all queuing up to ask for some of his money? Fuzz and her families, Barbie and Joshua and their churches, Ray Reeve and his ski school.'

And he told her, diffidently because it seemed such an insubstantial clue, about his thoughts on Ray Reeve and the powder snow. It was at any rate safer than discussing the Wayne–Tim dilemma. To his surprise, she was inclined to take it seriously. Perhaps she wanted a way out as badly as he did.

'You're right, powder snow does cling. And another thing, remember what Barbie and Joshua said to you about the crossbow.'

'That they saw Tim with it, but we . . .'

'Yes, but what did they tell Tim to do with it?'

He thought for a second, then, 'Bloody hell, they told him to give it to a teacher.'

'Exactly. And Tim, wouldn't you say, is the kind of boy who does what's he's told?'

'But if Ray was skiing over in the powder snow, how would Tim get a chance to give it to him?'

'If he really was over in the powder snow.'

Birdie walked the next few steps in silence, warm with the hope that the choice between Wayne and Tim needn't be made after all. Ray, a bitter man with the great dream of his life ended by Hent, miraculously handed a crossbow. Ray on the chair lift ahead of Hent, turning and firing into his chest. But at that point it fell apart.

'He'd be too far away.'

'Yes, but let's go and check it.'

So they retraced their steps back up the hill and past

148

the hotel to the chair lift and stood there at the bottom timing it with Birdie's stop watch. They'd agreed that they'd been standing there for about five minutes between Ray's arrival and the descent of Hent's body; certainly no less than four minutes. So they counted the chairs that arrived at the bottom in four minutes: twenty-six of them with a gap of around twenty yards between each pair of chairs. Birdie put his stop watch away with that hope obliterated.

'Twenty-six chairs, that makes more than five hundred yards. With a crossbow that's just not on.'

Nimue took his arm and they trudged back down the hill. But he wasn't abandoning the hope of a way out so easily.

'What we're forgetting all the time is the people up at the top. It's just within the bounds of possibility that somebody loaded him on to that chair already dead.'

'But what a risk. Whoever it was couldn't have known the lift attendant would be having a screaming row on the phone at just the right time.'

'But what if somebody was hiding inside the shed waiting for a chance?'

'They couldn't have waited more than a few minutes because he hadn't been dead long when he got to the bottom.'

'Perhaps they were lucky. They could even have winched the body down the ramp in a crate.'

She said: 'Are you thinking of Aeneas Campbell?'

'Aeneas Campbell, yes – or your friend Allana.'

She smiled. 'Allana's hardly capable of getting a Yorkshire terrier downstairs, let alone a body down a bit of mountain.'

'People do impossible things when they're desperate. And remember, she's got those snow shoe things.'

'But they're just toys. She bought them in the shop

149

that morning when I met her and asked me if you could get down the mountain on them.'

He stopped in his tracks. 'You're telling me Allana bought the snow shoes just a few hours before her husband was murdered?'

'Yes, but she bought a whole lot of other things too, silly things. Allana always tends to go a bit mad in shops.'

He began walking again, but her arm was no longer linked through his.

He said, 'You know the big problem with this business? Everybody's trying to protect somebody; you and Fuzz protecting Wayne, you quite sure it can't be Allana . . .'

'And you protecting Tim.'

There it was again. They were pacing faster and faster down the main street, back at the same problem. He began to say he wasn't protecting Tim then stopped, not sure of his own motives any more.

They walked in silence until they got to the village square and the church and Nimue asked, 'What are we looking for now?'

'Underpants.'

She laughed and took his arm again, glad of anything that lessened the tension between them.

'Didn't you pack enough?'

'I thought I did, but I can't have.'

One pair at least seemed to be missing, although he was usually a methodical packer. They went into the small supermarket and took a wire basket, but there was no sign of what he was looking for. Nimue found a large middle-aged woman in an overall and began talking to her in Italian and, to Birdie's acute embarrassment, the two of them plunged into what was obviously a hilarious female conversation, with sidelong glances from the

150

woman in his direction. Nimue came back to him grinning.

'They've sold out. You'll just have to wash some in the washbasin.'

'Sold out of underpants?'

'Yes, they've had a run on them, if that's the expression I want. She said a little English girl came in yesterday and bought the last three pairs of them.'

'A little English girl, three pairs of men's underpants?'

'That's what she said.'

As they walked back up the street Birdie asked, 'Did you get a description of the little English girl?'

'I didn't ask for one. Why?'

He said darkly, 'I'll bet it was something to do with Brenda.' He'd told Nimue about Brenda's invasion of his room, and felt she'd taken it rather lightly.

'I shouldn't be at all surprised. Perhaps I should have asked her who'd been buying Superglue recently as well.'

He'd almost forgotten the humiliating Superglue episode and didn't enjoy being reminded of it. And yet, once in his mind, it refused to go away. He thought of the chair carrying him into the dimness of the long shed, the wheel revolving. Then he pictured the same chair, still with this strip of anorak attached to it, motionless in a siding with other chairs awaiting attention. Dimly he had an idea that these two pictures were linked in some way with the questions he was asking himself, but he didn't yet understand why that should be so.

At the hotel they found Aeneas Campbell waiting for them, pacing up and down the lobby in his overcoat. Birdie was surprised to see him there, remembering that it was the big day for the start of the Hent empire's satellite transmission, but his problems were even more immediate than that.

'It's Allana. She wants you to stay with her up there

151

tonight.'

He was talking direct to Nimue.

'Why, what's wrong?'

'She doesn't want to be on her own. I stayed with her last night, but I've got a reception down at the hotel tonight for some of the advertisers.'

And they drew out of him a list of woes. The road up to the satellite station still hadn't been cleared and nobody seemed to know how long it would take. Allana was firm in her refusal to have anything to do with the chair lift but went nearly hysterical at the idea of spending a night up the mountain with only the satellite technicians for company.

'And God knows I can't ask them to babysit Allana. They'll have enough to do this evening.'

Nimue sighed. 'When does she want me there?'

'We thought you could go up about half past four, before they close the lift.'

It didn't seem to have occurred to either of them that Nimue might refuse. Birdie felt angry at the way they were all heaping their problems on her.

'We'll both go up.'

An evening in Allana's company struck him as no treat, but he was damned if he'd let Nimue go up there without him. Aeneas looked ill at ease.

'The fact is, she made a point of only wanting Nimue. I'm afraid she seems to have taken an irrational dislike to you.'

Great, Birdie thought. Yet another person in this bloody case taking a dislike to him. Fuzz, Allana, Joe and Sidney. Superglue, avalanches and snubs from copper-haired mental cases on snow shoes. Nimue was looking at him anxiously, biting her lip, and he could tell she was torn between resenting her friend's attitude to him and the wish to go up and help regardless.

152

'Oh, go on. You can have a nice cosy evening sitting up there discussing everything that's wrong with me.'

'Birdie, you know it won't be like that.'

Aeneas seemed, at last, a little conscience stricken. He said to Birdie, 'You could come along to the reception at the hotel. I could do with an extra human being among the advertisers.'

Birdie accepted his consolation prize as politely as possible and Aeneas left, looking like a man who still had several loads on his mind. As they went upstairs to their room Nimue said: 'I didn't want to go off again. Allana is an idiot.'

But he wished she'd said it with a little less tolerance in her voice.

153

CHAPTER TEN

After the school party austerities of the Hotel Soldanella, the lounge of the Montagna Bianca seemed a
haven of middle-aged comfort. There were deep plush
armchairs, trollies with bottles of champagne, small
tables scattered with vases of pink rosebuds so plump
they looked edible, and plates of canapés too delicate to
eat. Even with its head cut off, the body of the Hent
empire knew how to stage a launch. The opening of
satellite transmissions from the mountain was probably
the biggest event in the village since the war and the
party had a quota of local notables. Birdie could pick
them out because they wore good suits and anxious
expressions, in contrast to the cashmere casualness of the
advertisers. He felt woefully distinct from either group in
his chainstore sweater and ski trousers and was still
angry with Aeneas, Allana and the whole organisation
for separating him from Nimue for the night. Aeneas
had pressed a glass of champagne into his hand in an
abstracted way when he came into the room, then
dashed off to talk fast German to a group of men in a
corner.

Transmission was due to start at seven, he'd been told:
a live show from the studio in Milan to celebrate the
opening, and there were still ten minutes or so to go.
People were beginning to drift towards the huge televi-

154

sion screen at one end of the room, though it was
showing only the double H symbol that Hent had already
stamped on the life of three continents and had paid so
much to launch into space. Paid, finally, with his life.
Birdie sipped champagne and stared at it, thinking of the
body swinging down in its mottled coat, of Nimue up at
the satellite station with Allana.

He'd panicked just before she went, thinking suddenly
that she'd be vulnerable up there on her own with only
Allana and the preoccupied technicians for company,
that somebody had, after all, tried to kill him under an
avalanche and might do the same for anybody asking too
many questions. She'd listened, then pointed out in that
case she'd be safer up the mountain than anywhere else.
Her friend needed her, and that was that. After a while
he'd given up arguing but taken a few precautions of his
own. He'd travelled up with her on the chair lift,
carrying her skis so that she could come back to him as
soon as it got light in the morning, and walked with her
up the snow path and along the tunnel to the door in the
rock wall. Not trusting himself to be polite to Allana,
he'd parted from her there and skied back down to the
village as quickly as possible. By the time it was dark
he'd made a census to his own satisfaction: Barbie and
Joshua, heads together in their hotel coffee shop, Sidney
and Joe in the disco, Ray Reeve drinking grappa with his
ski school friends as usual. (He'd scowled at Birdie when
he looked into the café, and Birdie had scowled back.)
Aeneas was here at the reception, filling the customers
with champagne and, for the sake of completeness,
Birdie added Tim to his list, still in bed but reported by
Fuzz to be taking light nourishment. It was some
satisfaction to him that with the road blocked and the
chair lift closed for the night, none of them could get
near Nimue till morning.

155

He found that somebody was pressing another glass of champagne into his hand and all the attention of the room was concentrated on the big television screen. There was a rising of tension, as if the party were caught up in the invisible line that was harnessing the mountain above them and the studio in Milan to its satellite twenty-two thousand miles away. Birdie had to fight an unscientific impulse to go outside and look up into the darkness, and for the first time the excitement of the thing gripped him. It wasn't, after all, simply a financial shenanigan involving an unlikeable set of people. It was all that but more than that, a conjuring trick on a cosmic scale, a risky juggling act of communication using the orbiting planets themselves. And what he already thought of as their local mountain – although it had been doing its best to kill him the day before – was calling to the satellite. He looked at the screen over the heads of advertisers and village dignitaries, wondering if Nimue was watching in the room up the mountain.

'Oh God,' said Allana. 'Will we turn it off? It's a crime against space.'

In the foreground of the picture three girls and two men were doing inventively sinuous things while a tenor in the background sang something about remembering. Allana and Nimue were sitting on the big leather sofa in what had been Hent's mountaintop office, watching the opening of the show.

'I don't mind; we'll switch it off if you like.'

'No, we'll leave it on after all. It might get better.'

Allana had been in a difficult mood, or rather a succession of difficult moods, ever since Nimue arrived, with the shock of her husband's death and her own self-imprisonment on the mountain bringing her at some times near hysteria, at others to an unrealistic

156

self-confidence. She'd just informed Nimue that she'd had enough, that she'd go down the mountain with her as soon as it was light. No, not on the chair lift, she'd walk down. All right then, if the snow was too deep for walking she'd ski down with Nimue. After all, skiing wasn't very difficult, was it? Didn't you just point your skis down and lean forward and there you were? When Nimue pointed out that where you were was probably face down in the snow with two broken legs, Allana raged at herself for not being able to ski and at all the people in her life who'd neglected to teach her. Then, disconcertingly, she was calm again, asking, 'Do you think people make a lot of money running ski schools?'

Surprised, Nimue asked what made her think of that.

'Ray. You know, Ray the teacher. He's staying at your hotel.'

Which was even more surprising. Nimue thought Hent would hardly have been likely to involve Allana in his business discussion with Ray Reeve.

Allana said, 'He came up here this morning to talk about it.'

'He what?'

Allana laughed at the shocked expression on her face. 'What's so surprising about that?'

'You mean the day after your husband had been murdered Ray Reeve came up here to ask you to put money in his ski school?'

'What's wrong with that?'

'There's a hell of a lot wrong with it. For one thing, he shouldn't have been bothering you at all. For another, it's a thoroughly nasty try at getting money out of you while you're still in a state of shock.'

But she couldn't, until she'd thought much more about it, tell Allana why she was so disturbed. Up to then, the case against Ray Reeve had been only a half serious one, more of a diversion from the battle over Wayne and Tim. There was his bitterness against Hent, the absence of the powder snow, the remote possibility that Tim really had passed the crossbow to his teacher. But if you added to them the fact that before Hent's body was out of the mortuary Ray was putting the ski school proposition to his rich young widow, the case was strong enough to be alarming. She wanted urgently to discuss it with Birdie and felt resentful that Allana's dislike had kept him down in the village. She was remembering how often in the past she'd had to resist strong temptations to shake Allana till her teeth rattled. She resisted them again, saying as casually as possible, 'I think you should be careful with Ray Reeve. He's an obsessive man.'

But Allana wasn't deceived by the casual tone. 'It's no use, Nimue. I like him. You know how quick I am at summing up people.'

Quick, and usually disastrous. Allana's Friday night tirades of fury and insult as Monday's latest prince turned out to be yet another frog were legends among her friends. Hent, it seemed, had turned into a frog long before his death, but the middle-aged school master seemed an unlikely new prince.

'And he's over fifty,' Nimue said.

It was a grossly unfair tactic, but justified if it helped to warn Allana off. But yet again she'd under-rated her friend's stubbornness.

Allana flared up, 'Well, what about yours? He's over fifty as well.'

'He is not. He's forty-three.'

And she bit her tongue, thinking it was beginning to sound like a classroom scrap. But Allana was well into the attack.

'Anyway, I don't like him. And you shouldn't have told him about Getting Back at Hent.'

158

'I tell Birdie everything. And I'm honestly not too bothered whether you like him or not.'

A sudden penitent look on Allana's face. Tears began forming in her eyes.

'You . . . you really like him, don't you? That makes me feel awful. Awful.'

On the screen the sinuous dancers had been replaced by a plump American comedian talking about his bank manager. The tears were running down Allana's cheeks now, quite unchecked.

'I wouldn't have . . . not if I'd known you really like him.'

Nimue sighed, finding quick mood changes less easy to take. 'Don't worry, love, you haven't said anything so terrible, and there's no law that says you have to like him too.'

'Oh, it's worse than that. Oh, it's much worse than that.'

'Come on, Allana. It's not as tragic as all that.'

'But it is, it is.'

Nimue went to the television and turned the sound down, and the comedian mouthed his lines in silence.

'All right, what's so terrible about it?'

And Allana, looking her full in the face, said, 'I nearly killed him.'

'You . . . you nearly killed Birdie? How?'

'I changed the signs at the top of the ski runs so he went down the one with the avalanches. I was just . . . just so angry you'd told him about it and he was all . . . cold and disapproving. So I saw him go in the café, then I went along on my snow shoes and changed them round.'

Nimue sat frozen, struggling for words.

'You deliberately sent Birdie down the Cascata? You were trying to kill Birdie?'

159

'I wasn't thinking about killing him. I was just so furious because he knew about Getting Back at Hent. And I heard the skiers talking about avalanches. Oh Nimue darling, don't look like that. I wasn't really trying to kill him.'

And she sat there looking at Nimue with the tears running down her cheeks, waiting to be forgiven just as she'd waited to be forgiven in the old days for borrowing her silk blouse or using up the last of the coffee.

Nimue said, 'You're mad.'

In the old days she'd often said that too, but in a tone that carried forgiveness with it. Hearing that wasn't the case now, Allana sank her face in her hands and rocked to and fro.

'Oh, what'll I do? What'll I do?'

A few minutes ago Nimue couldn't have watched this without putting an arm round her and comforting her, but now she sat quite still, looking at Allana and thinking hard.

When the sobbing quietened enough for her to be heard she said. 'Listen Allana, is there anything else you've been hiding?'

'Anything else?'

'Yes, about who killed your husband for instance?'

Allana began sobbing hard again. 'I didn't kill him. I swear to God I didn't lay a finger on him.'

'But you did try to kill Birdie.'

'I told you, I didn't mean to. I didn't mean to. If I'd known you really liked him . . .'

On the screen the sinuous girls and boys were back again, gyrating in a pattern of lights as the first part of Hent's satellite show came to its end.

Birdie watched the gyrating girls, finding them less stimulating than Nimue at the washbasin. He wondered

160

what she was doing in the mountaintop office with Allana. Probably giggling over their coffee like a couple of schoolgirls and comparing notes about the shortcomings of the men in their lives, especially Birdie Linnet.

Again there was this feeling of being shut out, by his age, by his sex. He gulped his third glass of champagne, not enjoying it, and watched the lights on the screen splinter into kaleidoscope patterns.

Aeneas said loudly, 'Advertisements coming up.'

And this was the signal for guests who'd drifted talking into various parts of the room while the show was on to congregate again in front of the screen. There was a feeling that the serious part of the evening had arrived, that this was what the cosmic juggling act was really about.

For the first few seconds it was what everybody expected. A low silver car sliced like a razor along the kind of mountain road reserved for mules and the makers of car advertisements, and an American voice talked about power and acceleration. Then, quite suddenly, the screen went blank. One of the guests muttered a question in German and Aeneas replied sharply in the same language as he made a sideways leap towards a telephone. Before he'd finished dialling a number the screen was alive again, but not with the silver car or anything like it. Instead the party guests were staring, at first silent and uncomprehending, then rustling with questions, at a message in large white letters on a purple background. The message was a Biblical quotation in English. 'The Lord will come down in the sight of all the people upon Mount Sinai.' This lasted for a few seconds, followed by film of a red mountain in a desert that might have been anywhere from Sinai to Nevada, followed by another written message, accompanied this time by a sonorous voice-over: 'Since the time of Moses, men and women have searched for God upon the mountaintops of the world.' By now the guests were flinging questions at Aeneas in several languages and a plump man, possibly the representative of the firm advertising the silver car, was having a choking fit after swallowing his champagne the wrong way. Aeneas disregarded them, intent on what the telephone was telling him. Other telephones had started ringing in various parts of the room but nobody answered them and they went on adding to the general din. By now the picture on the screen had changed to a small white church on top of a hill, then an even smaller church clamped like a barnacle to a lump of grey rock. Yet another telephone began ringing on a table next to Birdie.

Aeneas commanded him, 'Answer that. Tell them I'll be on in a minute.'

Then he bounded across the room to one of the other phones, sending a tray of champagne glasses crashing as he went. Birdie found himself listening to an English voice gabbling incomprehensibly about cables, monitoring points and something called TVRS.

'TVRS?'

The owner of the voice grasped that he wasn't talking to Aeneas himself.

'TV Repeater Station. Tell him they've bypassed the alarm and the monitor, so they must be in one of the repeater stations.'

Birdie crossed the room to Aeneas, who'd just put down his own phone and was looking shell-shocked.

'It's not coming from Milan. They're monitoring the output and say they're putting out the Cinzano ad as scheduled.'

'This sure as hell ain't the Cinzano ad,' said one of the guests.

'No, but it's what the satellite's getting.'

162

Birdie, not knowing the technicalities of the thing, was only just beginning to realise its enormity. The studio in Milan might think it was sending out advertisements, but what the satellite was getting and relaying to wide swathes of Europe were all these mountaintop churches.

He said, anxious for Nimue, 'Has somebody got at the transmitter?'

'No. I've just phoned them. They're as puzzled up there as we are.'

Birdie delivered the phone message.

'Yes, of course, they've got into a repeater station, but what repeater station? There are dozens of them on the cable between here and Milan.'

Birdie might not know much about telecommunications, but he recognised the work of Joshua and Barbie Jones when he saw it.

'Then I'd say it must be the one nearest here. I saw Joshua and Barbie Jones round the hotel a couple of hours ago.'

It took a few seconds for that to register with Aeneas.

'You mean those religious nuts who wanted Hent to hand the whole thing over?'

'That's right. They told me they run a television channel of their own back in the States so they must know all the technicalities.'

The film was coming to its end, with another message about seeking Him in the world's high places and an address in Plains, Georgia, to which contributions should be sent. A short gap of screen blankness followed, then they were back with the variety show in a close-up on the navel of one of the dancing girls.

Aeneas said to Birdie, brushing aside the advertisers, 'If you're right, they'll be packing up now. Let's go and get them.'

And without even time to collect his anorak, Birdie

163

found himself out in the cold moonlit night, running with Aeneas up the hotel drive.

'Where are we going?'

'The nearest repeater station is by the road into the village. If you're right, that's where they'll be.'

They ran without slowing down, out of the drive and on to the main road. The moon was bright enough for the trees to cast shadows. Above them, invisibly, the mountain station poured out its interrupted message to the satellite.

'We'll sue them,' said Aeneas, 'through every court in Europe.'

Nimue had been staring blankly at the screen when the advertisements began, listening to Allana's sobbing and aching to get away from the claustrophobic room. She watched the silver car, sat up and took notice at the sudden break in transmission and, when the churches film was substituted, made the same connection that Birdie was making down in the valley.

'Barbie and Joshua Jones. They've hijacked the satellite.'

This jerked even Allana out of her misery. 'What's happening?'

'Somebody's broken into the transmission. They're feeding the satellite their own programme instead.'

As the film went on, Allana kept glancing first at the screen then at Nimue and seemed to be on the verge of saying something. She looked faintly puzzled at what was going on, but not very surprised.

With her heart sinking even lower, Nimue asked, 'Did you know this was going to happen?'

Allana shook her head, but unconvincingly, and she was blushing.

'You did know, didn't you? It was all part of Getting

164

Back at Hent.'

'Not like this,' said Allana.

'They must have had inside information from some-body; plans, circuit diagrams.'

It would be a surprise to her if Allana even knew what a circuit diagram looked like. But what was certain was that Barbie and Joshua's hijack plans must have depended on some inside information.

Allana said, 'I didn't think it would be all that about churches. I thought it would be about the rubbish he put out . . . about him using people.'

'You helped them do this because you thought they were going to criticise Hent? How long have you been planning it?'

'Nimue, it wasn't like that. It wasn't like that at all.'

But the technical success of the hijack seemed to have pumped some vitality and confidence back into Allana, pushing the guilt over Birdie into the background. The tears had dried and she was walking around the room with a gleam of devilment back in her eyes.

She giggled suddenly. 'Oh, but it will have surprised them. Won't it have given them all a surprise down there?'

It was as if her husband were still alive for her to score off him.

Nimue got up abruptly, taking her anorak from the back of a chair. 'I've had enough of this. I'm going down.'

'You can't get down. The road's closed and they don't start the chair lift till morning. You've got to stay here with me.'

Nimue began buckling her feet into ski boots. 'It should be nearly a full moon. I'll ski down.'

Allana ran over to her. 'Nimue darling, don't go off and leave me. I've said I'm sorry about Birdie. I'll make

165

some more coffee for us, nice and strong the way you like it.'

'You'll be all right.'

It had struck Nimue in the past few minutes that Allana always would be all right. She had a child's capacity for separating her actions from the consequences of them.

'Nimue, you can't leave me up here on my own.'

'There are the technicians if you get lonely.'

Nimue finished buckling her boots and walked to the door. Allana followed her halfway down the tunnel.

'Nimue, don't leave me. What'll I do? Oh, what'll I do?'

'Frankly, my dear, I don't give a . . . Oh, never mind, you'll be all right Allana.'

Along the straight Birdie set the pace and Aeneas kept up with him. The repeater station he said was near a car lay-by. You'd pass it every day without noticing it, but though small and earthbound it was a vital part of the satellite link, boosting the signal as it came up the cable from Milan to make its leap into space.

Birdie asked, 'So how did they know it was there?'

Aeneas didn't slacken pace. 'That's one of the things I'll be asking them in a few minutes.'

The pine woods were thick on either side of the road, with the occasional glint of a frozen waterfall. It struck Birdie that the saboteurs might avoid them altogether by keeping to wood paths, rather than coming up the road, but Aeneas didn't think there was any risk of that.

'They'd need some equipment. They probably took it as far as the lay-by in a car.'

But when they got to the lay-by there was no sign of a car.

Aeneas groaned. 'We've missed them.'

But Birdie shushed him and pointed into the trees. They listened for a moment then, unmistakably, the sound of low voices not far away. He asked, as low as possible, 'Is that where the repeater station is?'

Aeneas nodded.

'Carefully from here, then. I'll go first.'

Admittedly Barbie and Joshua didn't look dangerous. But they had after all been the next ones down on the chair lift after Hent's body – although as far out of crossbow range from behind as Ray Reeve had been from in front. This was in Birdie's mind as he followed a trail of footsteps up a broad snow-covered path. Aeneas, less cautious, was treading on his heels but Birdie wouldn't be hurried. Then, sooner than he expected and no more than a few dozen yards from the road, he was in a clearing with a building like a small brick garage in the middle of it. And Barbie and Joshua Jones, drinking coffee by moonlight.

They hadn't needed a car after all. They'd solved the problem of transporting their equipment by borrowing from somewhere a stout wooden toboggan. It stood there, beside the repeater station, giving a domestic touch to the scene. And, equally domestic, there were the two spiritual climbers sitting side by side on a pine log, with a vacuum flask at their feet. For just an instant Barbie was surprised to see them, but recovered at once.

'Mr Linnet, Mr Campbell. Isn't it a glorious night?'

Aeneas was struck speechless. Barbie Jones produced two more plastic cups from a bag at her feet.

'Would you care for a coffee?'

'No!' yelled Aeneas, in a voice as sharp as a fox's bark. 'No, I would not care for a coffee.'

She looked hurt. 'It's decaffeinated, Mr Campbell. We never drink anything but decaffeinated.'

Aeneas said, 'You realise what you've done?'

167

Joshua Jones, who had gone on sipping his coffee, said, 'What have we done, Mr Campbell?'

'Wrecked our opening transmission, wasted months of work on our advertising, made us a laughing stock on a European scale, endangered the biggest investment we've ever made . . .'

As Aeneas fired fusillades of figures at him, Joshua calmly drained his cup and stowed it tidily away in a bag. When the list of charges had run its course he looked at Aeneas with polite interest and asked, 'Why do you say we have done all these things, Mr Campbell?'

'Because you're here and the film was all about your ridiculous churches.'

'If the Lord chooses to use His own mountaintops to advance His own cause you can hardly blame us for it, Mr Campbell.'

'And another thing: I want to know who's been working with you.'

'The Lord is working with us, Mr Campbell.'

'The Lord told you where to find the repeater station, did he? The Lord told you how to by-pass the alarm system, did he?'

Joshua said nothing, just went on looking sadly at Aeneas. This infuriated him even more.

'I hope your Lord knows as much about bankruptcy as he seems to know about telecommunications, because we're going to sue you for more money than you're ever likely to see.'

Barbie said, still holding the vacuum flask and plastic cups, 'I think you'll find the law in this field is very complicated, Mr Campbell. Joshua and I have been into it quite thoroughly.'

Joshua nodded. 'Nobody owns space.'

'We're not talking about space. We're talking about the nonsense you've just fed to our transmitter.'

168

Barbie seemed ready to argue the legal niceties but her husband was sticking to fundamentals.

'If you send a signal into space, Mr Campbell, and it comes back in a way that surprises you, don't you think you might be dealing with something a law court doesn't recognise?'

As his angry breath hit the cold air, Aeneas looked like a dragon hissing smoke.

'Are you planning to convince a court that God personally leaned out of heaven and sent down your nonsense instead of our advertisements? Are you saying all this had nothing to do with it?' He gestured at the equipment scattered round the toboggan: the video recorder, a small television monitor, a metal box the size of a toffee tin.

'Who knows the causes of things, Mr Campbell?'

'Well, I know the cause of this!'

Aeneas made a dart at the video recorder and took a cassette from it. Birdie, who'd been guiltily enjoying the sight of Aeneas wasting his anger, assumed it was the video of the churches and that he intended to keep it as evidence. Which might have been a good idea, if he'd remembered to keep an eye open for Barbie. Joshua let out a protesting cry when Aeneas grabbed the cassette, but it was Barbie who acted. She simply got hold of the toboggan and pushed it with great force at Aeneas' shins. One moment he was standing there flourishing the cassette, the next he was flat on his back in the snow. And the moment after that, with a speed surprising from such a solid and contemplative man, Joshua Jones was on top of him. Before Birdie could do anything, or even work out what he wanted to do, the two men were rolling over and over, down the slope and on to the lay-by. Birdie's first reaction was relief that it was somebody else's turn to hit the snow. He wondered whether he should intervene but as far as he could see, after its violent start, the contest looked non-lethal and evenly balanced. Aeneas was fit and sinewy but the spiritual climbing guide was showing a fair instinctive talent for wrestling. There was much grunting and, from the side of Aeneas, bad language, but neither seemed to be doing the other serious damage. And when Birdie thought about it he was damned if he could see why he should wade in on the side of the Hent empire and the peremptory Aeneas Campbell.

When Aeneas began rolling over he'd dropped the video cassette in the snow and Barbie was on it at once. She wasted some moments looking down on the struggle in the lay-by, then seemed to conclude, like Birdie, that it wasn't going to end in serious harm. She went off at a fast walk along a path through the woods, taking the cassette with her. Aeneas, who was looking up at the time because Joshua had him flat in a shoulder hold, saw her go and yelled to Birdie to stop her. When Barbie heard that she started to run, as neatly as a deer. Birdie went after her, not because he cared one way or the other who had the cassette but in case she should do herself harm alone in the woods at night. He didn't want to be blamed for another bad case of exposure.

She was making good speed, the back of her grey and pink jacket bobbing along about fifty yards in front of him. The path they were on was a reasonably firm track in the snow, probably used for daytime strolls by visitors needing calmer recreations than skiing. There were even wooden benches at intervals and way-markers nailed to trees. But for all that it was difficult by moonlight, with pine branches snapped off by the weight of snow lying across the path to trip the unwary. And Birdie was handicapped because wiry little Barbie Jones, at probably less than two-thirds of his weight, could skim the

170

surface of the snow while his boots sank inches into it. He contented himself with keeping her in sight and not trying too hard to close the gap between them. The path began to edge slowly uphill and although Barbie's pace hardly slackened, Birdie was beginning to feel the effects of a bruising two days and not enough sleep. Several times Barbie glanced behind, and he called to her to stop in a voice as unalarming as he could make it, but without result. They might have gone on for miles like that, except a whippy willow bush converted itself into a snare for Birdie's feet which he saw just too late. He pitched forward and his cartilage registered a red-hot protest. After a few minutes of massaging and swearing he began the pursuit again, but at a pace that was slowed to a limping walk, with Barbie Jones well out of sight. As far as he was concerned, the Climbers of Mount Tabor could keep their precious cassette, but he still wanted to ask them a few questions.

As soon as she'd left the mouth of the tunnel, Nimue began to realise she was being less than wise. She'd skied by night before and enjoyed it, but that had been with cheerful parties by torchlight. To go down on her own by moonlight was something she wouldn't have committed herself to in saner moments, but her anger with Allana, the cloying closeness of Hent's office, had made her desperate for snow and cold air. She stood for a moment looking down at the lights of the village, then back to where the top of the satellite station was just visible above the pass. When she began to ski she went cautiously on the red run, sticking to the side of the piste and offering this time no challenges to the moon-shadowed moguls. Through the trees the skiing was easier but there was less light than on the open snow field, and when she stopped to rest the loneliness and silence closed in on her. She jumped when an owl flapped from a tree with an alarmed yip of a hoot, watched as the branch it had left swung up and down, scattering its snow with a pattering sound. And there, looped above the pine trees, were alien shapes, black and motionless against the sky: the chairs hanging from their silent cable. By day in spite of what had happened she could travel on the chair lift quite happily but, looking at it now, she understood for the first time something of Allana's fear. She shivered and skied on down, thinking of Birdie and of curling up warm for the night in their little pine-panelled room. When the cold thought of Tim and Wayne tried to float in she shut her mind against it, concentrating on missing the ice patches that gleamed bright as glass on the more worn parts of the piste. Turn and turn down the gleaming track of snow, with the pine trees closing in. She felt as if they were moving, nudging closer and closer to the piste, and if she stayed too long they'd swallow it completely, leaving her in a maze of trees and darkness. Then she told herself not to be daft and skied on. It was a relief to see the lights of the village again, much closer now, and know she was almost back at the nursery slopes.

She rested, leaning on her ski poles, before tackling the final stretch. Another few turns and she'd be clear of the trees, running over bright open snow. But as she waited the feeling began to creep up on her that there was somebody else close by in the trees, not an owl or a fox but a human being, waiting there quite silently as she was waiting, and staring at her. It was a feeling she'd known before in higher and lonelier mountains than this, the strong conviction that there was another person present, out of sight but so real that climbers had been known to divide up their rations to share with a non-existent companion. But she hadn't expected to meet it

172

here, not now the village was in sight and the worst of the journey over. Her first impulse was to ski off at once, to leave the imaginary thing out on the mountain where it belonged, with the moonlight and the dark hanging chairs, but she wouldn't give ground to it so easily.

'Don't be daft,' she said to herself, but out loud this time.

And at that the imaginary thing was no longer imaginary. There was a sound from the pine woods on her left, of a branch moving and dropping snow, but no whirr of owl wings to explain it this time. Then, quite unmistakably, the muffled sound of feet moving on snow and light, regular breathing.

She called, 'Who's there?'

Every muscle in her body was tense. A man had died on this mountain sprawled dead by the hut she could just see below her, and she knew neither the face nor the name of his killer, any more than she knew the face or name of whoever it was in the trees.

'Who's there?'

Still no answer, but the steps were coming in her direction, though the person making them was hidden by the trees. Then, just below her, the branches nearest the piste began to rustle and sway. She slid her wrist from the strap of the ski stick and held it as a weapon, bracing herself to thrust down the slope against whoever was coming at her. Then the branches parted and out on to the piste, neat in her ski suit and padded cap, stepped Barbie Jones.

She didn't seem surprised to see Nimue, didn't appear to notice the threatening ski stick. They might have been meeting casually in the village square.

'Miss Hawthorne, would you do something for me?'

And she advanced towards Nimue, holding nothing more threatening than a video cassette. Nimue let the point of her ski stick drop back on to the snow and tried

173

to stop her knees shaking.

Barbie went on, 'Would you look after this for me? Mr Campbell thinks he can use it as evidence and I don't think so myself, but it might be as well if we kept it from him.'

Without thinking, Nimue put out her hand to take it, then she hesitated, realising that this must be the video that had sabotaged the satellite show. As Barbie stood there waiting with the cassette held out and a hopeful expression on her face, like a charity flag seller, Nimue did some quick thinking. She came to the conclusion, as Birdie had done a little earlier, that there was no obligation on her to take the side of the Hent empire.

'Yes,' she said, 'I'll look after it. But only if you answer a few questions.'

Barbie looked surprised to find conditions attached to a simple favour, but agreed at once.

Nimue asked, 'It was you who took over the broadcast, wasn't it?'

Barbie admitted it at once, adding modestly, 'With the help of a top rope from the Lord.'

'But you had to know a lot about how the thing worked, didn't you? You couldn't just go in and do it.'

Barbie said modestly, 'On my fiftieth birthday I qualified in communications electronics. Joshua and I decided the Lord would want us to use what was available.'

'Even so, you'd need to know how this system worked, diagrams and so on?'

This time Barbie didn't answer quite so willingly, but she was still holding the cassette and Nimue had made no further move to take it from her.

After a few seconds she said, 'Yes, we needed them.'

'Who gave them to you?'

'The Lord provided them.'

174

Trying to keep her temper, Nimue asked, 'But how exactly?'

'In a large brown envelope at our hotel reception desk.'

Nimue crushed an irreverent mental picture of a giant Old Testament arm stretching from the mountaintop to the Hotel Montagna Bianca.

Barbie said, 'Diagrams, and a programme schedule for the opening night.'

'But who left them there?'

'We don't know. We didn't need to know. Our guiding principle, Miss Hawthorne, is to use what the Lord sends, however He sends it.'

'And when did this envelope arrive?'

'Saturday. We found it when we got in on Saturday afternoon.'

Two full days before Hent was murdered. Nimue realised that Barbie was still holding out the cassette, and this time she accepted it and stowed it away in a pocket. Whether the story of the brown envelope was true or not, she thought she'd got all the answers she was likely to get from Barbie for the present. And at that point there was another rustling in the pine trees, louder and longer than the sounds Barbie made, and Birdie, red-faced and breathing heavily, joined them on the piste.

Later, when Barbie had trotted off without signs of undue anxiety to see if Aeneas was still fighting her husband, Nimue showed Birdie the cassette and told him about the brown envelope. They were walking down the hill back to the Hotel Soldanella, with Nimue carrying her skis and Birdie helping out his injured knee with one of her ski poles as a walking stick. They wondered whether to accompany Barbie back to the scene of the

175

conflict, but Birdie's view was that no great harm was likely to have been done there.

'The worst of it will be in court, if Campbell gets them to court.'

'I'll hang on to the cassette for now, I think.'

'What makes Campbell so mad is he's convinced they had inside help.'

'Well, judging by the envelope story, he's right.'

And she told him too, though with some reluctance, about Allana's reaction to the sabotage.

He stared. 'Bloody hell, you think Allana's responsible for that?'

'A few hours ago I'd have said she wasn't capable of anything half so organised, but I'm beginning to wonder about Allana.'

'So am I.'

His tone suggested that, far from wondering, he'd already made up his mind. They walked on a few more paces, Birdie limping heavily, Nimue shifting her skis from one shoulder to the other. She didn't look forward to what she had to tell him next.

'Birdie, that time you went down the Cascata . . .'

'Yes?'

'I . . . I know who changed the signs round.'

He stopped dead in the road. 'You know . . . ? Oh ye gods, she didn't, did she?'

She nodded, biting her lip.

'For goodness' sake, why?'

'She was annoyed because I'd told you about Getting Back at Hent.'

'Annoyed. Bloody hell, she tries to kill me and you tell me she was annoyed.'

He began limping again, faster.

'Any more girlish confidences? She didn't happen to mention that she'd put an arrow through her husband or

176

anything like that, did she?'

'There was something – Ray Reeve.'

And she told him about Ray Reeve's visit, and Allana's sudden interest in ski schools. He listened without interrupting, his anger giving way to something more serious.

When she'd finished they walked on for several minutes in silence before he said, 'That looks like it then. She wanted her husband's money, and Reeve wanted his share.'

It was just what she'd feared.

'No, I just won't believe Allana would do that. I know she sent you down the Cascata, I know it was mad, but it was just the first thing that came into her mind. She's like that. She couldn't plot. She couldn't think far enough ahead to plot.'

'Somebody did.'

'Somebody did, but not Allana.'

He said stubbornly, 'But suppose somebody had a hold over her, somebody who could plot and think ahead?'

'Ray Reeve?'

He nodded.

'But we've already proved Ray Reeve couldn't have shot him. He was too far in front of him.'

Birdie took a deep breath. 'I've been thinking about that. Remember the Superglue? Well, what did they do with the chair afterwards?'

'They put it into the sidings, till they could get the glue off.'

'Yes, and what do you think they do when they want to get it out of the sidings?'

She looked at him, frowning a little.

'I don't know.'

'Nor do I. But first thing tomorrow I'm going to find out.'

177

CHAPTER ELEVEN

At the Soldanella the disco music was thumping from the basement and the Alderman Kibbalts poker school had taken over the common room. But for once the phone at the reception desk was unattended and there was no sign of any of the teachers. Agreeing to give the bar a miss, Nimue and Birdie decided to go straight up to their attic room. To get to the narrow staircase that led to it they had to walk the length of the corridor inhabited by the school party. The doors to Tim's room and the one shared by Sidney and Joe were closed, with no sound coming from inside them. They were level with the last door on the corridor and Birdie already had his foot on the staircase when they heard a girl's voice, loud and tearful, 'I never did it. It's not true, I never did it.'

Birdie froze, and Nimue whispered, 'I think that's Brenda's room.'

They listened for a moment and though they could hear murmurs of voices inside, the shouted denial was not repeated. Birdie tried to signal to Nimue that they should leave whatever adolescent drama this might be to look after itself. After Allana herself, Brenda had a fair claim to be his least favourite female, and even with Nimue as a chaperone he didn't intend to tangle with her again. But Nimue either misread his signals or disregarded them. She gave one brief tap on the door and

178

walked in. Reluctantly he followed.

It was a small room, with one divan bed and two bunks, cluttered with anoraks and Mars-bar wrappers, shampoo and talcum powder and all the other detritus of teenage girls on holiday. But it was cluttered with other things that should have had no place in the holiday baggage of three female sixteen-year-olds. He took them in gradually, puzzled at first, then with rising hysteria as he saw the scale of the collection. The first three pairs he noticed were hanging over the end of a bunk: three pairs of nylon jockey-style in light blue, royal blue and mauve. And, laid out flat on the divan bed, another dozen or so in assorted styles – briefs, Y-fronts and one pair of thermal long-johns in all colours from the fluorescent nylon shades to the depressed pinkish-grey of the man who always put the wrong things together in the launderette. Like the time he'd put four pairs of his own Y-fronts in with his second-best tracksuit. Then it dawned on him that one of those four pairs was present and staring him in the face – was an exhibit in this unbelievable, intolerable collection. He closed his tired eyes, opened them, and there they all still were, plus another five or six pairs he hadn't noticed before, drooping along the windowsill. And, to make things worse, every single one of them was tagged with a neat cardboard label and each label had a name written on it. And just like the rest, the pinkish-grey pair had a label and that label said, in neat and precise capitals that might help its perpetrator to pass in geography or biology CSE, 'Mr Linnit'. And Birdie, unable to take his eyes off it, knew that Nimue must have seen it too.

His immediate urge to explode, to explain, to demand explanations found no outlet because something else was going on in the room and everybody else's attention was concentrated on that. The quietest girl of the appalling

179

trio, Cathy, was sitting hunched on the bottom bunk, sobbing her heart out. Her face was crunched up with misery and she didn't even register the arrival in the room of himself and Nimue. But the other two girls were cut off in mid flow. Brenda, who'd found a place to perch on the windowsill alongside the underpants, was struck with her mouth wide open and the other girl, Monica, was sprawled on the floor with her face still frozen into a grin at her friend's misery.

Nimue moved into the centre of the room and shut the door. 'What's the trouble?'

For a moment Brenda and Monica just stared at her, and at Birdie, who was standing with his back to the door trying to find somewhere to look that wasn't festooned with underpants.

Brenda recovered first, ignoring him and looking straight at Nimue. 'We're holding a trial.'

Cathy opened her eyes, realising for the first time that there were other people in the room, and made an immediate appeal to Nimue.

'I haven't done anything wrong. I haven't done anything they didn't.'

And she broke down again sobbing.

Birdie was scared to make a move. One part of his mind told him he should pick Brenda up by the ears and shake her till she told him what his underpants were doing there. But above that was a dawning sense that something more important was at stake. The atmosphere in the room was savage. Nimue obviously sensed it too because she moved and spoke as carefully as somebody dealing with scared but dangerous animals.

She said, 'What's the trial about?'

And, without waiting to be asked, she stepped across Monica and sat herself on the bed, carefully putting aside some of the pants collection to make a space.

Birdie noticed that she gave the pinkish-grey pair labelled 'Linnit' no more attention than the rest. He remained standing by the door, fearing to attract too much attention to himself if he tried to find somewhere to sit, but for all the notice the girls took of him he might not have existed. All eyes, Brenda's challenging, Cathy's tear-brimming, and Monica's curious, were directed on Nimue.

When they didn't answer her she asked again, 'What's the trial about?'

And Brenda said, 'She's been cheating.'

'Because of the underpants?'

In a room in which every surface was draped with them it seemed a reasonable guess, but all three girls looked surprised at her knowledge. Brenda nodded.

Nimue glanced at Cathy and asked, 'Which are hers?'

Birdie's eyes opened as wide as Brenda's and he just stopped himself from speaking.

Monica said, 'Those are,' and pointed to the pants hanging over the end of the bunk.

'Thank you. And yours?'

Monica pointed this time to the underpants on the windowsill beside Brenda.

Nimue gave Brenda a long, direct look. 'So these on the bed are yours?'

'That's right.'

Brenda wasn't surrendering power easily. Her tone was defiant, but some of her bravado was dented when Nimue said, 'Go on.'

'Eh?'

'You heard me. Go on with the trial.'

Cathy began sobbing harder and Brenda looked at a loss. This was clearly the last thing she'd expected.

Nimue said calmly. 'You said Cathy cheated. How did she cheat?'

181

And Monica said in a rush from the floor, 'Because she bought hers at the shop. She didn't get them properly.'

Birdie by now had caught up with what Nimue seemed to have understood by instinct and he realised they could give damning evidence against Cathy if they chose.

Nimue asked, 'And how was she supposed to get them?'

A level insolent look from Brenda.

'You know.'

'I don't know till you tell me. How was she supposed to get them?'

'From blokes.'

Monica, at Nimue's feet, snorted and collapsed into nervous giggles, but Nimue and Brenda remained entirely serious. Birdie recognised it as a power struggle – and a power struggle in which he knew nothing of the battle ground, the rules or the fighting weights. A tough young woman of nearly thirty against an unabashed sixteen-year-old, and both of them as remote from him as if the fight were taking place on the surface of the moon.

He heard Nimue's voice: 'So you have to ask the blokes to give them to you?'

Another explosive giggle from Monica and a slow smile from Brenda, perhaps thinking that Nimue wasn't so formidable after all.

'Of course not. You have to take them after.'

'After what?'

Monica was nearly choking and Birdie wondered how long it would be before that and Cathy's continual sobbing brought a teacher to see what was happening. But when it came to noise, the alarm threshold among the Alderman Kibbalts group was a high one.

'Oh, you know,' said Brenda, with a smile like the

opening betwen the shells of a boiled mussel.

'You tell me. You've said you have to take the pants from the blokes after. After what?'

And Brenda said, 'After having it off with them.'

This time Birdie did make a noise, a wordless grunt of protest, and moved towards the divan, although whether to get closer to Nimue or his stolen underpants he couldn't have said. Nimue, hearing it, held up her hand warningly and he subsided against the door.

She pressed on. 'So for this competition, you're only supposed to collect the pants of men you've had it off with?'

Brenda nodded, and Monica stopped giggling just long enough to say, 'And Cathy didn't. She bought them at the shop. They've all got Italian labels.'

Nimue turned seriously towards Cathy. 'Is it true?'

The girl nodded miserably, but she seemed to regard Nimue as a possible protector from her two friends.

'They kept on at me. They kept asking how many pairs I got, and I couldn't . . . I didn't . . .'

She sank her damp, red face between her hands. Birdie thought Nimue might go across to comfort her, but she kept her position on the divan and her judicial tone.

'So Cathy's collection is disqualified. That's what the trial was about, was it?'

Brenda nodded. 'And for telling lies to us.'

'I see. You and Monica, you collected yours fairly under the rules, did you?'

Monica said between giggles, of course she had. Birdie had counted five pairs on the windowsill, and wondered.

'And what about you, Brenda? Did you keep to the rules?'

'Course I did.'

But this time she sounded just a fraction uneasy. Up

183

to this point she probably hadn't appreciated the problems Birdie's presence could create. Possibly, he thought, she hadn't even remembered. Apparently casually, Nimue picked up a particularly hideous pair of nylon briefs from the bed beside her. They were pale blue with a pattern of dart-boards in navy and red, and the label attached to them said 'Zonk'.

'So you got these from a bloke called Zonk after having it off with him?'

Brenda said, 'Behind the bike sheds at the youth centre in September.' She added, as if it made them more of a trophy, ''E's a glue-sniffer.'

Nimue picked up another pair, chaste white Y-fronts. 'These?'

'Nobby Norris, when we were on the geology project.'

Monica and Cathy had stopped giggling and crying and were looking fascinated. It was clear that the game was another way for Brenda to keep dominion over her friends. Nimue's hand went to another pair. She held them up while Birdie wished the entire mountain, chair lift, satellite station, the lot would fall on top of him.

'And these? I see they're labelled "Linnit".'

A warning glance at Birdie, telling him not to intervene. He was sweating and furious, wanting to crash heads together, but he kept still.

'When did you collect these?' Nimue asked.

By now, if not before, Brenda knew she was on dangerous ground. Her glance went first to Birdie at the door, then Nimue on the divan, and Birdie could see the decision forming to try and brazen it out. He hoped Nimue could see it as clearly.

Brenda said, 'Yesterday. The evening after that bloke was murdered.' And she added, seeing how far she could go, 'The night you were away.'

But if she'd expected to get any reaction from Nimue,

184

she failed.

'Where?'

''is bedroom.'

'After you'd been to bed with him?'

A glance at Birdie, a glance at Nimue, then, 'Yeah, after I'd been to bed with him.'

At last Nimue turned towards him. She asked him in exactly the same voice she'd used on the girls, 'Is it true?'

'No, it damned well is not true. This little scrubber came to our room, as I told you. I didn't throw her out as quickly as I should have done because she was pretending to know something about the murder, and I didn't touch her – though looking back I wish I'd wrung her fat little neck.'

It is difficult to see whether Brenda was more gratified at having managed to provoke such an explosion of rage from an adult or hurt at the reference to her plumpness. It was enough to send Monica off into giggles again.

Nimue, still judicial, asked Birdie, 'These are your pants?'

'You know damned well they are.'

Which, before an audience of three school girls, might not have been discreet, but this trio didn't need pro- tecting from anything. Nor, come to that, did Nimue.

'Then how do you account for their presence in Brenda's collection?'

'They were on the chair and soaked from that ava- lanche. The little tart must have picked them up on the way out.'

'Well, Brenda, what have you got to say to that?'

Birdie reflected later when he was a shade calmer that if Brenda had been really poisonous she'd have persisted in her story. Perhaps Nimue's approach had subdued her, or perhaps she felt she'd won the game by making

Birdie angry. At any rate, she gave in.

'Yeah, all right. But the rest are real, though.'

It would surely have been the opportunity for Cathy and Monica to have jumped in and destroyed their leader but Birdie noticed that they were looking at Nimue with some hostility. Brenda, hung about with her trophies of underpants, was clearly their flagship and they resented seeing her paintwork damaged. Perhaps Nimue realised that, and it led her to make her first wrong move in the game by trying to fire a final disabling shot. She picked up another pair of pants from the bed, apparently at random, but when Birdie saw the label on them he knew the choice had been deliberate.

'Who's Bruin?'

'Bruin the Ruin,' said Cathy and Monica in reviving chorus. The sobs and giggles sounded very much alike now.

Brenda said, more sedately, 'You know, our bloody teacher.'

'Did you pinch them from his room too?'

But this time the answer came from Cathy and Monica. Their 'No she didn't' was spoken in chorus, shaken but triumphant and Birdie knew that something in the atmosphere had changed. Brenda's mouth was wearing its confident mussel-smile again and all three were staring at Nimue as at a teacher about to fall into a trap.

Cathy said, 'She got them fair. We saw it.'

It took even Nimue a while to adjust to that. After a few seconds she said, 'You want me to believe you were both of you in his bedroom watching?'

'Not in his bedroom,' said Monica. 'In that place up in the tunnel.'

And the expression on Nimue's face told Birdie, a second before his own brain got there, that something to overturn all their ideas might have happened.

She said, talking directly to Brenda, 'This isn't a joke now. If you've been making it up, this is the time to stop.'

Some of her seriousness got through to Brenda. When she spoke again, she was defending herself for the first time.

'He's always been, you know, sort of looking at us. You know, at netball when he thinks we're not looking, and touching you if he gets the chance. You know, hand on your shoulder, and so on.'

Birdie thought of plump, worried Bruin with his hang-dog loyalty to Fuzz and tried to fit him into this picture. Cathy and Monica had been nodding as Brenda talked.

She went on, 'And when we came here he was doing it even more. So I sent him this note telling him I'd meet him at that store place in the tunnel. You know, the one where they keep the stretcher.'

Birdie remembered it, just inside the tunnel entrance, not far from the path that led down to the chair lift hut.

He asked sharply, 'When was that?'

But Brenda just stared at him. His remark about her fat neck was still rankling, and Nimue had to repeat the question before she'd answer it.

'After lunch. About three o'clock.'

'Yes, but three o'clock what day?'

She stared at them both as if they should have known. 'The day the bloke was murdered.'

Cathy put in, 'You know, you were there when the three of us came down together in the chair. When that attendant bloke made the big fuss.'

Nimue said, 'You'd been with Bruin just before we saw you at the bottom of the lift?'

'Yeah. I'd put in the note to come at three o'clock and

187

we got there a bit before that so they could hide.'

Monica added, 'There's that sort of notice board thing. We got behind that.'

Birdie remembered a large faded board with a map of the various ski runs, probably stored there until it could be repainted. He was sweating, partly at the idea that anyone could be fool enough to make love in what was no more than a large niche without a door when anybody was liable to walk past, partly at the thought of those two other teenage fiends acting as spectators. In his old police days, shut in a room with a grievous bodily harm practitioner, he'd never felt as menaced as by these three girls. Could Bruin have been so mad? But Brenda was now enjoying her story.

'And he came, a bit after the time I told him, looking ever so nervous. And I made him take his ski pants off and . . .'

Monica exploded into giggles, 'And they had it away on the stretcher.'

'Yeah,' Brenda said. 'It was just like being in a boat. I nearly got seasick.'

The other two giggled and Birdie hoped Nimue would ask the necessary question. She did.

'How long did all this take?'

Monica said instantly, 'Until the bloke came along.'

'What bloke?'

She took a deep breath, pleased to have Nimue's attention on herself instead of Brenda. 'The bloke in the tunnel. She'd told us to keep a look out in case anyone came along the tunnel. You can hear them a long way off because it echoes.'

And this, like all the other details they'd given, squared with what Birdie remembered of the tunnel.

'So we heard these two lots of steps coming along, then they stopped, and we heard one lot going back towards the satellite place and the other lot of steps coming towards us.'

And that, surely, corroborated the story of Aeneas Campbell: about how he'd walked some way along the tunnel with his employer before parting from him.

'So what did you do then?'

'I whispered to Brenda that someone was coming.'

And what the effect of that would be on Bruin at a crucial moment, Birdie dreaded to think. If the story could be believed, there he was having it away with a pupil on a ski stretcher at the top of a mountain and another of his little pupils suddenly started whispering from the shadows. It gave him the horrors to think about it.

Nimue asked Brenda, 'What did you do?'

'Pulled the blankets up over us and stayed where we were.'

'And you two?'

Monica said, 'We stayed where we were as well.'

Birdie was trying to picture exactly where the old notice board had been.

'You must have been very close to the tunnel.'

Monica gave him a direct answer this time. 'I could've touched him. He walked straight past us and I could've touched him.'

'Who?'

'The bloke who got murdered. Horace Hent.'

He took a deep breath. 'You're saying that Hent walked straight past you when you were behind the notice board. What did he look like? Was he behaving normally?'

She stared. 'He was just a bloke, walking along.'

And at that point, even allowing for the missing eight minutes, Hent must have been no more than twenty minutes or so from his death. But if that thought had

189

struck them, it obviously mattered less than their own drama.

'And was anybody with him?'

'No, we told you. The other bloke went back the other way.'

'And Hent, he didn't stop in the tunnel, didn't hang about at all?'

'No, he just walked.'

So that was one possibility ruled out – that Aeneas had murdered his employer during that walk through the tunnel together and somehow managed to spirit his body on to the chair lift unseen. By the girls' testimony, Hent had left the tunnel alive and alone.

He heard Nimue's voice. 'What did you all do then?'

Brenda said, 'He went mad. Bruin was just standing there with the blanket from the stretcher wrapped round him, telling us all to get out. He went mad because them two were there.'

'So what did you do?'

'We went.'

Snatching up the poor man's underpants on the way. Birdie wondered how long Bruin had looked for them before bundling himself back into his ski trousers.

'Did you see anything more of Mr Hent? Think carefully.'

By now it was getting through to them that there was more than their seduction of Bruin involved. They all three shook their heads seriously.

Birdie asked, 'Where did you go when you came out of the tunnel?'

'We looked in the café, but there was nobody from our lot there so we came out again, then we came down on the chair lift.'

'Are you sure you didn't see Mr Hent in the café or near the chair lift?'

190

Another triplicate headshake. Nor did they know where Bruin had gone after they left him in the niche off the tunnel. One thing certain was that he hadn't taken the chair lift, or he'd have been among those arriving immediately before or after Hent's body. Birdie thought a serious talk with Bruin was the next thing on the list.

Nimue seemed to think they'd got all there was to get from the three girls. She stood up.

'If you think of anything else, let us know.'

They seemed surprised she was going so casually. Probably they'd expected a moral lecture, or the immediate summoning of Fuzz to deal with their sins. Nimue went and Birdie followed, pausing only to pick up his pants from the now disorganised collection on the divan. He didn't look at Brenda.

Back in the safety of their room, Birdie was annoyed to find how lightly Nimue took his embarrassment. She flung herself down on the duvet, eyes closed, and his first thought was that she was trying not to cry, until he realised it was laughter she was suppressing. Nervous laughter probably, laughter in reaction – but still, it seemed to him, inappropriate.

'It damned well isn't funny. It could ruin somebody's life, that kind of thing.'

'If you could have seen your face . . .'

'They're playing with bloody dynamite. At one time girls that age collected match-box tops.'

'Oh come off it, Birdie. I'll bet you knew some sixteen-year-old girls who didn't collect match-box tops.'

'For goodness' sake, I'm old enough to be their father . . .' And that was part of his shock. He pictured his daughter as a child still, but when he thought of Brenda's round eyes and mollusc lips he felt there was yet another area of ground that didn't seem quite as firm as it had once been.

191

'Little tarts.'

Nimue said, more soberly, 'The point is, were they telling the truth?'

'They certainly weren't telling the truth about me.'

'I know that.'

To his relief, her words came almost absent mindedly. She hadn't thought of doubting him and, if he'd been less disturbed by what had happened, that might have pleased him.

'The point is, were they telling the truth about Bruin?'

He sat down heavily on the bed beside her, aware of how tired he was. The sabotaged television show, the champagne and canapés, the chase through the woods, seemed days rather than hours away. But he remembered how, when the girls' story came to Bruin, the whole atmosphere had changed. There'd been an excitement, combined with the apprehension that this time they might have gone too far. He said, reluctantly, 'I got the feeling they were speaking the truth this time.'

'So did I.'

They looked at each other, not wanting to face it.

Birdie said, 'I quite like Bruin.'

'So do I.'

He kicked his shoes off and lay down on the bed beside her. Since the disagreement over Tim there'd been a feeling of physical as well as mental tension between them, but his tiredness, his need to rest near her, was stronger than that. She stroked his hair back.

'I think you'd better speak to him.'

'What, now?'

The disco music was still thumping below them. The thought of having to plunge into that, through a maze of girls like Brenda and boys like Wayne all gyrating to the mind-assaulting rhythm, to face Bruin with the story they'd just been told, seemed harder than anything the mountain could throw at him.

She relented. 'Tomorrow then, before breakfast.' She added, 'And I'll talk to Fuzz.'

'Ye gods, yes.'

He'd been so preoccupied with the Bruin angle that he'd missed that aspect of the story. Bruin and Fuzz had told the police and everybody else that they'd been skiing together down the blue run at the time of the murder, out of sight of the chair lift and the tunnel. But if the girls' story were true, Bruin couldn't possibly have been with Fuzz all the time.

Nimue said, 'I'm getting a bit annoyed with Fuzz.'

'So am I. Everywhere you turn, she's there trying to protect somebody.'

They undressed and slid under the duvet together. His arms went round her and her firm body fitted easily against his. But though she felt as exhausted as he was, sleep didn't come easily to either of them.

He said after a few minutes, 'Has one thing occurred to you?'

'What?'

'Supposing Tim gave that crossbow to Bruin?'

A picture was beginning to develop in his mind of Tim, penitent and confused after his meeting with Barbie and Joshua, meeting Bruin on the way to his assignation with Brenda. He imagined the teacher lumbered with an entirely unwanted crossbow at such a delicate point.

'But what would he do with it?'

'He could have hidden it, I suppose. There was enough stuff in that store place.'

But a worse picture was forming: Bruin scurrying off after the event in a frenzy of guilt and embarrassment from the tunnel, meeting Tim and almost abstractedly accepting custody of the crossbow.

Nimue, following his thoughts, said, 'If Hent had seen

193

what was happening . . .'

And that fitted all too well. Hent, to judge by his films and papers, might have been amused by the idea of a teacher being seduced by one of his pupils. Suppose, in hurrying past that niche in the tunnel, he'd seen what was going on there, met Bruin a few minutes later and let him know he'd seen it. Suppose Bruin, holding the crossbow, panics and . . .

He said with relief, 'But it still doesn't work, does it? Bruin wasn't on the damned chair lift at all.'

She sighed. 'We keep coming back to it, don't we. Either Tim was telling the truth when he says Hent passed him alive, or he wasn't.'

And he sighed too, and lay awake beside her until the circling of his thoughts shaded into a dream in which Ray Reeve and Allana, Barbie and Joshua, Bruin and Brenda circled endlessly on a chair lift like a circus roundabout, with the pale and incomprehensible faces of Wayne and Tim watching from the snow below them.

CHAPTER TWELVE

He woke just before seven in the morning, still feeling tired, to find Nimue already awake beside him. He suspected that she hadn't slept at all. They could already hear steps and voices from the corridor below them as the earlier risers among the Alderman Kibbalts group prepared for their descent on the huge jugs of milky coffee and baskets of fresh bread that were being prepared in the kitchen. Knowing that their teachers would have to be there to supervise them, Birdie dressed hurriedly, arranged to meet Nimue downstairs later and went down to the lower corridor. No sound came from the room shared by Brenda and her friends, which was a relief. He remembered that Bruin had a small room of his own at the far end of the corridor, overlooking the hotel porch. But before he got to it he was confronted by Sidney and Joe, already in ski clothes and on their way downstairs.

Sidney said, 'Here, we've been thinking. Suppose somebody climbed up one of those pylons with a crossbow?'

Perhaps the thought that they were due to return to England in just over a day's time, leaving Wayne in custody, had stirred their thought processes, but the last thing he wanted was more wild theories. As patiently as possible he explained about the deep trackless snow, but

195

this puzzled them for only a few seconds.

'Yeah, but supposing somebody swung down the cable hand over hand?'

Rather less patiently, he asked how anybody could have carried out such a Tarzan act without being seen by everybody on the slopes. When he left them they were starting to put together another theory involving a specially trained monkey. By lunchtime it would probably be bug-eyed monsters from Mars. The delay they'd caused meant Bruin was just coming out of his room as Birdie got to it, in baggy ski pants and a Fair Isle sweater, with the usual worried expression on his face.

Birdie said, 'I'd like a word with you. Can we go back inside?'

Bruin protested gently that he was supposed to be seeing fair play at the breakfast table, then he saw from Birdie's expression that it was serious. He led the way into the small tidy room, closed the door and propped his buttocks against the windowsill. His eyes were growing more worried by the moment and his plump face was creased like a puppy's. Birdie, not enjoying it at all, straddled the spindly chair by Bruin's bed.

'We were talking to Brenda last night.'

'Oh,' said Bruin. And again, 'Oh.' His eyes were fixed pleadingly on Birdie's, his body stiff.

Birdie said quite gently, 'I think you'd better tell me about it.'

'It wasn't her fault,' said Bruin.

Which, from a teacher of twenty-eight or so talking about a pupil of sixteen, should have been self-evident. But Birdie, with his recent experience of Brenda's tactics, had his own ideas on that even if it wasn't the right time to express them.

Bruin said, staring at him as if he expected Birdie to find some answers, 'Women my own age . . . I can't seem to . . . They don't seem to take me seriously.'

Birdie said, as coldly as he could, 'So you made the first approach to Brenda?'

The eyes were screwed up now, and Bruin gave a quick little nod of the head. 'I'd . . . I'd noticed her in class, looking at me. And after that I couldn't help looking at her, and she didn't seem to mind.'

'Did you have sexual relations with her before this holiday?'

A shake of the head so quick it was almost a flinch. 'No. I didn't mean to, then she sent me this note and . . .'

'And what?'

'And I thought she wanted to have a talk, to discuss what we felt about each other.'

And somehow that was much worse than a teacher going for a quick piece of satisfaction with an available pupil, the idea of this earnest man sitting down with a sixteen-year-old to discuss their feelings for each other. At least, when it came to it, Brenda had spared Bruin that.

Birdie said, 'But that wasn't what she had in mind?'

Now Bruin's eyes were open again and there was a shade of aggression in them. He seemed to have realised that Birdie had a pretty clear picture of what had gone on in the store room – a picture that showed him as the victim rather than the seducer.

'We . . . I got carried away.'

And so did your underpants, Birdie thought, but didn't say it. He asked instead, 'Did you see Horace Hent going past?'

Eyes screwed up again, as Bruin re-lived the embarrassment. 'No. I heard the steps, and one of the other girls, Monica, saying it was him. She said, "It's the satellite bloke".'

And the worst part of that moment, Birdie thought, was not the fear of discovery but the knowledge that Brenda had brought her friends along to spy on him.

'What did you do then?'

'I . . . we put the blanket over ourselves and waited . . . waited till he'd gone past.'

'Then?'

'Then I told them to go away.'

It was said with an awful simplicity. He'd gone in there wanting to lay his feelings at Brenda's ski-booted feet. He'd ended up as the teacher ordering out three erring pupils – and three erring pupils who could wreck his life.

'What did you do when they'd gone?'

'I . . . sat there for a bit. Then I started looking for my clothes, then I collected my skis and . . . skied down.'

He looked drained of his whole story, but as far as Birdie was concerned the important part was still to come.

'So how long was it between the time Hent passed and when you were back outside the tunnel?'

'I don't know. Five minutes, ten minutes.'

'And did you see anything of Horace Hent after he'd walked past you in the tunnel?'

'I never actually saw him, not even in the tunnel. And no, I didn't see him afterwards either.'

'Not at the tunnel entrance, not on the path down to the chair lift or anywhere?'

'No, not anywhere.'

Bruin seemed genuinely puzzled.

'But I wouldn't, would I? I mean, when he passed us in the tunnel he must have been going for the chair lift. By the time I'd got dressed and got out of the tunnel he'd be on his way down, wouldn't he? He'd be . . . he'd probably be dead.'

'When did you hear he was dead?'

198

Again, puzzlement.

'When Fuzz and I got back to the hotel.'

'Did you see Tim in the tunnel or at the top of the chair lift or anywhere else?'

'Tim? What's Tim got to do with it?'

A tone of panic, but perhaps in his shaken state Bruin was imagining that Tim might have been another watcher behind the notice board. Then his face cleared.

'But Tim would still have been on his way up in the chair lift.'

Birdie noticed that in spite of Bruin's misery he was managing to keep a clear head about the events of the afternoon. But, after all, he must have heard at least a dozen pupils going through them when he'd been sitting in on their interviews with the police. Almost at random, Birdie asked, 'Did you see anyone else from Alderman Kibbalts?'

To his surprise, Bruin nodded. 'Yes, I saw Ray.'

'Ray Reeve? Where?'

'Waiting by the down side of the chair lift. He was just standing there watching the chairs go past.'

And as they both knew, Ray Reeve had got on the chair lift. The problem was that he'd arrived at the bottom more than twenty chairs in front of Hent's body.

Birdie said, 'But if Ray hadn't got on the chair lift by the time you came out of the tunnel, that means Hent hadn't got on it either.'

In spite of Bruin's mental clarity, he took time to work that out.

Birdie had to explain. 'Ray got off that chair lift at the bottom about four minutes before Hent's body, so Hent must have got on about four minutes after him, right? But when you came out of the tunnel and saw Ray standing by the lift, Hent had passed you five or ten minutes before.'

Bruin frowned. 'Yes, I suppose that's right.'

'So where did Hent go between walking past you in the tunnel and getting on that lift?'

Bruin stared at him. 'I don't know. I told you, I didn't see him.'

He was obviously a long way from making the connections that Birdie was making, but then he'd probably never noticed the chairs waiting for repair in their siding.

'Did Ray know you'd seen him?'

'No. I was up above him, remember, and a fair distance away. And . . . I didn't want to draw attention to myself just then.'

The sounds in the corridor, the crashing of feet on the stairs, were growing louder. Bruin twitched, probably envisaging a breakfast riot in full swing below them, but Birdie wasn't letting him go.

'Right, you're standing there near the tunnel with your skis on. You haven't seen Hent, you haven't seen Tim, but you have seen Ray Reeve. What did you do then?'

'I've told you, I skied down.' In his humble way he was getting near impatience. 'I waited a bit to get my bearings, then when I started off I was a bit . . . unsteady. I kept falling over. Then I lost a ski and it took me a long time to get it back on again.'

Birdie could imagine it all too well. Even at the best of times Bruin lacked the confidence to make an averagely competent skier. Badly shocked as he was, he'd hardly have known snow from sky.

'It didn't occur to you to go down on the chair lift?'

A vehement shake of the head. Of course not. He'd have guessed that Brenda and friends went that way.

'Which run did you go down?'

'The blue. I skied down it with Fuzz, just as I told the police.'

200

'Where did you meet her?'

'About halfway down. I knew she usually went that way and I thought I might catch up with her.'

After what had happened, you'd think Fuzz would be the last person Bruin wanted to see, but like the Alderman Kibbalts kids he'd gone straight to her in a crisis. Looking for what? Comfort, forgiveness or somebody to explain the workings of Brenda's mind?

'And how did Fuzz react?'

Bruin screwed his face up. It looked as if he was still trying to work that out for himself.

'She was concerned about Brenda mainly. She said we shouldn't get her all mixed up with guilt.'

'But you'd admitted to her you'd just made love to one of your pupils. Wasn't she worried about that?'

'That was part of not making Brenda feel guilty. She said the education system in this country set up artificial and unnecessary age barriers and we shouldn't always go along with them.'

Birdie's private view was that Brenda, Wayne and the rest of them could do with a few age barriers, artificial or not, but it wasn't the time to go into that.

'In other words, Fuzz wasn't too bothered about what had happened.'

'She was bothered about Brenda. Apparently there'd been . . . something before with an older man and she was afraid Brenda might get taken into care if it happened again.'

A sympathetic nerve throbbed when Birdie heard Bruin say 'an older man', trying it experimentally for size on his tongue. Not thirty yet, but Bruin was already finding himself consigned to the other side.

He asked, 'So Fuzz wasn't going to report you or anything?'

Bruin seemed shocked at this. 'Good heavens, no.'

'So what happened after you'd told her?'

'We just skied on back to the village together, quite slowly because I still wasn't doing very well.'

'And you got back to the hotel together and found everything in a turmoil because Hent had been murdered. Was that when you decided to lie to the police?'

Bruin looked even more miserable at hearing it put so baldly.

'We realised quite soon that the police would be wanting to know where everybody was at the time. And this had nothing to do with the murder so . . .'

'So you both agreed to say you'd been together on the blue run all the time?'

'Fuzz thought it would be traumatic for Brenda if she had to tell the police, and we weren't sure about the law on that sort of thing in Italy.'

'And Fuzz, I suppose, had a quiet word with Brenda and friends and said they needn't tell the police about it?'

Birdie sighed, and Bruin said defensively, 'But it didn't matter. It didn't make any difference.'

'It made quite a lot of difference. If you'd come up with this story before it would have cleared one person at least.'

Aeneas Campbell, who really had parted from his employer alive in the tunnel. But he didn't tell Bruin the thought above all others in his mind – that this evidence pointed yet again in the direction of Ray Reeve and those missing eight minutes near the end of Hent's life.

Bruin, who was looking at him closely, asked, 'Don't you think Wayne did it, then?'

It was a shock to Birdie to be reminded that Wayne's guilt, which seemed less and less real to him, was still an established fact as far as most people were concerned. It brought back the unwelcome pictures of Wayne with his motor cycle magazines in the hostel room at Milan, of Tim's frightened face in the moonlight, of the strain lines on Nimue's face.

'Would you be glad if it wasn't Wayne?'

'Yes, of course I would. But . . .' His voice trailed away and he looked into Birdie's face, waiting for him to say something else.

Instead Birdie got up and opened the door into the corridor. 'You'd better be getting down to breakfast.'

As they went out, Bruin asked, 'Are you going to tell anybody about this?'

'If I have to.'

But the expression on Bruin's face made him add, 'I'd tell you though, before I did it.'

That proviso wasn't meant to include Nimue. He found her in the common room, drinking a solitary coffee among the cards and discarded magazines, and told her Bruin's story.

Her first comment was, 'For an intelligent woman, Fuzz can be quite shatteringly stupid.'

He nodded. 'Wayne's got to be protected and Tim's got to be protected, and now even bloody Brenda's got to be protected.'

Nimue said thoughtfully, 'And protecting Brenda means protecting Bruin too.' She stared out of the window at the early skiers walking up to the lift. 'If it weren't for the chair lift problem, I'd say Bruin could have done it.'

'Go on.'

'A nervous man, badly panicked, a weapon unexpectedly to hand.'

He said, 'But then he'd have to get the body on to the chair lift somehow. And remember to take the crossbow and drop it under the lift, where the police found it. Can

203

you imagine Bruin being that cool?'

'Probably not.'

She went on staring out of the window and he wondered how he could make her share the excitement that was building up in his mind.

'What do you make of Bruin seeing Ray Reeve standing by the chair lift?'

'We knew he had to get on the lift at some point.'

'But according to Bruin he wasn't getting on it, he was just standing there. And you know you agreed with me that this business about the powder snow is odd.'

She drank coffee, looking as if her mind were elsewhere. Without answering him directly she said, 'You know they go home tomorrow?'

Go home, leaving Wayne in custody in Milan, taking with them Tim, guilty about something and stubbornly silent.

She said, 'I'll have to talk to Fuzz.'

He went cold with unhappiness. The events of the last twelve hours or so had convinced him that the situation had changed, had moved on from the Wayne–Tim dilemma that threatened to do so much damage.

'You mean, tell her about Tim?'

And it might be Wayne or it might be Tim who stayed in custody in Italy, but the rest of them would go, including Ray Reeve with so many questions unanswered. And Birdie Linnet would go with them on his cheap charter ticket but Nimue had work to do in Milan so the next time he'd see her would be weeks later when she got back to England, in some weekend he'd managed to snatch from his work rota. If she wanted to see him again. The misunderstandings that had grown between them over the past few days made him uncertain even of that.

She was talking quickly and he was half hearing. 'I

204

know you don't want to do it to Tim, but we can't play judge and jury. If we can shake the case against Wayne . . .'

'And throw them Tim instead?'

Tim the frightened, Tim the guilty, Tim the confused. The trouble was, he didn't know now whether he was pleading for the boy or for himself.

He said, 'There must be another way. Just give me time.'

'But that's just what we haven't got.'

The memory of Tim's inert body over his shoulder, of Tim's childishness against Wayne's insolent youth.

'Just give me a bit more time.'

'I've got to see Fuzz. Now, after breakfast.'

He turned away, hands clenched in his pockets, neck bent, and walked slowly towards the door.

'Where are you going, Birdie?'

'Back up the ruddy mountain, I suppose.'

The clouds had moved on to the tops of the mountains, threatening more snow. On the nursery slopes under the chair lift instructors were putting up poles with red and blue flags for the beginners' slalom races. Looking down at them, Birdie in his black mood resented even that reminder that the week was nearly over. They'd race and the ones who didn't fall over would get medals to take home, and Hent's death and everybody concerned with it would become for most of them as remote as the mountains. He wanted to keep them where they were, to shout at them all that he must be given time, but time was running out on him as inevitably as the lift was carrying him upwards. At that moment Nimue might be telling Fuzz about the crossbow and however much Fuzz might want to protect Tim, she couldn't sacrifice Wayne for his sake. He imagined the two women walking down the street together to the small police station beside the church and he felt he was being shut out of all the decisions that mattered. And yet part of him, the ex-policeman part, knew that their decision would be right, that guilt or innocence were no responsibility of theirs, but withholding information certainly was. The trouble was, he couldn't shake off his feeling of responsibility for Tim and his instinctive hostility towards Wayne, and he felt if only he could be given time it was a choice which needn't be made. The case building up in his mind was taking shape, but it needed a process of wearing down and waiting that might take days or weeks. But stubbornly, because there was nothing else to do, he'd plod on with it until time ran out on him completely. One obvious thing was to check whether Brenda and her friends had been telling the truth when they claimed to have seen and recognised Hent from their hiding place. The question of where Hent was in that missing eight minutes towards the end of his life was vital to his case, and if they could be believed, he didn't spend them in the tunnel with Aeneas Campbell. But could Monica and Cathy really have seen Hent from where they claimed to be hiding? He thought they could, but wanted to make sure for himself.

He tipped himself off the chair lift, left his skis by the shed, and began to walk up the path to the tunnel mouth, head down and preoccupied. Then about halfway up he was aware of voices above him and looked up to see two people standing at the top of the path, just outside the tunnel. One of them was Allana Hent in an emerald green ski suit, bright hair loose and flaring around her shoulders. And the man with her, square-shouldered and reassuring, keeping a guiding hand on her elbow, was Ray Reeve. Birdie caught his breath and stopped. It was more than he'd hoped, meeting them together. He'd assumed that Ray would be trying to keep his negotiations with Allana over the ski school secret, but here they were in full view of the ski slopes, apparently not caring who saw them. And Allana had a leather bag over her shoulder, as if her seclusion on the mountaintop was over and she was out for a day's shopping. They started down the path and Allana slipped and nearly fell, but she was giggling and stayed leaning against Ray Reeve for a few seconds more than seemed necessary.

Ray's eyes, looking out over her head, met Birdie's as he came up the path towards them and instantly there was a hostile look in them and his body stiffened. Allana must have felt something was wrong because she stopped giggling and looked first up at Ray's face, then down the path where she saw Birdie.

'Oh,' she said, and her face went pale and still.

He walked up a few steps towards them so that he could speak without raising his voice. He said to her, 'You've forgotten your snow shoes today.'

Perhaps she'd hoped Nimue hadn't passed on the story about changing the signs round. If so, he was pleased to let her know that in this respect at least Nimue hadn't shut him out.

'I don't need snow shoes today.' But she didn't look at him when she said it.

He turned to Ray Reeve. 'I'd like a word with you.'

'I'm sorry, we're leaving for Milan.'

'Milan?'

He'd assumed that Ray Reeve, like the rest of the school party, was a fixture in the resort till the coach arrived to take them to the airport. Allana, who was keeping very close to Ray, saw the doubt in Birdie's face and seemed encouraged by it.

She said defiantly, 'I'm driving Ray to Milan in my

207

car. We're seeing some financial people about his ski school.'

Over her head Ray Reeve looked at Birdie with an arrogance that hadn't appeared on his face when he thought he was tied for ever to Alderman Kibbalts.

'Mrs Hent has decided to finance us. When you see Fuzz, will you tell her I shan't be travelling back with the rest of the party.'

'That's all very nice for you, but I want a talk first.'

'We're in a hurry. We want to get there before the offices close.'

Reeve clearly expected Birdie to move aside, but he went on blocking the path and said to Allana, 'How are you getting to Milan? I thought you wouldn't even go to the bottom of this mountain?'

'Not in the chair lift, no. But Ray's thought of a way.'

He nodded and, realising Birdie wasn't going to give way, stepped off the path, trampling a way for Allana in the softer snow at the side. She followed, stepping cautiously in her fur boots, clutching her shoulder bag. Birdie put out a hand to try to stop Ray.

'Why were you standing at the top of the lift the day Hent was killed?'

'What are you talking about? I was waiting to get on it, of course.'

'Bruin said you were just standing there.'

'What's Bruin got to do with it?'

Allana said, 'Oh come on, he's mad.'

And Ray Reeve pushed past him with Allana following. The only way to stop them would have been to knock Reeve down and although Birdie was sorely tempted to do it he was still calm enough to see that it wouldn't help matters. Ray Reeve flat in the snow was even less likely to tell him what he wanted than Ray Reeve upright and arrogant. He could only watch them as they walked on down to the top of the mogul field where Ray Reeve clipped on his skis and Allana swept her hair up into a knot on the top of her head. He still couldn't work out how Ray proposed to get her down the mountain and hoped that an attack of hysterics at the last moment might still keep them there. But Reeve finished fastening his skis, straightened up and said something to Allana. She nodded and, without hesitation, he swept her up and arranged her across his shoulders like a Highlander carrying a shot deer, her legs tucked under one arm. Then off he went, skiing carefully but quite fast between the moguls, not at all unbalanced by the weight of Allana across his back. It was a virtuoso performance and there were shouts, laughter and even some applause from other skiers on the slopes, even though most of them probably didn't appreciate that they were seeing Hent's widow ending her mountaintop seclusion. As for Allana, she stayed as quiet as if she were unconscious. But there was just one sign of nervousness. In the hurry of leaving, she'd forgotten to fasten her shoulder bag. It hung over Ray's back, gaping open to show a yellow cardboard file inside. And as Birdie watched from above the file plopped out and slithered into one of the dips between the moguls. He knew from the time it would take him to collect his skis and put them on that he'd have no hope of catching Ray Reeve and Allana. They'd be driving down the valley to Milan before he could get to the bottom of the mountain. As a consolation prize, for want of something better to do, he went after the file.

CHAPTER THIRTEEN

After Birdie had gone, Nimue sat over her cold coffee in
the common room, wondering whether she was more
angry with herself or him. She decided after a while that
the anger was mostly against herself for being so
reluctant to do what had to be done. She knew she must
go to Fuzz, tell her about Tim and the crossbow and
decide how, not whether, they should pass that information on to the police. Admittedly it was easier for her
because she found Tim an unappealing child, but even so
she daren't let herself picture him shut in that hostel
room where she'd visited Wayne. But her chief pity was
for Fuzz, in spite of her annoyance over the way she'd
acted in the Bruin affair. Fuzz identified fiercely with
every one of the kids in her care and Wayne's freedom in
exchange for Tim's would seem no bargain to her. She
kept telling herself, as she'd have to tell Fuzz, that the
decision was out of their hands.

As for Birdie, when she thought of him blundering
away at something up the mountain, trying anything to
escape from this stark problem he'd presented them
with, she didn't know whether she wanted to burst into
tears or shout with rage. As it was she did neither, but
returned her coffee cup to the kitchen and went to find
Fuzz. But it soon became obvious that she'd left it too
late. Most of the school party had already left for the

nursery slopes to watch or take part in the races and a couple of girls she found hanging around in the lobby thought Fuzz must have gone there as well. She collected her anorak from her room and set off up the hill, hearing the public address system trying to muster starters for the first races.

There was a modest carnival air on the nursery slopes, with red netting marking the edges of the course and a large banner, bought second-hand from a richer resort, strung above the finish. At the bottom of the ski lift where the snow that had been freshly shovelled to hide Horace Hent's blood no longer stood out from the rest, groups of competitors with numbered bibs over their anoraks were waiting to be carried up to the start. The public address system was pumping out Tyrolean music between its announcements. Nimue noticed Sidney and Joe among the competitors, drawing on cigarettes and looking narrow-eyed at the opposition. And at the end of the queue, helping a girl to tie on her bib, was Fuzz. Nimue waited until the girl had been attended to and then said hello, noticing that Fuzz looked half dead with exhaustion and not enjoying the thought of heaping another worry on to her.

She said quietly, 'We've been hearing about Bruin.'

Fuzz looked at her for a few seconds, then, 'Brenda's been talking about it, I suppose.'

Nimue gave her an account of the tribunal of the underpants, which didn't seem to surprise her very much.

At the end of it Fuzz said wearily, 'How can men be such idiots?'

'Well, young Brenda's not exactly a wise virgin.'

Fuzz was instantly defensive. 'Brenda's not a bad kid. She's just had a lot to cope with.'

'Fuzz, you can't protect all of them, not all the time.'

211

'I'm not trying to. I just wish somebody would give some of them a fair deal occasionally.'

It was a bad prelude to raising the problem of Tim. At that point the music stopped and the public address system, in English and Italian, urged spectators to get behind the nets as the races were about to start. Nimue and Fuzz walked together to the less crowded side of the course, under the pine trees.

'Is Tim here?'

Fuzz pointed immediately to a figure with woollen hat pulled well down and anorak collar turned up, standing a little apart from the other spectators on the opposite side of the course.

'I said he could come and watch if he wrapped up well. His temperature was back to normal this morning.'

'Has he said anything to you about why he ran off that night when Birdie wanted to talk to him?'

'I haven't asked him questions. He's got enough to worry about.'

Although Tim's face was turned towards the slalom course along with the rest of the crowd, Nimue had the feeling that he'd been watching them. Just as Fuzz had known at once where to look for Tim, so he was conscious of their presence.

She said, 'He looks miserable.'

'He needs to go home. I'm glad it's nearly over.'

Fuzz was still taking it for granted, as she had every reason to do, that when the Alderman Kibbalts party piled into its coach the next day Tim would be going with them. Nimue, her eyes on the muffled-up figure across the course, wished she could leave things as they were. Then she thought of Wayne as she'd last seen him, sitting on his hostel divan and asking for his leather jacket, and made herself look away from Tim. She'd been so preoccupied with looking for Fuzz that she'd left

212

the hotel without her gloves and, feeling her hands cold from standing around, she pushed them into the deep pockets of her anorak. Or at least, the left hand went in deeply but the right hand struck something hard and solid, blocking the pocket completely. Before she remembered what it was, Nimue drew out the video cassette that Barbie Jones had thrust on her the night before.

'What the . . . ?'

But Fuzz, recognising it before she did, said: 'It's that churches film.'

By daylight Nimue could see there was a picture of a church on a mountain glued to the plastic case, but she was surprised that Fuzz should have known immediately what it was. She stared at her, then remembered.

'Of course, you've seen it haven't you, when you thought they were going to show the kids a skiing film?'

'That's right.'

But Fuzz was looking at her as if there were more to it than that.

'They got it on to that satellite transmission last night, didn't they?'

Again Nimue was surprised. She didn't think Fuzz would have had a chance to see the sabotaged broadcast, but then news about it would travel fast round the village.

'Yes,' said Nimue. 'I saw it. They must have been pleased with themselves.'

The way Fuzz was staring made her uneasy, as if she was asking for something but Nimue didn't understand what it was. Then an idea began to take shape, the missing link in the chain that had brought circuit diagrams from Hent's office up the mountain down to Joshua and Barbie Jones' hotel pigeon hole in the village. Around them the crowd cheered and cat-called as the first competitor whizzed ambitiously down the course and wrapped himself round one of the posts, but Nimue didn't notice.

'You've met Allana, haven't you? You got her to take those diagrams so that you could pass them on to Barbie Jones?'

Fuzz said nothing, just stared at her, and Nimue's mind raced, trying to find the key she needed. She found it hard to come to terms with the idea of Fuzz as a concealed religious enthusiast.

'You're one of . . . what do they call themselves? The Climbers of Mount Tabor?'

Fuzz looked startled and angry. Her reply was loud enough to make some of the spectators turn round.

'I certainly am not. I'm an atheist.'

'But . . . but you helped them sabotage the broadcast, didn't you? You got the circuit diagrams from Allana?'

Fuzz said, her voice lower, 'Barbie Jones may be a religious nut, but she's a religious nut who knows about communication electronics.'

More cheers, whistles and cat-calls from the crowd as an Alderman Kibbalts girl sped under the finishing banner in a racer's crouch that would have looked good in an Olympic finish. Usually Fuzz would have been cheering her on more loudly than the rest but this time she wasn't even watching. Nimue, looking into her tired, unblinking eyes, thought she was beginning to understand at last.

'I see. You didn't mind what the film was as long as it made Hent's opening broadcast look stupid.'

Fuzz nodded, but there was still an intentness about her that disturbed Nimue and angered her when she thought of Allana's impulsiveness and how it had been used.

She said bitterly, 'You've got rather a selective sense

214

of responsibility, haven't you Fuzz?'

She expected anger, but there was none. Instead Fuzz asked her, 'You've known Allana a long time, haven't you?'

'We lost touch.'

Fuzz said, 'She needs help. I . . . I'm afraid Allana's involved in something really serious.'

At the words and the way Fuzz was looking, Nimue felt her whole body go cold. She'd been horrified yesterday when Allana admitted sending Birdie down among the avalanches, but that was nothing to what she was fearing now. Supposing Hent found out that Allana had been stealing diagrams from him and guessed why. Suppose he'd tackled her about it. If she could so casually decide to change the warning signs round at less provocation, what else could she have done on the spur of a moment?

'Oh no,' she said, and watched Fuzz's face becoming a shade less strained as the burden was shared.

'I'm afraid so.'

At that point the spectators further up the course began to make a different sort of noise, cheering and shouting as for all the competitors, but laughing too, laughter that grew and swelled as more of the crowd saw what was happening. But the voice coming over the loudspeaker was angry, demanding in English that somebody should get off the course, with the laughter growing stronger at each demand. Nimue wished they were all a thousand miles away, but against her will her head turned with all the other heads up the course to see what was going on. The slalom poles were all in place and a competitor was weaving among them, stylish but slow. Nimue thought at first from his odd shape that he was crippled or deformed and couldn't understand why any crowd could be so heartless as to laugh at him. Then she

215

saw it was not one person but two, that the skier was slow because he was carrying somebody over his shoulders, head and legs hanging down. A ski casualty perhaps, being rescued in an unusually flamboyant way. But if so, why were the crowd laughing? Then the figure across the skier's shoulders lifted her head, responding to the crowd's noise, the red-brown hair fell loose and Nimue recognised Allana. She heard a gasp from Fuzz at her side.

'Allana and Ray! What are they doing?'

Perhaps Ray was already thinking in terms of publicity for his ski school because, finding himself on the slalom course, he was giving the crowd a show of skill they wouldn't forget in a hurry, turning elegantly between each pair of poles and on the last straight run down to the finishing banner, beginning to lift Allana off his shoulders as he glided so that as they came under the banner he set her feet gently down on the snow, more like an ice skater than a skier. And for an instant they stood exactly like that, panting and smiling with the whole crowd laughing and applauding them. Nimue had to restrain herself from dashing out to Allana there and then, asking what she was playing at, trying even at this moment, though far too late, to force some sense and caution into her. But Fuzz understood and caught her by the wrist.

'It's all right. Look, they're going to the car park.'

And with the crowd still laughing and the voice on the loudspeaker appealing to everybody to clear the course for the next competitor, Ray was walking away with his skis over his shoulder and Allana beside him.

'Come on,' said Fuzz.

They raced across the snow, dodging round spectators and competitors. Several of Fuzz's pupils called to her but she didn't reply. When they got to the car park Ray and Allana were standing in the far corner of it beside a green sports car, and it was clear even from a distance that they were arguing. As they got nearer they could hear Allana's voice.

'Oh, what'll we do? You'll have to go back for it.'

Ray said something to her in a lower voice, but if it was meant to be calming it didn't succeed. She thrust the leather bag at him, showing its emptiness.

'It must have dropped out over those bumps at the top. I've got to have it.'

Her car keys must have been more safely zipped in a pocket because they'd survived the journey and she was holding them in her hand but making no effort to open the door. Ray Reeve tried to take them from her, urging the need to get to Milan before the offices closed, promising to ring up and ask the ski patrol to keep a look out for the file. Neither of them took any notice of Fuzz and Nimue standing a few yards off.

'No, I want it to go with me. You'll have to go back up and get it.'

And, probably aware that the chances of finance for his ski school depended on it, Ray Reeve gave in, though with bad grace. He began to unclip his skis from the rack on the top of the car, but she wasn't standing for any delay.

'You won't need your skis. I told you, it must be near the top on those bumps.'

He might have stayed and argued, but he registered at last that Fuzz and Nimue were watching. They could tell from his expression when he saw them that it hadn't been part of his plans to stay around and discuss things with his fellow teacher. He began to say something to Fuzz, turned to Allana instead, then abandoned both attempts and set off at a fast walk for the bottom of the chair lift.

217

Allana called after him, 'Be quick. I'll wait for you.'

Then she saw Nimue and Fuzz closing in on her.

'The file,' she explained. 'The file fell out of my bag.'

Afterwards Nimue could never decide what she'd have done if left to herself, any more than she could explain why she let Fuzz take the initiative. But at the time there was a force of determination, of absolute will, about Fuzz that made it as unthinkable to oppose her as to stand against an avalanche itself. Fuzz simply stepped up to Allana, took the car keys from her and opened the door.

'Get in. Off you go.'

'But . . .' said Nimue.

'But . . .' said Allana.

Fuzz repeated to Allana, 'Off you go.'

'But I've got to wait for Ray,' Allana said. 'He's getting the file.'

'I'll look after the file. Now, get into that car.'

And, after one glance at her face, Allana sat in the driving seat and allowed the car keys to be forced into her hand.

'But what'll I do about Ray?'

'I'll see to Ray. Now, you're to drive down to Milan and get the next plane to London or Dublin. You've got your credit cards?'

Allana nodded. From force of habit she'd fitted the ignition key into it's slot, though without taking her eyes off Fuzz.

Nimue protested, 'Allana, you can't just go off like this. We've got to talk.'

But the look she got was a cold one. Allana hadn't forgotten that she'd been deserted at the top of the mountain.

Fuzz said, 'She can go and she's going.'

And, still looking at Fuzz, Allana turned the ignition

218

key and started the engine.

Fuzz slammed the door shut and shouted through the window, 'Careful on the bends, and for goodness' sake remember you're driving on the right.'

A little nod, white-faced, from Allana and the car began to move. Nimue ran after it for a few steps with some desperate idea of standing in front of it, of forcing Allana to stop and talk, but she'd left it too late. The car wheels raced a little on the ridges of ice at the exit from the car park, then gripped and gathered speed. The car turned into the village street and Nimue watched it driving too fast – of course Allana would drive too fast – past the Hotel Soldanella, past the shops, past the Montagna Bianca and down the main road into the valley until it was out of sight.

She turned to Fuzz. 'Why did you make her go off like that?'

'Why should she have her life ruined because of him?'

Now that Allana had gone the force of Fuzz's determination was waning. She walked aimlessly beside Nimue back towards the nursery slopes, looking more tired than ever but not so tense. They walked in silence, with Nimue wondering at the impossible web of loyalties into which Fuzz had woven herself, asking herself what values dictated who, in the end, might be sacrificed.

They were almost back with the spectators before Nimue said, 'They'll have to let Wayne go anyway. You know he never took that crossbow out of his room.'

Fuzz nodded, hardly seeming to hear.

Nimue went on, 'It was Tim who took it. The police will need to question Tim again.'

She looked for Tim on the far side of the course, but this time didn't see him. 'We'll have to tell them.'

A nod from Fuzz. 'Just give Allana a bit more time, then we'll tell them.'

Another competitor wavered down the course and fell in slow motion, legs and skis splayed out. Various anatomical suggestions came from the Alderman Kibbalts group. The clouds were moving down from the top of the mountain and small nodules of snow began to fall.

CHAPTER FOURTEEN

Birdie found the file in a dip between two moguls with all its papers still tucked inside it and carried it to the side of the piste so that he could look at it without risk of being mown down by passing skiers. Since Allana had tried to take this with her, above all her other possessions, he assumed it must be important. The initials on the outside said simply 'G.B.H.' which gave him a shock until he remembered what Nimue had told him about the alliance of ex-wives. G.B.H. meant simply Getting Back at Hent. But when he looked inside there seemed nothing sinister about the contents. They consisted of letters, about twenty of them, written on various kinds and colours of notepaper, on airmail forms, some typed, some handwritten, some stapled to press cuttings about Horace Hent's activities with felt-tip exclamation marks in the margins. The puzzle was, not one of the letters was addressed to Allana herself. All the ones he read were addressed to somebody called Catherine P. He picked out a few at random.

In shiny black ink from an address in Geneva, on notepaper with a magnolia on the top of it:

Dear Catherine P,
    Welcome to the bunch. I saw that TV interview while I was in America and I could have strangled

him. Catherine A says he's going into satellites now. Wish they'd book him on the space shuttle and forget the return ticket. Hope to meet you sometime. Sisterhood is powerful.

Yours in G.B.H.,
Anne B.

Erratically typed on an airmail form from Los Angeles:

Dear Catherine P,

Thank you for the cheque. His lawyers are being as bloody as ever, but it's not my fault the dog hotel idea didn't work. How was I to know how much Afghans eat for heavens' sake?

Anyway, when it comes to your turn, you get yourself the best lawyer you can get and tell him to watch the small print because that bastard's mean with money as well and a million dollars doesn't go as far as you think it will.

Love and G.B.H.
Jane

Then there was a whole series of messages on white file cards in neat Italic handwriting, with no addresses or dates on the top. They were all signed Catherine A, and they were mostly concerned with plans for a meeting between Catherine A and Catherine P in the near future. One of them read:

Dear Catherine P,

I'm looking forward very much to meeting you in Italy. I'm glad you like my G.B.H. idea, but don't let's underestimate the practical problems. Anyway, we'll talk about that when I see you. Wait for me to

222

make the first contact.

Yours,
Catherine A

Snowflakes pattered on the letters as he read them and shouts and cheers drifted up from the nursery slopes. He puzzled over the names and the question why, since none of the letters seemed to be addressed to Allana, she'd been so determined to carry them away with her.

But they helped in their small way to build up the picture for him. Catherine P, Catherine A, Anne B and Jane were clearly people who were not friendly towards Hent, and Allana was closely enough involved to be carrying a file of their letters around. He almost felt sorry for Hent to have been the target of such vengefulness, and wondered whether he'd really been bad enough to deserve it. But that was beside the point. Allana had disliked her husband and talked happily to Nimue of plotting against him. Allana was now a rich widow and Ray Reeve, showing in such surprising colours when away from his pupils, was first in the queue for some of the money. And if Allana was so happy to dream up plots against her husband, what was there to stop her constructing one with Ray Reeve? He could picture the two of them in the darkness inside the chair lift shed, could imagine what Allana's part in the proceedings might be. The big problem was the girls' evidence that Hent had been alone when he walked along the tunnel, but couldn't Allana have followed him a few minutes later, when the girls had gone giggling off to look in the café and Bruin was too shaken to notice what was happening? Couldn't she have done that, in those missing eight minutes or so when Ray Reeve, on Bruin's evidence, was standing and waiting just outside the lift shed?

223

Birdie felt almost certain that it could have happened like that, and for a few seconds he was excited and happier at being so close to a solution. But then he had to tell himself that it was too late anyway. Ray and Allana had said they were on their way to Milan and, if they had any sense, they wouldn't stop there. They'd be on a plane and away within hours, and all he had to convince the police that they should be stopped was a theory with some of its pieces still missing and a certainty that if only he'd been given more time with Ray Reeve he could have broken him down. Perhaps when the police started questioning Tim again and he told them what he'd really done with the crossbow some of the story would come out. But a lot of damage would have been done by then and Ray, on Allana's money, could have got to somewhere that didn't have extradition treaties.

The snow was falling in larger flakes. He stood up slowly with the file under his arm, thinking of the last ride back down in the chair lift and what Nimue would have to tell him at the end of it. Then, from only a few yards up the slope, somebody spoke to him.

'She wants that file.'

He turned round, not believing the evidence of the voice, having just imagined its owner on the first stage of a journey to South America.

Ray Reeve glared down at him. 'She wants that file,' he repeated.

He looked furious and, although less tall than Birdie, was standing on top of a mogul and towering over him.

'I'm sure she does,' Birdie said, 'but she's not getting it. This file's evidence.'

'You're mad,' said Ray Reeve.

He began to scramble down towards Birdie. He was breathing heavily and, without his skis, was as clumsy as anybody else trying to walk on steep, hard-pack snow. Birdie watched and waited for him, aware that they were very much on their own. With the weather closing in, most of the skiers had gone down to watch the races and, even if the two of them were visible from the chair lift, nobody could intervene from there. Ray came within grabbing distance and tried to take the file but Birdie twitched it away and side-stepped. Ray almost over-balanced but kept his footing and swung round to make another grab. This time Birdie was holding it behind him and Ray grasped him by the arm until Birdie put the other hand against his chest and pushed.

'Try that again,' Birdie said, 'and I'll flatten you.'

Ray Reeve glared at him but stood still. 'That belongs to Mrs Hent. She wants it and you've got no right to keep it.'

Birdie took a step up the slope, staying just out of his reach. 'I might just give it to you if you answer a few questions.'

'Such as what?'

'Such as how long you and Mrs Hent have been working together.'

'We haven't been working together. I spoke to her for the first time yesterday about the ski school.'

'And when did you speak to her about killing her husband?'

'Killing her husband? You're crazy, certifiable.'

Ray Reeve rushed at him, head down. Birdie side-stepped again but not quite quickly enough and Ray's head caught him in the stomach. He staggered back-wards and felt Reeve's arms locking on to his, twisting them and trying to wrench the file free. They both lost balance and slithered down the side of a mogul, Birdie on top, but his arm was awkwardly twisted and he could feel his grip loosening. Then the file slipped from his

225

fingers entirely and Ray was up and walking away with it. Birdie flung himself at his knees, bringing them both down again, and they wrestled and kicked in the icy dip between the snow humps in silence, apart from their heavy breathing and the snow that landed with small whispering sounds on the back of whoever was on top. But Birdie had the advantage of training as well as size, and after a few minutes of this Ray Reeve tired and lay there panting and glaring, with Birdie pinning him down by the shoulders. They'd dropped the file in the struggle and Birdie got to his feet quickly and picked it up. Ray Reeve, wriggling into a sitting position, adopted Birdie's own tactics and tried to hook him round the knees. Unfortunately for them both he got the knee with the cartilage trouble, and a reflex action from the pain brought it crashing up against his chin. He slumped back against the mogul, looking groggy, and Birdie was anxious for a while at what he'd done. But Ray was not only conscious but still doggedly combative, struggling to get to his feet in spite of dizziness.

Birdie did some quick thinking, then began scrambling as fast as he could back uphill, towards the shed at the top of the chair lift about three hundred yards away. He hoped Ray would realise where he was making for and follow him. Far from escaping the man, he wanted to go on questioning him, but on ground he'd chosen himself. He was trying to work out how to manage this when he saw Joe and Sidney skiing towards him over the mogul field, wearing numbered bibs. For once glad to see the pair of them, he waved and waited until they came to a halt beside him. With Sidney and Joe, he decided, the direct approach was best.

'Mr Reeve's looking for me. I want you to wait for him and tell him I'm up there in the chair lift shed. Only don't tell him I told you to say it.'

226

They seemed to grasp this and didn't even look surprised. It was probably tame stuff compared with their fantasies.

Sidney objected, 'But we're supposed to be racing.'

'Never mind racing, this is to help Wayne. You want to help Wayne, don't you?'

'Yeah, but Joe's the favourite to win. I've got five quid on him with Groggy.'

Joe said, 'It's OK though if it'll help Wayne.'

He supposed that was, by their standards, a heroic sacrifice for a friend's sake and decided to build on it.

'Another thing: can you wait till Mr Reeve's on his way up to the lift shed, then find some way of getting the lift attendant out of the way?'

Seeing the eager look in Sidney's eyes he added hastily, 'Don't hurt him or anything. Just fake an accident so that he has to come out of his box.'

They were both showing signs of curiosity now but he had no time to waste because any minute Ray Reeve would recover from his giddiness and appear over the moguls.

'Have you got that then? Tell him where I've gone, then do something to distract the attendant.'

'Right, boss,' they said as he hurried away.

What he'd done in the way of encouraging their criminal tendencies didn't bear thinking about but, like Barbie and Joshua, he could only use what the Lord provided. He laboured on uphill as best he could, his knee twinging at every step, and managed to slip inside the lift shed while the attendant was helping somebody onto a chair on the other side. So far so good.

From where he was standing in the darkness just inside the shed with the chairs clanking in from the daylight towards the great wheel, he could watch it all happening. He could see the dark figure that was Ray

227

Reeve toiling up over the mogul field, stopping now and then to get his breath or look round for him. He watched as he drew level with the two boys and Sidney pointed enthusiastically in the direction of the lift shed. He hoped they weren't overdoing it. Then, as Ray plodded up the last stretch towards him, Birdie watched Sidney and Joe spring into action. Joe went first, skiing straight down over the biggest moguls in sight and coming down with a crash that even Birdie, who was expecting it, thought must be an accident. He sprawled on his back, groaning loudly. Almost as quickly, Sidney was down by his side, shouting to the world in general and, for some reason, in a voice from a Western film, 'He's hurt. He's hurt real bad.'

Birdie thought Sidney's acting talents weren't likely to save him from the dole queue, but they seemed good enough to convince the humane operator of the chair lift. He looked out of his hut and, seeing the tableau on the snowfield below him, clipped on his skis and went to help. Joe meanwhile writhed and groaned on the snow, miming symptoms that looked to Birdie more like snake bite than ski injury. But he could only leave them to it and hope they kept the man occupied for the time he needed. He looked around to check that nobody was watching and went to the back of the shed, stepping cautiously behind the wheel, to where the chairs that needed repair were hanging motionless in a line in their siding. Above the clanking of the machinery he listened for sounds from outside and watched the square of intense white light at the opening of the shed. Then, after a minute or so, there was a silhouette against the white. Ray Reeve stood there, uncertain, breathing hard and watching the chairs circle in and out. Birdie waited for a few moments and then called, so that his voice could be heard over the machine noise, 'I'm in here.'

228

Ray Reeve stepped out of the square of white into the dimness of the shed.

'What are you doing in here?'

He sounded angry, but alarmed too at the darkness and the noise. As he walked behind the revolving wheel and came closer, Birdie could smell the sweat on him.

'I thought it would be a good place to have that talk.'

'There's nothing to talk about. Just give me that file.'

Birdie was worried in case the boys' acting abilities couldn't keep the attendant away for long enough, but he didn't want Reeve to guess that.

'There's no hurry. Why don't we sit down?'

Birdie led the way to one of the motionless chairs in the siding and Ray Reeve followed him, protesting.

'I don't want to sit here and discuss your fantasies. I want that file.'

'Sit down!'

And, to Birdie's surprise and relief, Ray Reeve gave an angry shrug and sat down in the chair beside him.

Birdie said, 'Did you sit and talk to Horace Hent like this?'

'Did I . . .'

He didn't seem to understand the question at first, but when he did he answered in a voice to humour a madman.

'Of course not. I talked to him in his office along the tunnel there.'

'That was in the morning when he wouldn't back your ski school. What about the afternoon?'

'Afternoon?'

'The afternoon just before he was murdered. Did you sit and talk to him like this then?'

And at last, unmistakably, he saw something like uneasiness in Ray Reeve's face. But he still insisted, 'I didn't see him at all in the afternoon, only in the

229

morning.'

'But a witness saw you waiting at the front of this shed only a few minutes before Hent was murdered.'

'Are you accusing me of murdering him?'

'Are you denying you were standing there?'

A pause, then, 'No, I'm not denying it. I was waiting to get the chair lift down, you know that.'

'But my witness says chairs were going past and you weren't getting on them.'

'Who is your witness?'

It was Birdie's turn to hesitate, but it would have to come out at some time anyway.

'Your colleague, Bruin.'

Silence. Birdie watched Reeve's face closely in the dim light and followed up his advantage.

'Another thing: you said you took the lift down because you'd broken a binding in the powder snow.'

'So?'

'So how come you didn't fall over? How come you weren't covered with snow?'

Ray seemed to have forgotten about the file. He was looking straight ahead at the square of white light and the chairs disappearing into it and breathing more heavily than when he arrived. After several seconds of silence he said, 'I wanted that ski school. I wanted it very much.'

Birdie hardly dared to breathe. The chairs went clanking by them at regular intervals but he wasn't conscious of anything except the man sitting beside him. He prayed the attendant wouldn't come back and find them until this had been said.

'He'd refused to finance us in the morning, you knew that.'

Birdie nodded.

'I'd . . . I'd been thinking it over since then. I came to

Checkout Receipt

03/31/04 11:53AM
****

P is for peril /
32140001248414   DATE DUE: 04/21/04

Murder makes tracks /
32140000216701   DATE DUE: 04/21/04

The cat who knew Shakespeare /
32140001404231   DATE DUE: 04/21/04

TOTAL: 3

the conclusion that Hent himself quite liked the idea, but he'd been persuaded against it by that side-kick of his, Campbell. I thought if I could have a talk with Hent on his own, without Campbell there . . .'

A silence. Birdie could hear shouting in the distance and hoped it didn't involve Sidney and Joe.

'So you arranged to meet Hent in here?'

Ray said angrily, 'No, that's just the point. I hadn't arranged to meet him anywhere.'

He looked desperately worried now, talking not so much to Birdie as at that square of white light.

'It's not easy to meet people like Hent, is it? They're protected, bundled up, not like us.'

'So what did you do?'

'I'd worked out the one place where I could get him to myself was on the chair lift. If I waited till he got on, then jumped on beside him at the last minute . . .'

Birdie thought that if you wanted anything as badly as Ray Reeve wanted his ski school the whole horizon of madness and sanity was disrupted as if earthquakes had smashed it.

Twelve minutes alone with Hent, swinging down over the snow and pine trees. Twelve minutes to persuade that parcelled-up man to unwrap a few layers of wealth and rescue him for life from Alderman Kibbalts.

Ray said, 'It was basically a very sound idea.'

Twelve minutes – and your pupil thrusting into your hands a crossbow that will pierce through parcels, however cosily wrapped.

Birdie asked, 'How did you know he was going down in the lift then?'

'I didn't. I'd been skiing around there and keeping my eyes open and I saw him go out of the tunnel and down to the shed.'

'You actually saw him go down to the shed?'

'Yes, he walked in the back of it. I thought he was going to walk through and take the chair down and I'd missed him.'

'But you hadn't?'

'No. I skied over there, and he still hadn't come out of the shed. Then I had to wait a bit because three of our pupils were messing around and I didn't want to . . .'

'Which three?'

'Brenda and two of her friends. Then they went down, and Hent still hadn't appeared, so I just went over and stood outside the shed on the down side and waited.'

And all this time – the missing eight minutes or so – Horace Hent had been inside the lift shed where they were sitting.

'So you just stood outside the shed and waited. And then what?'

Ray Reeve turned towards him, every line on his face deeper than Birdie had ever seen it.

'Nothing. I just waited and nothing happened.'

'But when he came out . . . ?'

Ray said fiercely, 'I'm trying to tell you he didn't, not while I was there. I saw him go in the back of this shed and I was waiting for him to come out the front, but he didn't.'

'So you went in to look for him?'

'No. I told you, the whole idea was I was going to jump in the chair beside him when he came out.'

Birdie asked, as calmly as he could, 'How long did you wait?'

'About five minutes.'

Birdie pounced. 'You'd been looking for him all afternoon, but when you got your chance you only waited five minutes. Why was that?'

Ray looked away again.

'Because I heard him talking. Or rather, I heard him

232

shouting.'

Birdie almost jumped out of his chair.

'You're telling me you heard him? What was he saying?'

Ray shook his head.

'I couldn't hear that. Just listen to the noise these chairs make. If he hadn't been shouting I don't suppose I'd have heard him at all.'

'So you're waiting at the front of the shed and you hear Hent shouting inside. What did you do then?'

'I . . . I got on the next chair and went down.'

Ray tried to look away, but Birdie twisted round in his seat to face him. Their arms were touching and he could sense a tension running through Ray's like the throbbing of the steel cable over their heads.

'Hent was being murdered in there, and you're trying to tell me you just got on the next chair and went down?'

Ray shouted at him, 'I didn't know he was being murdered. I just knew he was in there having an argument with somebody.'

'Who?'

'I don't know who. It didn't matter. The point was, if he was having an argument he'd be in a bad mood when he came out and that wasn't any use to me. It was none of my business so I just left.'

Birdie took a deep breath, so near success but with a few dangerous steps still to take.

'And why didn't you tell the Italian police about this? You realise it would have been the best bit of evidence they'd got.'

'Would you have done in my place?'

Birdie knew he couldn't give an honest answer to that, but luckily Ray Reeve went on without waiting for one.

'I hear later he's been murdered. The whole village knows by now I've got a grudge against him. I'm one of

233

the last people to see him alive. You know damned well what they'd have thought.'

'You could have told them what you've told me.'

'Oh yes, Ray Reeve, skulking around chair lifts trying to catch a few crumbs from a rich man's table. Do you think I enjoy talking about that?'

Birdie said as calmly as he could, 'Anyway, that wasn't the truth was it? You didn't stay outside and hear him shouting. He may have been shouting, but it was at you when you went inside with the crossbow.'

Ray made a movement to jump out of the chair, but stopped when Birdie caught him by the arm.

'I never touched the damn crossbow. I never saw it.'

'I think Tim gave it to you.'

There were more shouts from outside, shouts of anger, but Birdie was hardly conscious of them.

'And you'd got an arrangement with Allana, hadn't you? You dispose of the husband and she gives you your ski school, wasn't that it?'

Ray said, despairingly, 'What's the use of talking to you? I never even spoke to her before yesterday.'

He was making no more attempts to get away and his anger seemed to have given way to sad puzzlement.

'So your idea is that I walked in here with a crossbow and shot Hent as he sat down in one of these chairs?'

'Yes.'

'Then perhaps,' said Ray quite gently, 'you can explain how I got to the bottom several minutes before his body did?'

This was just what Birdie had been waiting for, why he'd gone to the trouble of decoying Ray Reeve into the ski shed. He got up suddenly and, keeping his eyes on Ray, walked to the end of the line of stationary chairs.

'I think he was sitting in one of the chairs in the siding here, just like you are, or was dumped in it. I think you told Allana to wait until you were on your way down, then pull this lever and . . .'

He'd already noticed the red hand grip on a chain above their heads. He pulled. Nothing happened. He pulled harder.

'. . . these chairs in the siding would start moving . . .'

The trouble was, they weren't. It was beginning to dawn on him that the system must be harder to operate than it looked. Some kind of locking mechanism perhaps. He puffed, tugging on it with all his strength.

'. . . and Hent's body moves out, but by then you're about twenty chairs ahead of it . . .'

Ray was looking at him as at an unsatisfactory scientific experiment. He said again, but with more conviction than before, 'You're mad.'

Then he got to his feet and, before Birdie could even let go of the handle he was gripping, stepped neatly sideways and into the next one of the circling chairs on its way down. It scooped him up and carried him out into the square of white light, with Birdie chasing after it uselessly as it rose yards above the snow. And as Birdie abandoned the chase and turned, intending to jump on the next chair, he collided with the attendant on his way to see what was happening.

The man had obviously been hopping mad even before the impact of Birdie's twelve stone. By now he'd discovered that Joe was a bogus casualty and, as far as Birdie could tell from a stream of Italian with a few forceful English words intermingled, he was feeling vengeful. The sight of Ray Reeve mounting the chair lift at an unauthorised point hadn't helped, and Birdie was the last straw. He was a light man and went flying, grabbing Birdie by the anorak as he went. The next chair missed them by a few inches as it went over their heads. Birdie was the first up, pointing desperately out of the

235

shed at Ray's receding back. By now at least one empty chair would separate them.

'Murderer,' said Birdie, pointing. '*Assassino.*'

But the attendant obviously thought this was in the same line of country as Joe's accident. He grabbed Birdie's arm and tried to drag him towards his kiosk and the telephone. Despairingly, Birdie saw from the corner of his eye that two more customers were shuffling up to take their turn on the lift, putting yet another barrier between himself and Reeve.

'It's true. *E vere.* No joking.'

Yet another chair clanked past in the line that was carrying Ray Reeve down to Allana's car, to Milan, to God knows where. Birdie pulled himself free and leapt for the next chair with the attendant after him. He landed safely and was whisked up into space with the man shouting at him from below while down on the snowfield at a safe distance Joe and Sidney watched with a fascination that defeated even their world-weariness. Ray was now five chairs or about a hundred yards ahead of him, but with two other people on a chair in between. Birdie had hoped that the attendant might be furious enough to press the red stop button and bring the whole system to a halt. But he told himself this wouldn't be much help anyway, as whenever it started up again Ray would still have the same hundred yards start over him. The chairs were travelling at their same slow, relentless pace that made a mockery of his urgency.

There was just one possibility left. The chair had already carried him above the upturned faces of Joe and Sidney, but by twisting round Birdie could still see them. He yelled back to them, 'Joe, Sidney, ski down. Make him wait till I get down.'

They heard something because their heads were turned towards him enquiringly, but had they understood?

236

'Reeve. Mr Reeve. Don't let him get away.'

Too far away now to see their expressions, though surely they'd be registering surprise at what amounted to an invitation to carve up a member of staff. He watched, screwed round in his chair, until the larger figure of Joe began skiing down, followed immediately by Sidney, towards the piste that led through the pine trees. But that was a winding track whereas the chair lift went straight down, and Ray Reeve almost certainly had too long a start on them. He wondered whether Reeve had heard him shouting, but his view of the man was blocked by the pair of passengers in between, turning their idiot faces to goggle at him. He was annoyed with them, even before he realised who they were.

'Bloody hell.'

Not content with sending two people to block his view, the fates had decreed that they should be from the Alderman Kibbalts party. Worse than that, out of the whole party they'd chosen the two he least wanted to see again – Brenda and her friend Monica.

He tried to shut his mind to them and concentrate on what he should do when he got to the bottom. The tops of pine trees were under his boots now. That meant they were about halfway down the mountain. Six minutes to the bottom. Six and a half minutes and Ray Reeve and Allana would be scorching down the main street and away, with still nothing amounting to proof against them. No ski school in this place now for Ray Reeve, but plenty of snow in other parts of the world. Freedom of a sort for Ray Reeve, but for Birdie the closing of a trap that might in the end separate him from Nimue. And this bloody chair – to be a hundred yards or so from the man and yet powerless to do anything about it. He thumped his gloved hand up and down on the arm of the chair in frustration, trapped by a few feet of tubular metal and a

237

steel cable. The village was in sight now, the wide clearing in the pine woods for the nursery slopes, the wooden hut where Hent had flopped dead from the chair. Perhaps three minutes of the journey to go. And it was at that point that the lift stopped.

Birdie never discovered why. It might have been a delayed effect of his attempt to interfere with the mechanism at the top, or perhaps the attendant had decided to keep them hanging there in cold storage while he got on the phone and reported Birdie's misdeeds. The chairs were yo-yoing gently up and down, causing Brenda and Monica to cling together and scream. Birdie thought that if he'd been sitting next to Ray he'd have choked a confession out of him before they got off. Then an idea came to him so wild he immediately wished he hadn't thought of it, an echo of one of Joe and Sidney's more idiotic theories: if somebody swung down the cable . . . And if it hadn't been so suicidally mad to swing down the cable, hand-over-hand, until he got to Ray's chair . . . if it hadn't been so entirely unthinkable to stand up on that precarious seat in heavy boots a good twenty feet or so above the trees, to jump for that thick, grease-covered steel hawser, to swing down it like an acrobat . . . if it hadn't been so entirely unthinkable . . .

And as Birdie's heart and stomach muscles were agreeing how unthinkable the thing would be, he found his angle of vision on the pine tree tops had changed. They were several feet further below him and he could see more of them, the whole forest of them stretching past the village and down the valley. And they were behaving oddly, tipping this way and that as if involved in a series of slow earth movements. It took him a few seconds to understand the reason for this.

'Bloody hell. Oh bloody hell!'

Just as his mind had told him it was unthinkable to try

238

it, his body seemed to have decided to do just that. Somehow he'd scrambled up so that he was standing on the swaying seat of the chair, supporting himself with a firm grip on the metal pole that attached it to the cable. And from this distance, just a few feet above his head, the cable looked even less inviting. It was about half as thick as his wrist and gleaming with grease, slanting down in a black line towards the valley. It was bad enough now that it was immobile, but if the bloody thing started moving . . . His mind told him to sit down and stop mucking about but his body was tensing, weighing up the small leap it would have to make from the chair seat to get his hands round the cable. He tried to will it back, telling it that a jump from a base as insecure as the chair seat wasn't easy, that once it was made, even experimentally, the chances of getting back into his seat would be slim, that the pine trees would splinter like the matchwood they were when a man of his weight hit them from that height, driving sharp stakes into his body as fatal as the crossbow bolt itself, but probably less swift. He could see and feel all that, but he could no more call off what his body had decided to do than will back a dog from chasing a hare. His muscles tensed, his boots lifted from the seat and he found himself slipping sideways and down, hands curled round the greasy cable. He opened his eyes for a second, got snowflakes in them, and closed them again. Even through the thick leather palms of his ski gloves he could feel the friction. Another few minutes of this and they'd be burnt through. For those first few seconds even the thought of Reeve went and there was nothing but the feeling of sliding, of cold air on his face and sweat breaking out over every other part of his body. Then the slide was arrested with a suddenness that almost broke his grip and he found his hands were up against the metal sleeve that held the next chair on to the cable. That meant he was twenty yards nearer Ray Reeve and, thank the gods, the thing still wasn't moving. He opened his eyes and took some of the weight off his hands and arms by curling his legs round the pole that supported the chair. It would, with care, be possible to slide down that pole and on to the empty chair beneath but that would still leave him eighty yards behind Reeve. By now the first panic was over and mind and body were beginning to function together. He looked down the line of chairs, trying to ignore the alarmed faces of Brenda and Monica, and this time he could see his objective. Reeve was just sitting there, not turning round, as if he had no interest in what was going on above him. Perhaps it was just possible that he hadn't noticed, that when he landed beside him it might have the advantage of surprise. Encouraged by this idea Birdie launched himself on the next twenty yard stretch to the top of the next chair, bending his elbows more this time and bracing his shoulders to reduce the speed of his sliding. He arrived without damage except to his ski gloves, and a stickiness in his right palm suggesting that one of those had already given way under the strain.

But his real problem was that the next chair was occupied by Brenda and Monica. He'd been aware of their yelling as a background noise and was surprised that it hadn't made Ray Reeve turn round to see what was happening. But he must be used to outcry from his pupils. Now, resting against the pole, Birdie considered them in the light of an obstacle and decided their attitude was what mattered. If they'd only sit quietly he'd be able to swing over them, but quietness wasn't a quality he associated with Brenda. As he looked at them huddling together and wide-eyed it struck him that their attitude was mainly of fear. He was surprised they should be so concerned for him until he realised it wasn't his safety they were worried about. They'd actually got it into their thick little heads that he was doing all this with the aim of attacking them. In the last few minutes he'd been too busy to remember Brenda's collection of underpants but she hadn't forgotten, and as far as he could tell from her face she thought he was out for desperate revenge.

He called out, as low as he could because he didn't want Ray Reeve to turn round, 'Brenda, I just want to get past. I'm not trying to hurt you.'

'Don't you touch us,' she shouted. 'Don't you touch us.'

'I don't want to touch you. Just sit still and keep your heads down.'

'Go away.'

They were both shouting at him now and he thought it was useless trying to talk sense to them hanging twenty feet above the tree tops when the lift might start moving again any second. There was nothing for it but to go on, so he took several deep breaths and began to slide again, accompanied by screams from the two girls that must surely alert Reeve. The screaming got louder and his slide faster, until somebody grabbed his legs from below. He felt his fingers giving way, clutched, yelled, and kicked out. This freed his legs but set his body swinging from side to side, swaying the cable and the girls' chair with it. It increased the screaming still more but at least meant that they were too busy holding on to make another attempt to grab him. The trouble was, he couldn't move till the swinging stopped and when that happened Brenda would go for his legs again. Then he did what he should have thought of minutes before: tightened his stomach muscles and swung his legs up, hooking one knee over the cable so that he was hanging from it horizontally like a three-toed sloth from a

241

branch.

From that position he tried negotiating again, 'Look Brenda, you want to help Wayne don't you?'

'Go back to your own bloody chair.'

'How can I go back to my own bloody chair? It's bad enough going down. If you'd just keep still and . . .'

'You said my neck was fat. It's not fat. I've got big bones.'

'So have I, and they're going to be big broken bones if you don't let me past.'

Perhaps she misunderstood it as a threat of violence. There was no spoken response, but the cable he was clinging to began to sway violently again and the girls' chair rocked backwards and forwards. Then he saw they were doing it deliberately, working their legs backwards and forwards like children on a playground swing. He didn't know whether they actually intended to throw him off – perhaps they hadn't thought it through that far – but he couldn't wait around to give them the benefit of the doubt. Still imitating the sloth, in posture but not speed, he fumbled his way across the top of their chair as quickly as he could and launched himself down the cable again. He got as far as the next empty chair safely, with the sloth posture taking some of the strain off his arms, but the angle it gave him on the pine trees, upside down and slanting, was such an unpleasant experience that for the next twenty yards he switched back to the Tarzan mode. But by now he knew that his strength was giving out. His cramped fingers wanted desperately to uncurl and he dreaded the vibration in the cable that would tell him the thing was about to start moving again. Although he knew it was a bad idea he couldn't stop himself speeding up. And now Ray Reeve was watching him. The violent swinging of the cable had alerted him, even if he'd disregarded the noise, and Birdie slithered the

242

last ten yards at increasing speed feeling those cold eyes staring at him. If Reeve decided to throw him off the cable he'd make a more effective job of it than Brenda. Birdie's right hand crashed against the metal sleeve at the top of Reeve's chair, parted from the cable and gave a twinge that shot through his whole body as cold air hit the scorched and torn palm. He gasped and, at that point, Ray Reeve could have thrown him off with a fingertip. But he didn't; simply looked up and spoke as if he were facing a minor classroom rebellion.

'What is it this time?'

Birdie half slithered and half fell down the pole into the seat beside him. It was some time before he could speak, then, 'That thing does work. You know this place, know all the ski instructors. They'd tell you how to make it work.'

Either the chair ride had given Ray Reeve a chance to cool off, or he'd decided to pretend Birdie really was a mental case. He said quite calmly, 'I gather the idea is that I, or my accomplice, used some sort of delay mechanism to make sure I got down before the body. Is that it?'

Unnoticed by Birdie the cable above their heads was vibrating, then the chair lift began to move, slowly at first, then with increasing speed, beginning its last long stretch of descent to the nursery slopes.

'Yes,' said Birdie. 'That's exactly it.'

'I suppose I should find it touching you're so concerned about Wayne.'

'Me? Concerned about Wayne?'

Birdie was genuinely shocked at the idea.

'Yes, you must have been worrying about him a lot to dream up such a thoroughly crazy theory.'

'I'm not remotely concerned about bloody Wayne. All I'm concerned with is who killed Horace Hent.'

Birdie had noticed now that the chair lift was moving. There were two people travelling up towards them, waving and shouting to somebody. He wished they'd leave him in peace to finish the job that had to be done in the few minutes before the chair reached the bottom.

'And your theory depends on the idea that I was acting in conspiracy with Mrs Hent.'

'For a share of her husband's money.'

'And you refuse to believe I didn't meet Mrs Hent until I went to put a business proposition to her yesterday?'

'Yes, and today she wraps herself round your neck.'

Ray said, reasonably, 'I had to get her down somehow.'

The chair with the two people waving and shouting was almost level with them now. At least, the plump man was doing the waving and shouting. The boy beside him was muffled up and immobile. Bruin and Tim. Excited presumably because they'd seen his gymnastics on the cable. Well, explanations about that would have to wait until much later. He waved back from force of habit and turned to Ray, but Bruin wasn't giving in so easily. He yelled across the gap between the two lines of chairs, 'Birdie, Birdie, I've got to speak to you.'

'Later. I'll see you when I get down.'

Here was he, with perhaps two minutes of journey time left and Bruin doing his best to sabotage the whole interrogation.

'No, we've got to talk to you now. We were coming up to find you.'

Bruin seemed to be losing his wits as well. If there was a place not to hold a conference it was on a chair lift with one party going up and the other going down. Bruin's chair was already yards past them and moving steadily upwards, the gap widening with every second. Bruin

244

turned round in his seat, face pale and screwed up with anxiety.

'Tim wants to tell you something. He says he had the crossbow.'

A few minutes before Birdie had been willing the chair lift not to start and now, just as desperately, he needed it to stop, to keep Bruin and Tim there long enough to deliver what must be the final piece of the jigsaw. He screwed round in his seat, even forgetting that Ray was beside him.

'Yes. But, what did he do with it?'

Bruin shouted back, voice high pitched and desperate, 'I don't know.'

'But you said he wanted . . .'

Bruin had to shout at the top of his voice now to make himself heard.

'He won't tell me. He says he'll only tell you.'

'Tim!' Birdie bellowed. 'Tim!'

And the boy turned his pale face towards him.

'What did you do with it, Tim? Who did you give it to?'

But it seemed that whatever trust Tim had in him would only work when they were quiet and on their own, like the night he'd brought him back from the snow. Hopeless to expect that a scared and inward-looking child like Tim would shout his secret over nursery slopes and pine woods, over the ten, twenty, thirty yard gap opening between them. The chair carried Tim on up the mountain, still looking back but still unspeaking. And it carried Birdie and Ray down, over the nursery slopes, above the start of the slalom course.

Birdie, cheated of his trump card and with perhaps a minute and a half left to play, turned back to Ray Reeve.

'That's it then, isn't it?'

'What?'

245

'Tim. You know what he's going to tell me, don't you?'

'No, of course I don't.'

'He's going to tell me he gave you the crossbow, isn't he? You knew Wayne had got it and you told Tim to steal it and hand it over to you up the mountain.'

Reeve's precarious calm was going. He sounded angry again. 'This is the most utter nonsense. I'm not going to listen to any more of it.'

'But you've got no choice.'

In his eagerness, with the chair swinging closer and closer to the end of its journey, Birdie grasped Ray Reeve by the arm, pulling him round so that he could look into his face.

'He met you up there and handed over the crossbow. You'd already planned to put the blame on Wayne.'

Reeve might have intended no more than to free himself from Birdie's grip, but his violent push on Birdie's shoulders coincided with a lurch from the chair as it went past the last of the pylons. Birdie fell back against the side of the chair and grabbed for the safety bar, forgetting his skinned palm. The jolt it gave him when it made contact with cold metal made him slip further to one side, left leg shooting out into space, right boot scrabbling on the footrest. Ray Reeve leaned towards him and this time Birdie gripped him by the neck of his anorak, holding on grimly and snarling from the effort.

'He gave it to you, didn't he? That's what he's going to tell me: he gave it to you.'

'You're choking me,' Reeve gasped. 'You're choking me.'

They struggled, with Birdie half in and half out of the chair, as the lift carried them on over the slalom poles, over the spectators who had realised by now that what

246

was going on over their heads looked more interesting than events on the course. There were gasps and shouts from below, appeals from the loudspeaker for somebody to stop the lift, but none of this got through to the two men wrestling fifteen feet or so above them. Then, just as Birdie was managing to haul himself back into the chair, ignoring the choking noises coming from Ray Reeve, somebody did stop the chair and the suddenness of it unbalanced his attempt completely. He felt himself slipping under the safety bar and made a last desperate attempt to hook his arm round Ray's neck. Ray pushed the arm away and Birdie, with a surprised expression on his face, slid slowly under the bar and away.

For a moment he actually managed to hang by one hand from the footrest, but the hand had done too much already to hold him there. The last thing he saw before he plunged down was the upturned face of a competitor in the slalom race, numbered bib and red ski suit, ski tips crossed and an expression of total disbelief. When he fell he missed him by about ten yards and, although he didn't know it, Nimue by about fifty.

The first thing he was aware of was his own winded lungs making a tearing, crowing noise with the effort to draw air back into themselves, air jagged with snow crystals that pricked inside his nose and mouth.

The second was Nimue's voice. 'Birdie.'

Then, in desperately controlled tones, the same voice, 'Birdie, don't try to get up. Can you feel this?'

It took him some time to understand that by 'this' she meant her hand on his leg. He tried to nod, to make his lungs gasp 'yes'.

'And this?'

His other leg, but there were more urgent matters than that. How long had he been unconscious?

247

'Ray . . . getting off . . . getting off the lift.'

He could hear, above his head, the chairs moving again. He tried to will her to understand the urgency of stopping Ray from getting away, if he hadn't already gone. He noticed as his field of vision widened that Fuzz was standing beside Nimue and they were keeping the crowd well back from him. He tried to make both of them understand.

'Ray and Allana. He made Tim steal the crossbow for him and . . .'

Nimue said quietly, 'Don't worry about Ray now.'

'But he . . .'

Still quietly, 'We were coming to tell you. Fuzz killed Hent.'

At the bottom of the chair lift another crowd had gathered over an argument that was still raging. Nobody could understand why, as soon as Ray Reeve got off the chair lift, he was knocked to the ground and sat on by two of his own pupils shouting, 'Murderer!'

The three of them walked down the village street together for the last time, among people strolling back to lunch with skis over their shoulders, families souvenir shopping and children dragging plastic toboggans, for all the world as if they too had nothing more to think about than when to pack their suitcases. And Fuzz was talking all the time, pausing occasionally to raise a hand to somebody she knew, then going on in the same low tone.

'I hated doing it to Tim, hated it. He had enough guilt already without this.'

Birdie said, 'So he did give the crossbow to a teacher?'

She nodded. 'He didn't know what I'd do with it, of course. But at that point, nor did I.'

It had been an unwanted complication at the time,

248

Fuzz with nerves on edge already because Hent had telephoned at lunchtime to say he'd meet her secretly in the lift shed, then suddenly one of her pupils pressing on her a crossbow ready assembled. She'd carried it with her to the lift shed just as it was, not caring whether anybody saw it or not.

'He'd found out I was here, and he must have got something out of Allana about what we'd thought of doing with the satellite.'

Nimue said, 'She probably left some letters lying about. If you wanted to keep anything secret, you shouldn't have chosen Allana.'

Fuzz even smiled at that. 'I didn't choose, did I? I had to work with the wives he married. And after me . . .'

Nimue finished the sentence without irony. 'And after you, the others weren't quite so dependable.'

Fuzz was immediately defensive.

'It wasn't that, not really. I don't suppose I was so dependable myself when I married him. It was all part of the growing-up process.'

Birdie felt very distant from their conversation, as if it was all going on half-heard behind a pane of thick glass. He was still perhaps dazed from his fall. But his mind was moving on slowly and there were things it wanted to know.

'Those letters in the file, the names on them – they had nothing to do with you?'

Fuzz looked at him pityingly, and rattled off with teacher's efficiency, 'Catherine of Aragon, Anne Boleyn, Jane Seymour, Anne of Cleves, Catherine Howard, Catherine Parr.'

'Oh, Henry's wives.'

'That's it,' said Fuzz encouragingly, as to a dim pupil. But she did the explaining to Nimue.

'*Noms de guerre.* That was part of it, I suppose. Part

249

of the silliness of it, like the sugar round the almond. Even before this happened I was starting to wonder if I was using them, using his wives to get back at him, the way he used people.'

Perhaps she'd expected Nimue to contradict her, but when she was silent Fuzz went on more forcefully, 'Only it wasn't a personal thing. I married him, I got rid of him, I didn't want any money from him and that was that. But I'd seen the harm a man like that can do, seen it at close quarters.'

They were near the village square by now. A couple of Alderman Kibbalts girls, loaded with carrier bags, waved to them from across the street, but this time Fuzz didn't notice.

'Selling kids lies, unreality. Magazines, television then the satellite.'

Nimue asked, 'What did he say to you about the satellite, when you met him in the shed?'

'It was ironic. I think he thought our plans were much more formidable than they really were. I mean, you saw what happened in the end. He seemed to think we really were part of some great international conspiracy.'

'So what did he say?'

'He made threats about what he was going to do to us all. Prosecution for industrial espionage, cutting off alimony, and so on. As far as I was concerned he could go ahead and prosecute me and I never got any alimony in any case. It was the others – you see, I'd talked all of them into it. I felt responsible.'

Nimue asked flatly, 'And was that when you shot him?'

'He made all these threats, then he just sat himself down in one of those damned chairs as it came round the wheel and off he went. Off up into the air and away from reality as he'd always done. Then just as he'd passed me, while he was still inside the shed, he turned and gave this horrible gloating smile and I'd picked up the crossbow without knowing what I was going to do with it and . . .' She spread her hands wide. 'And that was that. I put the crossbow down on the next chair as it went past and I suppose it must have dropped off on the way down.'

Birdie said, more loudly than he intended, 'But why did you let Wayne take the blame? Why didn't you let Tim tell anybody about the crossbow?'

She looked resentful at his hostility, then the anger went out of her face and she explained quietly, 'I hated it. I've never hated anything so much. But you see, I had to get Allana out of the way before I told anybody, and she wouldn't come down the mountain.'

There was silence for a while, then just as they were in sight of the church and the grey stone police building beside it Fuzz said suddenly, 'That crossbow. It shouldn't have been so easy. It shouldn't have been so easy.'

They were opposite the entrance to the church now, with a few steps to go. The juke box was playing in the café across the square and there were several Alderman Kibbalts pupils at a table by the window. Only Birdie noticed them. The three of them halted in the square, by the statue of a mountain guide. Fuzz hugged Nimue, clung to her for a few seconds, then walked quickly up the steps and into the police station.

Later, sitting beside her on the bed, Birdie said, 'You might have told me.'

She went on winding bandage round his hand.

'I couldn't. She didn't tell me until you were away up the mountain.'

'Did you guess she'd been Mrs Hent Number One?'

'No, but . . .'

'But what?'

251

He was still resentful. He'd had a bad half hour with Ray Reeve who was disposed to blame him, unfairly he thought, for Allana's sudden departure and the various bruises inflicted by Sidney and Joe before they'd been pulled off him.

'Well, hadn't it occurred to you that when Brenda wrecked Bruin's alibi, she did the same for Fuzz? We knew Fuzz was a better skier than Bruin. She had plenty of time to kill Hent, get her skis on and be halfway down that run before he caught up with her.'

It hadn't occurred to him. He watched morosely as Nimue finished off the bandage and secured it with a safety pin.

'So when Ray Reeve was waiting outside the lift shed, Hent was shouting at Fuzz inside?'

'Yes. If he'd waited a couple of minutes more he'd have met Hent's body coming out.'

'And I was so convinced it was Reeve.'

Nimue said, not looking at him, 'It was suicidal, what you did on that chair lift.'

He said, 'I had to prove who it was before . . .'

'Before what?'

'Before it wrecked us.'

She moved over to the window and looked out. Dusk was settling over the valley and the mountain opposite showed as a dim white bulk, edged with a froth of light where it met the village.

Birdie said, trying to lighten the atmosphere, 'Reeve says he's staying on here for a bit. I don't envy Bruin getting this lot home single-handed tomorrow.'

'Yes.'

'I wonder if he's told them about Fuzz yet.'

'I wonder.'

'I can't get over the way she just walked . . .'

'Don't.'

252

Nimue turned from the window and he saw she was crying, tears running silently down her brown cheeks. He'd never seen her cry before.

'Love . . .'

She said, 'She doesn't understand yet . . . the consequences . . .'

And he understood that she meant being in prison. That she liked Fuzz and understood, probably better than Fuzz herself at that point, all that lay ahead of her.

'Love, we'll help with lawyers. We'll . . .'

And suddenly she was back beside him on the bed, her head on his chest, shivering as if all the coldness of the mountain had rushed into her.

'Love. Oh, love . . .'

He wrapped the duvet round her, held her tight. From the floor below the shouts and scuffles of Alderman Kibbalts doing its packing rose around them.